SECOND SLICE

....

A NOVEL OF SUSPENSE:
BOOK 2 IN THE DETECTIVES
DANIELS AND REMALLA SERIES

J. T. BISHOP

Eudoran Press LLC
PLANO, TX

Eudoran Press LLC
6009 Parker Rd Suite 149 #205
Plano, TX 75093
www.jtbishopauthor.com

Publisher's Note: This is a work of fiction. Names, characters, places, and incidents are a product of the author's imagination. Locales and public names are sometimes used for atmospheric purposes. Any resemblance to actual people, living or dead, or to businesses, companies, events, institutions, or locales is completely coincidental.

Book Layout ©2013 BookDesignTemplates.com
Cover Design by Chiara Girardelli

Ordering Information:
Quantity sales. Special discounts are available on quantity purchases by corporations, associations, and others. For details, contact the "Special Sales Department" at the address above.

Second Slice/ J. T. Bishop. -- 1st ed.
ISBN 978-1-7325531-3-2

To Jannin, Nichelle and Kerin, for keeping it goofy all the time. Life's not fun unless you're laughing, so thank you for making it fun. And, yes, you're all my favorite.

Other Books by J. T. Bishop

The Red-Line Trilogy
Red-Line: The Shift
Red-Line: Mirrors
Red-Line: Trust Destiny

Red-Line: The Fletcher Family Saga
Curse Breaker
High Child
Spark
Forged Lines

Detectives Daniels and Remalla Series
First Cut – A Novel of Suspense (Book One)

Coming Soon...Third Blow – A Novel of Suspense (Book Three)
Now available for pre-order

Interested in getting the first book in J.T. Bishop's Red-Line series for free? Go to
www.jtbishopauthor.com

ONE

....

"Anyone could have killed Karl. Maybe even someone at this table." Laura picked up the wine bottle and added more to her glass.

Madison smiled. "Really?" Her friend had a flair for the dramatic, but this seemed hard to believe. "Why would anyone here want to murder Karl?"

"You know my wife," said Preston. "She loves to stir the gossip. Hand me some more chips, Sam."

Sam Desmond picked up a bag of chips and handed them to Preston. "I think it's ridiculous. Knowing Karl, he was into something he shouldn't have been, and someone didn't like it."

"Oh, honey," said Sam's wife, Angela. "Just because he was wealthy, good-looking, in fabulous shape, and every woman around this lake ogled him, didn't make him a bad guy. You're just jealous." Angela took the last sip of her wine and reached for more.

"How many glasses is that for you?" asked Sam, raising a brow.

Angie glared. "Honey, we live on the lake. It's a ten-minute walk home. It's not like we have to be saints. You need to relax and let your hair down a little. Not that you have much to let down." She giggled, adding wine to her glass.

"Easy on the hair comments," said Thomas, who sat next to his wife, Lucy. He rubbed his bald head.

"Babe, you've shaved your hair for two years," said Lucy. "What do you care?" She picked up her burger. "Besides, I like bald men." The strap of her dress slid off her shoulder, and she slid it back up. "Something about the shape of a man's head just turns me on."

"Which head is that?" asked Angie, taking a swig of her drink.

The group laughed. Madison shook her head. She reached to take another sip of her water when she caught her husband, Donald, watching her. His passive face held a tension she recognized, and she gripped her glass.

Her husband picked up a grape and popped it in his mouth. "Whoever did it though was angry. I heard the killer carved up Karl pretty good."

"I bet it was his wife, Sharie," said Lucy. "Her husband was likely screwing everything that moved. I bet she found out and took care of business."

Madison held her water but didn't drink. She picked up a pickle spear though and took a bite.

"Karl was her third husband. She's no stranger to divorce," said Sam. "Why not do it again?"

"And how do you know he was cheating?" asked Thomas.

"Oh, come on," said Angie, slightly slurring. "How could he not be?"

"Just because he's good-looking doesn't make him a cheater," said Preston, Laura's husband. "I mean, look at me. I'm devastatingly handsome." He took Laura's hand. "And completely faithful."

Laura smiled. "That's just because I'm great in the sack. I make sure you don't look anywhere else."

Angie laughed mid sip and almost choked on her wine. "You tell 'em, Laura."

Preston smirked. "I can't deny that's true."

"Maybe you should work on that, honey," said Sam to Angie. "You could learn something from your friend."

"Ouch," said Lucy with a smile. "I think he just called you out, girlfriend." Her strap slid down again, but she didn't bother to put it back. Madison couldn't help but notice how Lucy's tube top barely covered the tops of her tanned breasts. Her husband couldn't seem to keep his eyes off of them either.

"Honey, the rate you're going, you'll be lucky to get some ever again," said Angie. "Besides, I give as good as I get." She finished her glass of wine with a healthy swig. Madison wondered if she'd even be able to make the walk home.

Sam watched his wife drink, and his face remained stoic.

"I wonder if Sharie thought the same," said Laura. "If he was cheating on her, the wife's the most likely suspect. She'd have good reason."

"Karl was wealthy and successful, and from what I could tell, he loved Sharie," said Madison. "They had a beautiful cabin on the lake and could do whatever they wanted, whenever they wanted. Why would you want to mess that up?"

"Jealousy and lies is all it takes," said Laura.

"Not everybody can have the perfect marriage like you and Donald have," said Lucy. Her second strap had fallen, and she'd left it. Madison noticed Sam eyeing her.

"You have all those things too," said Angie to Lucy. She reached for an available bottle of wine. "I hope none of you go killing each other."

Madison looked at Donald. Her heart thumped. "I don't plan on it. Do you?"

He arched a brow. "Why would I want to kill the most beautiful woman in the world?"

Madison caught Laura rolling her eyes. Lucy smiled, gazing at Donald.

Angie cackled. "I think I'm going to puke," she said, refilling her glass.

"I think you are too," said Sam.

"Oh, don't be such a downer. You could use a little more excitement in your life. If I wasn't around, you'd be dull and boring." Angie added more wine to his glass, too. "Here. Drink some more. You could use it."

Sam shook his head. "You are going to put me in my grave."

Angie nodded. "Damn straight."

Lucy sat back and stretched, raising her arms above her head, giving everyone a nice view of her cleavage. Laura glanced over at Madison, widening her eyes.

Lucy stretched out her toned legs too, and Madison noted how all the men at the table tried to watch her without being obvious. She was like Catwoman, luring in her prey, only these men were hardly prey. More like eager fans watching from the sidelines, wishing they could participate in the game, but knowing they could never compete.

Her husband, Thomas, watched her too, his face unreadable. Madison wondered what he was thinking.

"I think it's so exciting," said Lucy, continuing her stretch. "A murder. On Secret Lake. It's the perfect story for a good book. Don't you think?"

"Just so long as no one else is on the killer's list," said Thomas. "One murder is enough."

"You think there could be more?" asked Preston.

"I doubt that," said Donald. "Why would there be?"

"Maybe it's a serial killer," said Madison. "There was that guy they caught in the city a month or so ago. What was his name? The Makeup Artist? Just an hour from here."

"A serial killer. Really?" asked Donald. "Now, who's being dramatic?"

"Anything's possible," said Madison.

"God. A serial killer. Can you imagine?" asked Laura. She picked at the bean salad on her plate. "If that were true, then God knows who could be next."

"I think we're getting way ahead of ourselves," said Preston. "Serial killer is a bit much. It's likely an intruder, like Maddie says. There was jewelry missing, I hear. Maybe Karl just surprised a burglar. Or Sharie did it and made it look like a robbery. Those are the most likely options." He reached for a brownie from the plate on the table. "These brownies will be the death of me, Maddie. No pun intended."

"They're her specialty," said Laura. "Outside of her artwork, they're the best thing she makes."

"When's your next show, Maddie?" asked Sam.

"Next month," said Madison. "At an art gallery in town."

"Are we invited?" asked Angie. "Or are you trying to keep us hidden from the art folk?" She put her glass down and it almost fell over, but she caught it in time. "Whoops," she said. "That would have been devastating."

Sam shook his head. "Jesus," he said under his breath.

"You're invited. Why wouldn't you be?" said Madison.

"We know how those artsy, fartsy people can be," said Lucy. She'd sat back up in her seat and had adjusted her straps. "We don't necessarily fit in."

"I don't see why not," said Laura. "We liven up the party. You should see her latest work. It's gorgeous."

"I haven't even seen it yet," said Donald. "How'd you get to lay eyes on it?"

Laura grinned. "Because I'm her best friend. Besties get first dibs."

"Over husbands?" asked Donald.

"Appears so," said Thomas. Normally a reserved man, he grinned good-naturedly.

"Happens to the best of us," said Sam.

Donald didn't smile.

**

Laura rinsed a plate in the sink and handed it to Madison, who dried it with a towel.

"You did a great job with the potato salad," said Madison. "I don't think there's any left."

"Same with your brownies. Sam took the last one," said Laura. She picked up a wine glass and ran it under the water.

"Where is Sam? Did he leave?" Preston came up behind them and put a plate in the sink.

"He took Angie home, or should I say, carried her," said Laura.

"She was pretty drunk," said Madison.

"I wish she didn't drink so much," said Lucy, coming into the kitchen, holding a light sweater and sliding it on. Thomas came in behind her.

"She's been like that since I've known her, almost five years now since they bought their cabin," said Laura. She handed Madison a dish.

"Her liver's on borrowed time," said Thomas, rubbing his wife's shoulders. "You ready?"

"Yes," said Lucy. "We're heading out. Dinner was great, Laura. And a beautiful night to eat out by the lake. Thanks for a lovely meal."

"It was hamburgers. I didn't exactly kill myself," said Laura.

"Still, it was nice to get together," said Thomas.

Madison put a dried plate in a cabinet. "It was nice to see you two. It's been a while."

"I suspect you've been holed up, working on your latest project," said Preston. "Laura told us how busy you've been."

"Keep us posted on your show. I'd love to come," said Lucy. "If you can put up with us."

Madison smiled. "Of course. I'll give you the details once I have them."

"Did she tell you she's adding on to the cabin?" asked Laura. "Donald's building her a nice studio."

"Really?" asked Thomas. "I saw some workmen over there. Is that what they're doing?"

"Yes. They should start renovating soon." Donald walked in from the porch, a towel in his hand. "Outside is wiped down and clean." He put the towel in the sink.

"Thanks," said Preston. "You think the ghost will like the renovations?"

Lucy laughed. "Ghost?"

Laura picked up the last cup and rinsed it. "Maddie's place is haunted. Didn't you know that?"

"What?" asked Thomas.

"It's nonsense," said Donald. "Our place is not haunted."

"It's the oldest cabin on the lake," said Laura. "It's bound to have some secrets."

"It's just creaky and needs a few updates. Doesn't mean it's haunted," said Maddie.

Laura turned. "I've seen and heard a few things, and so have you."

"What things?" asked Lucy.

"That door swinging open. Remember?" asked Laura.

"That was the wind," said Madison.

"It was an interior door," said Laura.

"It's a drafty house," said Donald.

"That mirror broke. I know you didn't forget that," said Laura.

Madison recalled that day. She'd been having coffee with Laura in the front room and they'd been talking about the fight she'd had with Donald the night before when they'd heard a crash from somewhere in the house. They'd gone to look and found the antique mirror in the hallway bathroom smashed into pieces.

"Are you going to tell me that was an old mirror?" asked Laura.

"It was an old mirror," said Madison.

"It probably had a crack in it somewhere," said Donald.

"A crack?" asked Laura. "The mirror completely shattered. There's no explanation for it." She handed Madison the last cup and turned off the sink.

"I didn't know this. How did I not know this?" asked Lucy.

"Because it's silly," said Donald, his eyes on Madison.

"Your dad agreed," said Laura. "He said things were going on there since you were a child."

"You've had the cabin that long?" asked Thomas.

"My grandfather bought it," said Madison. "Then Dad got it and now I have it. It's been in the family for a while."

"That must be nice, Donald," said Thomas. "It's the best cabin on the lake. Maddie's not only talented, but rich."

"Donald does pretty well on his own," said Madison. She wiped the last glass dry and put it away. "I'm lucky myself." She dried her hands and walked over to Donald and put her arms around him. His hand went around her waist but his rigid touch made her tense in his arms.

"Well, honey, we should go," said Thomas. "All this silly talk of ghosts has got me ready to walk through the woods. Maybe we'll get lucky and see something." He wiggled his brows and made a sinister 'wooo' sound.

"Ha," said Lucy. "One sight of a ghost and you'd leave me to fend for myself."

Thomas shrugged. "You know me well."

"We should go too," said Donald. "It's late."

"Any more ghost stories, and I want to hear about them," said Lucy as they said their goodbyes.

"I'll let you know," said Madison. "But honestly, the house is just old." She hugged Laura and Lucy and followed Donald to the door. "Thanks again for dinner, Laura."

"You got it. Call me tomorrow. We'll do lunch this week," said Laura.

"Good night," said Preston, waving from the kitchen.

"Good night," said Donald, and following Lucy and Thomas, they left.

···

TWO

Madison followed her husband into the house. It had been a quiet walk home as they followed the wooded trail that circled the lake, her husband saying little. She'd sensed an underlying tension, and she'd said nothing, hoping he'd settle down.

They entered from the back, where large windows overlooked the placid lake. Soft lighting around the porch illuminated their path and Madison flicked the outside lights off and turned the interior lights on. The kitchen lit up and Madison tossed her purse into a dining chair. "It was a nice night," she said.

Donald went into the kitchen and opened the refrigerator. "If you say so."

Madison rubbed her head. "It was good to see everyone."

Donald grabbed some orange juice and opened it. "I suppose." He took a swig from the bottle.

Madison debated saying anything more. "It's late."

Donald recapped the orange juice. "And I've got an early morning."

"You do? It's Saturday."

He put the juice on the counter. "Not all of us can sleep in, get up when we feel like it, paint for a few hours, and sell what looks like child's scribble for thousands of dollars. Some of us have to work for a living."

Madison held her breath. "I never said you didn't work."

He closed the fridge abruptly. "Then stop questioning me. I have shit I have to get done. I'm going in to do it tomorrow." He cocked his head. "That is unless, of course, this latest work of yours will pay our bills, and all of this renovation you want on this decrepit old house. The latest work that apparently everyone else gets to see but me. That's nice."

"Only Laura. No one else."

He glared. "Not even your husband?"

Madison straightened. "You don't express much interest in my work. I didn't think you'd care."

He pointed. "I care when you embarrass me in front of our friends. I looked like an idiot."

"You did not. Nobody thought anything of it."

He shrugged. "That is so like you. You don't think of anything or anyone but yourself. It's always all about you, isn't it? This house. Your art. And then you have to go off on this whole haunted house thing. It's ridiculous. How much attention do you need?"

"I didn't say anything about that. Laura brought it up."

"And why did she do that? Because you've been spoon feeding her that crap from day one, and she eats it up. She just loves lording it over everyone about how she's such good friends with you. Like she's got some sort of secret access to the famous lady on the lake. And I'm second fiddle to her." He turned and flipped on the sink. "I hate that bitch."

Madison walked around the counter. "She's not like that and you know it. I've known her for years. She and Preston are good friends of ours. What is the matter with you? Why can't you ever be happy?"

Donald, who was rinsing his hands, abruptly shut off the sink and faced her, his lip curled in a sneer. "How can I possibly be happy with a woman who constantly makes me feel inferior? Who thinks she's better than me in every way? Who takes every chance she has to make me look like a fool?"

Madison's anger flared. "You do just fine at that all by yourself. You don't need me to do it."

His wet hand came up and grabbed her by the throat. Gasping, Madison grabbed his fingers. He brought his face close to hers. "If I didn't have some measure of self-control after living with you all these years, I'd snap your neck like a toothpick."

His grip tightened, and Madison's throat closed. Fighting to breathe, she clawed at his hands.

Glaring at her, he spoke. "You're lucky I still put up with you. I'd have gladly divorced you a long time ago."

A bang sounded in the kitchen and something cold splashed against Madison's legs.

Shoving her back, Donald turned toward the noise, and Madison gulped in air. Holding her neck, she massaged her skin. She looked to see the orange juice carton on the floor, and juice splattered across the tile.

Donald sneered at the mess. "Maybe that's one of your ghosts."

Madison cleared her throat, ignoring the juice. "You won't divorce me. You like my money too much."

His face went flat, and she waited to see what he would do. His words were his usual weapons, but she had known him to get violent. "You mean your daddy's money, don't you?" Walking closer, he grabbed her hair, and she flinched when he pulled it and leaned close. "If it weren't for him and his name, you'd be nothing. If I hadn't married you when I did, he'd have known the truth about you, and you'd have lost everything. Remember that."

His hot breath burned against her ear, and she shoved away from him. He let go of her and chuckled as she wiped away a tear.

"I hate you," she whispered. Shivering, she held her arms.

He stood there, his hands on his waist. "I really don't care." He watched her for a second before he turned away and, grabbing a towel, wiped his hands. "I'm going to bed now. You can sleep in the guest room tonight." Without looking her way, he tossed the towel on the floor, strode down the hallway, entered their bedroom, and slammed the door behind him.

Madison stood frozen in the kitchen. Another tear ran down her cheek, and she swiped it away. For the millionth time, she considered grabbing her suitcase, packing it, and walking out, and for the millionth time, she stopped herself. She couldn't bring herself to do it. The thought of her father's words echoed in her head. He's a loser. He'll never amount to much. You know he just wants the money. You always did know how to pick 'em.

Even though her dad had died two years ago, she couldn't bring herself to admit he was right. Again. Since her mother had died in childbirth, it had always been her and her dad. He'd always been hard on her, had rarely shown affection, and she'd rebelled from a young age. Doing the exact opposite of everything he'd wanted. To the point of getting pregnant at the age of twenty after a drunken night of sex with a drifter whose name she couldn't even remember. Telling her dad scared the hell out of her, and she knew he would use it against her. It would confirm everything he'd ever said about her. That she was stupid and would end up screwing up her life.

That's when she'd confided in Donald. He'd been a college friend who'd had a crush on her since they'd met. He was sweet and smart and promised her he'd take care of and protect her. He'd asked her to marry him and offered to claim the baby as his own.

She'd seen it is a chivalrous move and the only way out of an impossible situation. If her father knew the truth, he'd likely disown her. Had she been braver back then, and knew then what she knew now, she'd have walked out of her dad's life and never looked back. Raising a baby on her own would have been difficult, but she could have found a way. But back then, despite her rebellious nature, she was insecure and frightened, and Donald had offered a solution.

Madison sniffed and walked over to the windows, looking out over the dark lake and thinking back. Two months after marrying Donald, she'd miscarried. Her breath caught, and she swallowed. She couldn't help but think about how her life may have been different if her daughter had been born. But she also had to consider that perhaps it was a blessing. Would Donald have treated her child any better than her? She suspected not.

After losing the baby, Donald had said little, and her father— even less. During the most difficult and gut-wrenching time of her life, she'd had no one to turn to. That's when she'd dove into her art. She'd always enjoyed painting. It had been a wonderful release for her, and she'd taken an art class whenever she could when she was in school, despite her father's objections that it was a waste of time and money.

Once the pregnancy was over though, and she found herself in a strained marriage with a man she knew she didn't love, she couldn't paint fast enough. She threw herself into her work, allowing all her pain and agony out on the canvas. It was a welcome respite and not one she'd planned to share, until three years ago when she'd met Sharie, Karl Scott's wife. Sharie was an art director at a gallery in the city and when she'd heard that Madison painted, she'd asked to see her work. Madison had hesitated, but Laura had pushed her to do it, telling her it was time to come out of her shell and take a risk.

Sharie had loved her work and convinced Madison, after weeks of pestering, to do an art show at her gallery. Madison, terrified and excited, told herself not to expect much, and Donald said the same. But she'd sold every piece and had commissions for two more. Ever since, her work had been in demand.

At that point, she and Donald had moved into the cabin after her father's health had declined to where he'd needed assisted living. Her father had not attended the show and didn't seem to care about her success. Despite her dad's constant accusations that she would never be responsible enough to take care of anything, he'd turned the house on the lake over to her, with the stipulation that if she and Donald ever divorced, Donald would not get the cabin. She'd agreed, although never told Donald. She figured that was best left unmentioned.

Madison sighed as she stared out the window. That was another reason she found it hard to leave Donald. She wasn't exactly sure she could protect the home if they divorced, despite what she'd promised her dad. She and Donald did not have a prenup, and even though she'd inherited the house, if Donald fought her, he could make it ugly and possibly take quite a bit from her.

Sliding the glass door open, she stepped out onto the porch, and a breeze ruffled her hair. The irony of it all was not lost on her. She'd married Donald to stay safe, and now she was remaining with him to stay safe, despite all the warning signs. The same signs had been there when she'd married him, but she'd ignored them too. At what point, she wondered, would she listen? Her father's voice rattled in her head, and now Donald's voice took its place. Would she ever escape her father's shadow?

The lake called to her, and she walked down the small pier to the pontoon boat that sat silently on the water. This was her happy place. Being out on the water when it was quiet and peaceful provided the calm she craved. Stepping onto the boat, she undid the ropes and pushed away from the dock. After she hit the ignition, the engine rumbled to life. There were no restrictions on taking a boat out on the lake at night, but there was a no wake rule between the hours of seven p.m. and eleven a.m. The engine idled, and she gave it a little juice as she guided the boat slowly out into the quiet water. No one and nothing were out except the stars. Once she made it out to the center of the lake, she cut the engine. Silence greeted her, and she sat back in a cushioned seat and looked up at the blaze of lights in the sky, wondering about what was up there, maybe looking down at her.

Her gaze traveled back down to earth, and she eyed the homes around the lake. Laura's, five houses down from hers, sat back behind some shade trees. The porch where they'd had dinner was empty, and the house was dark, save for a few lighted trees. Angie and Sam's house was three houses down from Laura's, and Lucy and Thomas were six houses down on the other side of Madison's. Across the lake, almost directly across from Madison, sat Karl and Sharie Scott's cabin. While Madison's place was the oldest and most stately, Karl and Sharie's was definitely the biggest. Large columns connected two stories and a winding staircase traveled from the large patio on the first floor to the grand patio on the second floor. A large green lawn sprawled down to a small beachfront where the yard met the lake. A red speed boat was docked at their pier.

Madison recalled the few dinners she'd had there in the last few years. Some to celebrate her successes and others for holidays, and one she'd prefer to forget. It was after that particular party where she'd stopped drinking and hadn't touched a drop since, much to Donald's disappointment. Alcohol made her do stupid things, and most of it had to do with sex. Her pregnancy had just been the beginning. She was pretty convinced it was why she'd stayed married to Donald. After her miscarriage, she'd used alcohol to cope, and it made sex with Donald bearable, plus to be honest, exciting and impulsive. Donald liked her drunk, and they'd had plenty of fun together, even after the worst of fights. But she'd done a few other impulsive things as well, which Donald knew nothing about, and after one stupid night at the big house across the lake, she told herself she was done, and she hadn't touched alcohol since. She and Donald barely slept together now, and she wondered if he'd had affairs. To be honest, she wasn't sure she cared.

Swiveling, she put her feet up and lay flat against the seat. Watching the stars, she wondered again about the who might be observing from above. Pondering this unanswerable question, the warm gentle wind relaxed her, and she drifted off to sleep.

THREE

....

A murky fog obscured her vision, and she blinked to see, but it didn't help. Holding her hands out, she walked through the soupy mix, careful not to walk into anything. She saw and heard nothing.

Squinting, she stopped, focusing as the fog swirled and turned, and three figures became visible. They were only silhouettes, but she could see enough to tell one was a woman and the other two men. They didn't move, but just stared back. There was something about these three that intrigued her, and she took a step closer. The fog swirled, and as she reached out, she saw the woman reach out as well. But before their hands could touch, the fog thickened, a gust of wind blew, and shoved her backward.

Madison opened her eyes. The stars greeted her. Blinking, she sat up, holding her chest. Her heart thudded, and she could still see her hand reaching out to the other female, when something had stopped them.

Everything was still. Nothing moved on the lake. She had no idea how long she'd been asleep. The boat had drifted, but not far. Shaking off the strange dream, she stood and hit the ignition. The engine rumbled, and she steered herself quietly back home. Within a few minutes, she approached her dock. She cut the engine, and as the boat floated slowly toward the pier, she jumped out, grabbed the side rail, and pulled the pontoon closer. It bumped softly against the wooden deck, and she tied it to the posts.

The boat secured, she turned back toward the house. The kitchen light she'd left on was now off, and it was dark. She supposed Donald had returned to the kitchen. The glow of the moon though gave her sufficient light, and she walked down the dock to the patio. As she reached for the door, she paused, hearing something. It was faint, but in the quiet, it was easier to detect. She thought it sounded like a footfall, and maybe someone moving through the brush. Her heart rate jumped, but she saw nothing, just the bushes along the side of the cabin. Something cold moved through her and the hair on the back of her neck raised. Sliding the glass door open, she stepped inside and closed the door behind her. Locking it, she scanned the area, but there was nothing other than the distinct feeling she was being watched. Rubbing her arms, she shook her head. Karl's murder had spooked everyone around the lake. It had always been a place where everyone had kept their doors unlocked, and neighbors came and went. But now everyone thought twice about keeping their doors open.

Taking a deep breath and telling herself she was overreacting, she went into the kitchen and got a glass of water. She kept the light off, and after getting a drink, she realized she needed some things from her bathroom before going to sleep in the guest room. She didn't know if Donald really thought he was punishing her by forcing her to sleep elsewhere, or if he, like her, just preferred to sleep alone.

Considering how often she slept there, she should have just stocked the bathroom with her toiletries. She made a mental note to do that in the morning.

Moving slowly down the carpeted hallway, she stopped at the door to the master and quietly opened it. She knew that Donald would yell at her if she woke him, so she tiptoed into the bathroom. All she could make out in the dark room was the curve of his body beneath the sheets. In the bathroom, a soft night light gave her enough illumination for her to see what she needed. She grabbed a few things and opened a drawer to get her moisturizer when she kicked something on the floor. It clattered as it moved against the tile. Squinting, she tried to make out what it was, but couldn't see well enough. She found the shower light on the wall and flipped it on. The shower brightened, and the bathroom came into sharper view.

Finding the object, she froze, uncertain of what she was seeing. Her eyes widening, she stepped closer. It was a knife. She recognized it specifically as the knife she'd used earlier that evening to cut the brownies. She'd rinsed it and put it in the drainer next to the sink.

Her mind tried to comprehend why it was there. The blade was red with blood, and as her eyes looked around, she saw drops of blood in the bathroom. She followed their path and saw they led from the bedroom.

She stopped breathing, but her heart took a sudden leap in her chest. Everything went still, and a cold horror settled over her body. Her skin prickled. Where did that knife come from? Why was it in the bedroom? Why was there blood on it? Whose blood was it?

She tried to call for Donald, but nothing escaped her throat. She couldn't utter a word. She thought of the noise on the patio and wondered if someone had been, or was still in the house. Could he be waiting for her? Her hands shaking, she dropped what she held back onto the counter. She had to get out of the bathroom and get to a phone. Her cell was still in her purse that sat in the dining chair. There was a landline in the bedroom though. She had to get to it and call for help. And what about Donald? Was he okay? She had to warn him too.

Forcing herself to move and breathe, she took tentative steps backward, watching the knife, as if it might jump up and stab her at any moment.

Quivering, she made it to the bathroom door and pushed it open. Visions of someone standing there, waiting, made her almost throw up. But no one was there. The bedroom was dark though, and it terrified her that she may not be alone. The fear was so intense, she began to cry and tears ran down her cheeks. Forcing herself to move, she raced to the side of the bed, desperate for light, and flipped on the bedroom lamp. She began to reach for the phone when she saw Donald in the bed.

Nothing in the bathroom had prepared her for this. His lifeless eyes stared upward, and blood covered the headboard and the white sheets. His mouth was open in a silent scream and his throat was sliced open, the wound raw and seeping.

A scream caught in Madison's throat. The scene was horrifying and indescribable. She couldn't think. This was Donald, in their bed, murdered. She stepped back and stepped into something warm. Looking down, she saw it was blood. The shock finally hit her, and her throat unlocked, and she let loose a blood-curdling shriek. The sound of it catapulted her out of the room, and she ran. Expecting at any moment for the assailant to step out of the shadows and assault her, she made it to her purse. Grabbing it, she fell to the floor, her back against the wall, as tears ran down her face. Her hands shook so hard, she could barely grasp the phone.

Crying and shaking, she dialed 911.

**

Sheriff Rodney. T. Biggles arrived on the scene at the Vickers' cabin. It was five a.m., and he rubbed his tired eyes. He'd only been asleep a few hours when the call had come in. Another murder on the lake. He couldn't believe it when he'd heard it. What the hell was going on? His normal, peaceful days of going into the office around ten in the morning, having a cup of coffee while he discussed the relatively few day's events with his assistant, checking in on the locals during lunch and dealing with the occasional stolen bike, or neighbor complaint, had evaporated six weeks ago when Karl Scott had been found dead in his bed, stabbed multiple times. Since then, it had been sleepless nights, long days, loads of questions and multiple phone calls at the station from worried homeowners who thought they'd seen or heard something.

It was proving to be more than he could handle. His two deputies, Colin and Jeremy, were struggling with the workload, and Biggles knew this was way out of his league. The whole reason he'd taken this gig was to avoid all this mess. He'd worked for years as a police captain in a large city, and it had almost killed him, plus destroyed his marriage. Now he was facing it all over again. Murder cases took months of work and investigation, and he didn't have the manpower or the resources for it.

When Karl had been found, Biggles had called on the nearby county for help. They'd sent some officers, and he'd gotten forensic assistance and the coroner from the city. His friend and fellow captain, Frank Lozano, had been knee deep in the Makeup Artist murders, plus a series of bank robberies and had no officers to spare. The county had helped but now that a few weeks had passed and there had been no arrests, their time spent on the case had dwindled, and Biggles could see that they were leaving it up to him to handle the rest.

He sighed wearily and stifled a yawn. If this was another murder, then the shit would hit the fan. Every phone in every house along the lake was ringing right now. He could almost hear it himself.

Getting out of the car, he perused the scene. His two deputies were already there. Two cruisers were in the driveway and one had the lights flashing. The front door was open, and he headed toward it. There were a couple of neighbors standing on the front porch of their house, and he waved at them as he entered.

"Everything all right, Sheriff?" asked the neighbor.

Biggles recognized him. It was Keith Thomas, who ran the bait and tackle shop down the road.

"Not sure, Keith. I'm about to find out." He kept walking to prevent further discussion.

Once inside the home, his deputy, Jeremy, approached.

"What we got?" asked Biggles.

Jeremy's face was white. "It's a mess, Sheriff. Just like Karl Scott."

"Shit," said Biggles. "Where is he?"

"In the master. Down the hall. Madison, his wife, found him. She's in the living room."

Biggles nodded. "Got it. Where's Colin?"

"In the master."

"He touch anything?"

"Hell, no."

"Good. I'll get a forensics team up here soon as I can. The neighbors are going to hear about this soon enough. I need you to set up a perimeter around the house. Nobody gets in. Okay?"

Jeremy nodded. "There's one here now, though. Laura Benoff. Madison called her."

Biggles grunted. "Great. Word's already out then. Grab Colin and get started on that perimeter."

"I'm on it." Colin disappeared.

Biggles stepped through the foyer and into the living room. He saw Madison Vickers sitting on the couch. She held her head in her hands, and Laura was sitting next to her with an arm around her, looking dazed. Her eyes flickered to life when she saw him.

"Sheriff," said Laura.

Madison's head raised. Her eyes were red and tears streaked her face. Her nose was running, and Biggles could detect the shake in her fingers. More tears surfaced when she saw him. He walked closer.

"You all right?" he asked.

"No, she's not all right," said Laura. "She just found her husband murdered in her bed. She's terrified. So am I. What the hell is going on around here?" She hugged her friend and handed her a tissue.

Biggles shifted, unsure of what to say. "I wish I knew, but we'll find out." He watched Madison for a moment. He knew her well. A well-known and wealthy artist whose family had lived on the lake for years. Her father had been a royal son-of-a-bitch who Biggles had played poker with a few times until he figured out the man cheated.

"Can you tell me what happened?" he asked.

"What happened?" asked Laura. "Donald's dead. Slaughtered in his own home. What else do you need to know?"

Madison grabbed her friend's hand. "It's ok. He's only doing his job."

"If he'd done his job, they would have caught the guy by now."

Madison dabbed her eyes and nose. "I found him in the bed. We'd come home after having dinner at Laura's. He went to sleep. I took the boat out for a bit to clear my head. When I came back..." Her voice caught, and she bit her lip. "...I went into the bathroom, and there was a knife on the floor. I...I..." Fresh tears emerged. "I found Donald in the bed. He...he was dead." Her strangled words became a sob.

"That's enough," said Laura. "She's distraught. Give her a break."

"You know I have to ask these questions."

Laura glared. "We're not idiots, but do you have to ask them now? Isn't there something else you can do? Like fingerprints, or pictures, or I don't know, find a killer who's stalking our community?" She gently guided Madison's head into her neck, and Madison sucked in air as she tried to calm herself.

Biggles tried to keep steady. This was just the beginning. He knew Laura Benoff well enough to know that she'd be spreading the word and fanning the flames in a heartbeat. His job had just gone from hell to an even deeper pit of hell. One where he doubted even the devil himself had access to.

He paused. "Take your time, Madison. I'll be right back." Deciding that speaking to Madison while her pit bull Laura was by her side was a bad decision, he figured he needed to see the crime scene. Glancing out the back windows, he saw Colin cordoning off the backyard to prevent any additional neighbors from feeling the need to enter the house. The sun was up enough now that he could see people standing on their lawns, pointing toward the Vickers'.

He walked back toward the bedrooms and saw the door open to the master; stepping inside, he took a deep breath. Donald Vickers was in the bed, eyes open, throat slashed and blood everywhere. Biggles was glad he hadn't had breakfast yet.

The sheets had been pulled down to expose the man's bare chest, which was red with blood, as was the headboard.

Biggles didn't get any closer. He knew now that he would need a lot more than just the county's help. This was the second gruesome murder in six weeks, and this would require a bone fide task force.

Without thinking twice, he grabbed his cell and dialed a number. Listening, he heard a groggy voice answer. "Llo?"

"Lozano? It's Biggles. Sorry if I woke you, but I've got a hell of a mess here, and I need your help. Now."

FOUR

....

Madison blinked weary eyes. Seeing white walls and a big landscape painting beside the bed, she couldn't remember where she was. Next to her was a nightstand with a glass of water and a small digital clock. It read six p.m.

The memory of the last two days zoomed back, and her stomach clenched. Madison had spent her time either sleeping or barely coherent. Donald. The blood. Her terror. The sheriff. Laura had brought her back to her place and insisted she lie down. Madison had argued, but couldn't deny she'd had little rest, and her stress levels were so high, she could barely speak. Laura had given her a pill and brought her into the room, closed the shutters and told her to shut her eyes, if only for a few minutes. Madison had not expected to sleep, but she'd been in bed ever since. Laura had roused her to bring some food or water, but Madison didn't want either. She only wanted to try and forget.

Realizing she couldn't sleep forever, she sat up, her body aching. Donald's lifeless face came back into her thoughts and fresh tears surfaced. How could it be true? Her husband was dead, murdered in their bed. Who would do this, and why?

Wiping a tear from her face, she pushed back the covers and swung her legs out. She stood slowly, ensuring she had her balance.

She couldn't sleep this away. She had to do something, or find out what was being done. There was a box of tissues by the bed and she grabbed one and blew her nose, finger combed her hair, and smoothed her top. Laura had given her some pajamas to wear when she'd arrived and she still wore them. Once she got moving, she would need a shower.

Feeling a little more centered, she opened the door to the bedroom and stepped out. She was in the guest room down the hall from the main part of the house. Heading down the carpeted hallway, she heard voices.

Following the sound, she stopped at the end of the hallway when she heard her name. Laura was talking. Madison heard other familiar voices and recognized them as her friends Angie and Lucy.

"I just don't believe this," said Angie.

"I don't know why you're so shocked," said Lucy. "Donald was an asshole."

"There are a lot of assholes out there," said Laura. "And most of them live forever."

"I'm just saying," said Lucy. "There are people out there who aren't sad he's dead, and probably a few who wish they'd done it themselves."

"I'd fall in that category," said Laura.

"Really?" asked Angie. There was a pause. "Why? What do you know?"

"Nothing I have the luxury of talking about. Let's just say Donald wasn't an ideal husband."

"I knew it," said Lucy. "Was he abusive to Maddie?"

"I can't talk about it," answered Laura.

"I always thought there was something nasty about him. He gave off a vibe," said Angie.

"He stared at my boobs all the time," said Lucy.

"All men stare at your boobs, Lucy. So does Thomas," said Angie.

"And Preston. Not wearing a bra will do that," said Laura.

"Hey, if you've got it, flaunt it. I may get some looks, but Donald's was always creepy. Gave me the willies," said Lucy.

"I agree. To be honest, if we had to pick one of us as a killer, I would have picked him. But I guess someone else got to him first," said Angie.

There was a pause until Lucy spoke. "Do you think she could have done it? Did Maddie kill him?"

Madison froze, waiting to hear the answer. She heard Laura snort.

"Are you kidding?" asked Laura. "Maddie kill Donald? Never in a million years. He was a jerk, but she would have divorced him, not stabbed him."

"How do you know?" asked Angie. "Any woman can be pushed past their breaking point. Maybe Donald went too far."

"You know he'd have put her through hell if she'd asked for a divorce," said Lucy. "He'd have taken her for everything."

"Would you two listen to yourselves? This is Maddie we're talking about," said Laura. "The woman who will avoid stepping on ant trails when she walks. She wouldn't kill Donald. And even if she did, this would be the stupidest way imaginable."

"Would it?" asked Lucy. "Karl's murder six weeks ago, and now this? It would be easy to make people think someone's running amok on the lake."

"Maybe someone is running amok, taking out lake goers," said Angie. "I mean look who's dead. Karl and Donald. Both had enemies."

"They were ruthless in business. That's for sure," said Lucy.

"I heard the two of them had a big fight," said Angie. "A week before Karl died."

"I know," said Laura. "Donald barged into a dinner party at Karl's house. Sharie told me about it. They went into Karl's office and everyone could hear them yelling. Donald left not long after, but Karl never came back to dinner. Sharie was left to entertain her guests on her own. Karl never told her what they'd argued about."

Madison put her hand to her mouth. Donald had never mentioned his argument with Karl.

"There were rumors that Donald might have killed Karl," said Angie.

"I know. But he had an alibi," said Laura. "He was out of town the night Karl died."

Madison thought back to the weekend they'd found Karl murdered. Donald had gone to his corporate headquarters for a fundraising event, but that was only three hours away. She recalled when he'd returned home. He'd been distant and short and had barely spoken to her before he'd gone into the bedroom and closed the door. But that behavior was normal for Donald, so she had thought little of it.

"Well, considering Donald's dead now, and assuming Maddie didn't do it, I'm thinking they were both targeted by the same person," said Angie.

"It's possible," said Laura. "But let's be honest. There are lots of suspects. Even our own husbands."

Madison straightened.

"What are you talking about?" asked Lucy. "Thomas a suspect?" She chuckled. "Now that's funny."

"Is it?" asked Laura. "He lost a lot of money on that investment Karl recommended. Preston did too. I know they had a few contentious shareholder meetings. Preston said Thomas was furious with the way Karl was handling the funds. Preston wasn't too thrilled either."

"That doesn't make him a killer," said Lucy.

"Sam wouldn't have the balls to kill anyone. I can barely get him to argue with me," said Angie.

"He wasn't happy when you got drunk and flirted with Karl. And Karl flirted back," said Laura. "As I recall, you two got a little touchy-feely in the hot tub during the Fourth of July party."

Madison heard Angie gasp.

"What are you saying? Are you implying I slept with Karl?" asked Angie.

Madison held her breath.

"Did you?" asked Laura. "Lord knows you wouldn't be the first. Sharie knew he was unfaithful."

"That is ridiculous. I've never cheated on Sam." Angie's voice rose in anger.

"Oh, keep your shorts on. It's just us," said Laura. "It stays within these walls."

"I made out with him once," said Lucy.

Madison dropped her jaw.

'What?" asked Laura.

"Really?" asked Angie.

Madison heard Lucy sigh. "It was stupid. It was last year, during some picnic. I'd had a few drinks and so had he. I went inside to get more beer from the basement, and I dropped them and one can exploded. He'd come down to get some rafts for the lake and he helped me clean up the mess. We were laughing about something, and before I knew it, he was up against me, telling me how he'd always wanted to kiss me. Thomas and I, we were sort of going through a rough patch, so I let him. We made out for a few minutes before it started to get more intense, and I came to my senses and left."

"How come you never said anything?" asked Angie.

"It wasn't one of my prouder moments," said Lucy. "It was the closest I've come to cheating on Thomas."

Her heart heavy, Madison decided she'd heard enough and she should stop eavesdropping on her friends. She stepped out of the hall and into the main part of the house.

Laura saw her and stood. "Maddie, are you okay?"

Madison's legs still felt a little wooden, but she made it to the couch and sat. Laura went into the kitchen and got her some water.

"How are you?" asked Angie. "Did you get some rest?"

Madison rubbed her tired eyes. "I'm alive. That's about all I can say."

"You poor thing. I can't imagine what you've been through," said Lucy.

Laura brought the water and put it in front of Madison. "Here, have something to drink. You hungry? You've barely eaten."

Madison sipped her water. "No. I can't think about food."

"You should eat. You need to keep up your strength," said Angie.

"Maybe later," said Madison.

Laura sat beside her. "You're staying with me and Preston for now."

Madison shook her head. "No. That's not necessary. I'll be okay."

Laura cocked her head. "Honey. You can't go home. Your house is a crime scene."

Madison groaned. "Hell. You're right." She made a sad chuckle. "I guess I've got nowhere else to go." She swallowed. "You sure I'm not imposing on you and Preston?"

Laura smiled. "Are you kidding? Preston's the one who suggested it the moment he heard what happened. In fact, he even suggested I find you an attorney."

Madison raised her head. "What? An attorney? What do I need an attorney for?"

Laura's face dropped. "Are you serious? You found your husband dead in your bed with a knife from your kitchen. Unless the killer walks into Sheriff Biggles office sometime soon and confesses, you are likely the main suspect. You need a lawyer."

"But I didn't do it," said Madison.

"I know that, but they don't," said Laura.

"You have to protect yourself," said Angie. "It's the smart thing to do."

"And you don't talk to anyone without your attorney present," said Lucy. "I don't care what they tell you."

"Do you really think I'm a suspect?" asked Madison. Her heart thumped as she considered that possibility.

Laura met the gazes of Lucy and Angie.

"What is it?" asked Madison.

Laura sighed. "Biggles wants to talk to you. He's called in help from a captain friend of his. He's bringing in some detectives to help with the investigation. They'll want to talk to you, too."

"So you need an attorney," said Lucy.

Madison sat back. "Shit."

"With icing on top," said Laura.

"But somebody killed Karl too. Isn't it likely it was the same person?" asked Madison.

"It's likely," said Angie.

"But that doesn't help," said Lucy.

"Why not?" asked Madison.

The women hesitated and Madison waited.

"Not if they think you killed Karl, too," said Laura.

**

Biggles sat back in his worn leather office chair and sighed. He sipped on his strong black coffee, wishing it was something stronger. It had been a long, unpleasant seventy-two hours. It had taken three days to get the body transported to the city coroner and for the forensics team to finish their investigation of the house. Biggles had been there for most of it and when he wasn't, he was here in his office, filling out reports.

His friend, Frank Lozano, was sending two of his best detectives to help with the investigation. One of them had been injured in the Makeup Artist case and they'd needed a few days for him to get medical clearance, but Biggles was thankful for the help. This was more workload than he could handle, and his two deputies were not trained for multiple murder investigations. Lozano would get the results from the coroner and forensics as would Biggles, and Biggles would supply all the evidence from Karl's murder so Lozano's men would be up to speed.

He checked his watch. It was almost six p.m. Lozano's men were expected at any time. Lozano had mentioned that they'd helped crack the Makeup Artist Case, and they had his full confidence.

Biggles trusted Lozano. They'd been friends for twenty years and had worked together briefly before Biggles transferred from the San Diego PD and moved up to the lake. Lozano had owned a cabin on Secret Lake for several years, which is how Biggles had learned about the sheriff's position when it had opened up. It was the best move he'd made, and he loved the job. The community was small and the crime, minor. He could go fishing on the weekends and wave to his neighbors as they drove by on their boats. It was an idyllic lifestyle, until now.

Taking the last sip of his coffee, he eyed the machine for more, although he knew he should stop. He'd never sleep that night, but after the last few days, he didn't think he would anyway.

There was a rap on the door. "Come in," he said, putting his mug down.

The door opened and two men stood there. One blonde, tall, and muscular with khakis and a blue button-down shirt. The other had a slimmer, but similar build, had longer dark hair, and wore worn jeans and a loose-fitting red t-shirt.

"Sheriff Biggles?" asked the blonde one.

Biggles stood and extended his hand. "That's me. You Lozano's men?"

The blonde one nodded and shook his hand. "We are. I'm Detective Gordon Daniels. This is Detective Aaron Remalla."

"How you doing, Sheriff?" asked Remalla, shaking the sheriff's hand. "We hear you got some problems at the lake."

"That's one word for it," said Biggles. "Please have a seat. Can I get you something?"

"No, thank you," said Daniels.

"We're good. Thanks." said Remalla. "But I'm glad to see you have a coffee machine."

"Couldn't live without it. Caffeine is my drug of choice."

"Good thing. We should get along just fine," said Remalla.

"Rem can drink two-day-old microwaved coffee and come back for more," added Daniels. "It's disturbing."

Biggles smiled. "I got you beat. I once drank coffee that had been sitting for a week and had a bug floating in it."

"A bug?" asked Remalla, his face paling.

"I figure he wouldn't drink much," said Biggles, chuckling.

"You win," said Remalla, holding up his hands.

"I never thought I'd see the day," said Daniels.

Biggles relaxed. He liked these two. You never knew what to expect with cops. They could be hard-nosed, play by the book purists, or laid-back, play it by ear, freethinkers. Biggles figured these two were the latter. "You two been up to Secret Lake before?"

"We have," said Daniels. "Lozano's let us use his cabin a few times. It's nice up here. Which is why this is so surprising."

"Two murders in six weeks?" asked Remalla.

"It's crazy. If you'd told me this was gonna happen, I'd have laughed you off. This is a quiet community. Everyone knows everyone. There are no secrets around here," said Biggles.

"Maybe that's the problem," said Daniels.

"How do you mean?" asked Biggles.

"Maybe some secrets have yet to come out," said Remalla.

Biggles considered that. "Well, there're secrets and then there're rumors. I've heard 'em both."

"What's the difference?" asked Remalla.

"Depends which ones you want to believe," said Biggles.

"And which ones do you believe?" asked Daniels.

Biggles studied his coffee cup. "That, gentleman, is why you're here. I'm hoping you can help me figure that out."

Daniels and Biggles gave each other a look. "Then let's get started," said Daniels.

Remalla pointed at the coffee machine. "Then we better get that thing going because we're going to need it."

Biggles groaned and rubbed his face. He definitely would not be sleeping tonight.

FIVE

....

Madison paced the deck on Laura's patio, rubbing her shoulders. The day was warm, and the sun was out, but a chill swept though her. Madison still struggled to accept it. His pale, lifeless face flashed in her mind and she grimaced. Would she ever be able to forget it?

The lawyer Laura had found for her was on his way. Madison had not asked many questions about him, but Laura had assured her he was top notch and would represent her well. Madison could still not fathom needing an attorney. She'd done nothing wrong. But she knew Laura was right. The spouse was always the first suspect, and if they tried to link her to Karl's death, too, well that would be disastrous. She could be looking at life in prison. Her chest constricted at the thought.

The doorbell rang from inside. Madison stopped pacing and waited. It was only a minute later when the back-patio door slid open and Laura stepped out, a man behind her. He wore a blue suit and navy tie, with a white shirt. He was tall, had short dark blonde hair and wore black-framed glasses like Clark Kent.

Standing there, holding his briefcase, he stared at her. "Hi, Madison."

She narrowed her eyes. "Stevie? Stevie Webster?"

He put his briefcase on a deck chair. "Well, it's Stephen, or Steve. But yes, it's me."

Laura pointed. "You know him?"

"We went to high school together," said Madison.

He nodded. "Yes. Then you went off to that swanky private school, and I went to the local community college."

"That's right," said Madison. "I heard you made it to law school."

"I did. And I hear you're an artist."

"I am." She looked him up and down, trying not to be obvious. Stephen Webster had been a scrawny, shy kid who'd always turned red whenever she'd talked to him. But they'd occasionally shared a lunch hour together, and she'd sat next to him a few times. Video games and superhero comics were his favorite things to talk about if she remembered correctly. He'd turned into a nice-looking man.

"Well, I guess there's no need for introductions," said Laura.

"Not really," said Stephen. Loosening his tie, he walked to the railing. "You have a lovely home. The lake is beautiful."

"Thank you," said Laura. "You should see Maddie's place though. It's the granddaddy on the lake."

"I'm sure it is. You've always had good taste, Madison," he said to her.

Madison wasn't sure what to say. They were out here having light conversation when the reason he was here was to talk about her murdered husband.

"Can I get you something to drink?" asked Laura.

"Water would be great," said Stephen.

"Maddie?"

Madison nodded. "Water's fine. Thanks."

Laura went inside, and Madison walked up beside Stephen. "I'm guessing you know what happened."

"That's why I'm here."

Madison nodded. "Just so you know, I didn't do it. I didn't kill Donald."

He glanced over at her. "All I need you to do is tell me the truth, and I'll handle the rest."

"I am telling you the truth."

He held the gaze. "Ok. So why don't you tell me everything."

Maddie held her breath. Until that point, she had not considered what hiring an attorney would mean. The issues between her and Donald had been private, with Madison maybe telling Laura a few things, but not everything. But now she was standing here with a man who potentially held her future in her hands. A man she'd known since grade school. Biting her bottom lip, she turned and leaned back against the railing.

He sighed, slid his jacket off, and placed it on the back of a chair. "Listen. I know this will not be easy. No marriage is perfect. But if you and Donald had issues, I need to know. If they think you may have done this, I need to refute anything they could use against you. You will have to trust me."

"I haven't even hired you yet. How do I know you're any good?"

He offered her a satisfied smile. "Madison, I'm not that shy kid anymore who reads Spiderman comics. I'm a bad-ass criminal attorney who'll do whatever it takes to protect my clients. Laura didn't find me because I went to an ivy league school and graduated at the top of my class. She found me because I'm good at what I do. I'm expensive as hell, but I'm worth every penny. I don't lose, and if I do, I take it personally. So I make sure I don't. On top of that, I like you. I've always liked you. Full disclosure – I had a crush on you. I thought you were the prettiest girl in school. And I'll be damned if I'm going to let my grade school crush go to prison."

Standing there, with his arms crossed, he waited for her to answer. A million thoughts swirled through her head, and her heart raced. "You might not like what you hear."

"I'm not here to judge you. I'm here to keep you safe."

His words intrigued her. He could have said a million other things, but he told her he'd keep her safe. No man had ever said that to her.

Hugging herself and feeling strangely on the verge of tears, she nodded. "Ok."

He gestured toward the patio couch. "Have a seat and we'll get started."

Maddie sighed and did as he asked. He opened his briefcase, pulled out a pad of paper and a pen. Laura returned with the water and then left, giving them privacy.

Stephen tapped his pen on the pad. "Ready?"

She sipped her water. "As I'll ever be."

He waited, and she started with what had happened. The dinner, the return home, the argument, her boat ride, coming home and finding Donald.

He wrote in his pad, asking occasional questions, then asked her about her relationship with Donald. Madison hesitated, but knew she had to talk about it, so she started from the beginning. Her father, her pregnancy, marrying Donald, the money, the deterioration of the marriage, and the abuse. It was a long hard story to tell. Stephen made notes on his paper throughout, his face inscrutable.

When she finished, she ran her fingers through her hair and rubbed her scalp. Her head throbbed. "What do you think?"

He put the pad down and sat back. "Who else knows about your relationship with Donald?"

"No one, really. Laura knows some things, but I kept the worst of it to myself."

"Is there a life insurance policy on Donald?"

Madison cocked her head. She hadn't considered that. "You know, I don't know. He may have something through work. I never created one though."

He nodded. "How do you benefit from his death, other than the obvious?"

"Excuse me?" asked Madison.

"Sorry to be so blunt, but this is what the sheriff will look for. Donald was abusive, so that's a motive. Is there another? If there's a huge life insurance policy on him, that's important."

"I don't need Donald's money," said Madison.

"But what if you divorced? Did you have a prenup?"

Madison moaned. "No. We didn't."

"Then he could have taken quite a bit if he'd wanted. Could he have taken the cabin?"

Madison considered that. "Probably. He certainly could have made a claim on it. He knew how much I loved it and how long it's been in the family."

Stephen rubbed his jaw. "Okay." He paused. "Is there anything else I need to know? Anything else that might be pertinent to this case?"

Madison shivered. "I can't think of anything." She shook her head. "It doesn't look good, does it?"

"Depends. I need to talk to the sheriff. Find out what the crime scene shows. Get more information. Then we'll go from there. I hear he's got some outside detectives coming in to help."

"I hear that too."

"Are they going to talk to you?"

"Biggles called. They want to meet tomorrow."

"Ok. I'll be there. You answer only what I say to answer. Nothing more." He paused. "I'm guessing you're hiring me?"

Madison rubbed her hands together. "I'm guessing you're taking my case?"

"Absolutely. You want to know my fee?"

"Doesn't matter. I'll pay it. Even if I have to mortgage the house."

He leaned forward, his elbows on his knees. "Don't worry. I have no intention of letting you go to jail." He put a hand on her wrist. "Trust me."

Madison stared at her toes, considering everything, and prayed he was right.

**

Remalla bit into his cheeseburger and juice dribbled down his chin. Daniels grabbed a napkin and handed it to him. "You know, there are tribes in South America with more couth than you."

Rem wiped his face and spoke with a mouthful of burger. "Couth? What the hell is couth?"

Daniels picked up his turkey sandwich. "It's what you wish you had. Refinement."

Rem grunted and grabbed a fry. "Yeah, well, I'd like to see how 'couth' those tribesmen are when they haven't eaten someone all day."

Daniels stopped in mid-bite. "Someone?"

"Yeah. I read about this tribe that cannibalized strangers that walked into their camp. The locals kept wondering why all their tourists kept disappearing. Turns out the tribe was eating them." He took another bite of his burger.

Daniels looked at his sandwich, shook his head, and put it down.

"What? Aren't you hungry?" asked Remalla. He reached over and grabbed a chip off Daniels' plate.

"One of these days, I'll learn," said Daniels.

"Don't count on it," said Rem.

Daniels leaned back on the sofa. They'd made it back to Lozano's cabin a few hours after meeting with Biggles and crashed. After grabbing a quick breakfast that morning, they'd visited the crime scene at the Vickers' cabin and spent the next several hours speaking to neighbors and reviewing the reports on Karl's Scott's murder, comparing the two crime scenes. Hungry and tired, they'd stopped at the local diner on their way back to the cabin that evening since they hadn't eaten since breakfast. Daniels reached over and picked up a file folder. After flipping it open, he looked at the crime scene photos of Donald Vickers, and the picture of his wife, Madison. "What's your gut feeling about this case?"

Rem swallowed a bite of his burger. "It's interesting. Two murders on Secret Lake of prominent people in a six-week period. It's definitely not random." He pushed up from the ground where he was sitting cross-legged and sat next to Daniels on the couch.

"You think it's the same person?"

"Or two people working together."

Daniels scratched his head. He opened a second file and perused the photos of Karl Scott. "Scott was stabbed. Vickers had his throat cut, probably while he was sleeping. Why the difference?"

Rem licked his fingers. "I don't know. Maybe Scott pissed off our perp enough to cause him to react, and he gets stabbed. Now that our guy has killed someone, he's more comfortable with the next one. Plans it out. Goes for Vickers when he knows he won't fight back. Less risk."

"You make it sound like it could be a serial killer."

Rem shrugged. "Unlikely, but maybe. Stranger things have happened."

Daniels held up the picture of Madison Vickers. "What about her? You think she did it?"

Rem took the picture and studied it. Daniels picked up his sandwich and took a bite. "I don't know," said Rem. "She is the spouse. I suppose if we do enough shoveling, we'll find some dirt and a motive."

Daniels chewed. "Biggles didn't seem to think she did it."

Rem grabbed a fry. "Biggles knows her. She's a member of the community here. He fished with her dad once. He's not going to accuse her. That's why we're here."

"To be the bad guys."

"Yup." Rem popped the fry in his mouth. "The problem is Scott. Maybe Madison killed her husband, but why would she kill Karl Scott? Biggles couldn't tell us of any meaningful connection between the two."

"He might have. Donald Vickers had an argument with Scott not long before Scott was found murdered. They had some sort of business relationship."

"Nobody knows what the argument was about though. Was it about business, money, or the Knicks game?"

"Or a woman?"

Rem pointed. "Exactly. Biggles said Scott didn't always keep his hands to himself. Maybe Madison Vickers reciprocated."

"Well, if that's true about Scott, then all the husbands around here are potential suspects." He pulled out Karl Scott's photo. "Look at this guy. It's like he stepped out of a Tequila ad. Older, salt and pepper hair, virile, tan, in great shape, and wealthy as shit."

"It's like looking in a mirror," said Rem, smiling.

"You mean the fun-house mirror?"

Rem's face fell. "You're just jealous."

"I like my physique just fine. No need to improve on perfection." He popped a potato chip in his mouth.

Rem rolled his eyes. "Ok, Don Juan. I see your point. We need to keep our ears open for other potential suspects. Not just Mrs. Vickers. What about Sharie Scott, Karl's wife? She'd definitely have motive."

Daniels held his sandwich. "She wasn't home, remember? And if she hired someone, he sure did a sloppy job. No hit man would stab someone to death. Way too messy."

Rem nodded. "What about money? We can't ignore that. There's a lot around here."

Daniels flipped through the files. "True, but these women have plenty of money of their own. They don't need to kill somebody to get more."

Rem picked up the last piece of his burger. "Not unless a messy divorce could take it away, or maybe reveal secrets they'd rather keep hidden." He ate the last bite.

"Maybe. That's something to explore."

Rem took a swig of his soda. "My money's on Madison. Her story doesn't add up. She goes out on the lake in the dead of night after coming home from dinner with her friends? Doesn't make sense. Why not go to bed?"

"It's a good question. One we'll have to ask her tomorrow."

"There's more to that story. What if they came home after dinner and a few drinks, have a fight, he goes to bed, she takes out her anger and slices his throat open? She hopes Scott's death will make this seem like there's a crazy person stalking people on the lake. Then she hops in her boat, takes a ride, dumps any bloody clothes she was wearing, and comes back after an hour and 'finds' the body."

"Then why not dump the knife too? Why leave it behind?"

"I don't know. Maybe she thinks it looks better to leave it. Make it look more like an impulsive kill. Or maybe in her panicked state, she just forgets it."

Daniels munched on a chip and settled back on the couch. "It's definitely possible."

"I'd say probable."

"We can't assume anything though. It's also an easy way for a killer to make her look guilty. What if he's watching? Sees Madison go out on the boat, he goes after Vickers, and disappears, leaving Madison to explain it all."

Rem raised a brow. "Really? A supposed killer is watching the house as the couple comes home from dinner, on the hopes he'll get an opportunity to kill the husband and blame the wife. It's pretty thin."

"It's toast thin, but it's not paper thin," said Daniels, taking a drink of his water.

Rem eyed him. "Toast thin?"

Daniels shrugged. "Just something to consider."

"I'll use that next time I'm on the stand."

"You're welcome."

Rem shook his head. "What time are we meeting with Madison Vickers?"

Daniels checked his watch. "Ten a.m., at her friend's house. Biggles will pick us up at a quarter till. Her lawyer will be present."

"I figured." Rem stifled a yawn. "We better get some shuteye. It's gonna be another long day tomorrow."

"You want to update Lozano?" asked Daniels.

"Nah. It's late. We'll call him tomorrow."

"K." Daniels stood, crumpled his wrapper and tossed it in the diner bag. "How's your gut? Remember, you're supposed to be taking it easy. Doctor's orders."

Rem patted his stomach. "Feels good as new. Doctors worry too much."

"Well, considering the amount of food you've put through it, it's definitely working fine. Speaking of which, you want the bathroom first?"

A noise that sounded like a scrape against glass and then a bump against a wall made Daniels stop. Rem froze, his eyes widening. "What was that?"

Daniels looked toward a side window. The blinds were open, and it faced nothing but trees but in the room's light, all he could see was his reflection.

Rem stood. "An animal?"

"Doubtful, but maybe."

"Maybe?" Rem glanced toward the window. "Don't you watch reality TV? God knows what's out in the woods at night."

Daniels pulled his weapon from his holster and walked toward the front door. "Let's go find out."

Rem paled. "Are you serious? Are you going out there?"

Daniels face fell. "Come on, partner. You've faced down drug dealers, murderers, and serial killers. And this scares you?"

Rem took out his weapon and lowered his voice as he stepped closer. "I'm all for a little nature. I'll take a long hike in the woods anytime. But it's pitch black out there. I can handle a serial killer but a Big Foot is a different story. Did you know they've had sightings about an hour away from here?"

Daniels sighed. "If there's one thing I can promise you, it is not a Big Foot. Come on." He turned the knob on the front door and opened it. It creaked, but swung wide and Daniels stepped out, his weapon pointed down. Rem followed.

The wind blew softly and tree limbs swayed, but there was no other sound. Daniels continued out onto the small porch that wrapped around the cabin. Rem grabbed a flashlight from the front closet and flicked it on. He followed close behind. Reaching the edge of the porch that turned toward the side of the cabin where the sound had originated, Daniels peered around. Rem was so close, Daniels could hear him breathing. "Would you relax?" he whispered.

"Relax? With something out here? No way." He swiveled the flashlight.

Daniels saw nothing, and he walked toward the window.

"Where are you going?" asked Rem.

"It's called checking the area." He reached the window, looked in, and then turned and faced the trees. It was dark, but the stars were out and it was a peaceful night. He holstered his gun.

"Anything?" asked Rem.

Daniels pointed. "There."

He swung the light, but the beam did not penetrate the trees. "What? I can't see anything."

"Bear scat. A big piling heap." He pointed toward the ground.

"Are you kidding?" Rem squinted.

Daniels swore he could hear Rem's heart beating. "No, bonehead. It's a pile of leaves."

Rem's jaw dropped, and he relaxed the arm holding his gun. "You scared the hell out of me."

Daniels held back a grin. "Come on, Tonto."

Rem glanced at the small pile on the ground as a gust of wind blew and it scattered some of the leaves. "Very funny." He followed Daniels to the front door where Daniels paused, scanning the property.

Rem groaned. "What is it now, Kimosabe? Is Big Foot out there?"

Daniels glanced at him. "No, but maybe something with a smaller shoe size."

"What are you talking about?"

"Karl and Donald might not be the only two men who were targets. We might have drawn some attention."

Rem flicked his light back to look. "You think someone was here?" His demeanor shifted from fear to confidence when he realized he was dealing with a human and not an animal.

"There's no evidence of it. Nothing at the window, and it's too dark to check the woods, but my hairs are up. Something's not right."

Rem holstered his gun. "Good. I'll take that any day over Big Foot."

Daniels eyed his partner. "Come on. Let's get some sleep."

SIX

....

Madison rubbed her eyes. She'd had little sleep. Nightmares plagued her, and she'd had the disturbing feeling that she was being watched, even though she knew it was foolish. Her blinds were closed, and Laura's home was secure. Now that there'd been two murders, doors were locked, everyone's security systems were on, and outside lights were blazing. But Madison still got up during the night and looked out the window. She saw nothing. Secret Lake kept silent watch, and the trees were the only observers to her inquiry. Sighing, she'd dropped the blinds and returned to bed, only to stare up at the ceiling. Questions ran through her mind. Two detectives would question her soon. Would they believe her? Would they arrest her? Would Stephen be able to get her out of this mess? Was he single?

That last question made her snort in disbelief. That was absolutely the last question she needed to be asking. Her husband wasn't even cold, and she was curious about another man? She chalked it up to being exhausted and overwhelmed and closed her eyes, hoping to sleep.

Now, six hours later, she stifled another yawn. Her head felt like it was stuffed with feathers and she wondered how she would get through this interview.

"Tired?" asked Stephen. He'd arrived thirty minutes earlier to help her prepare. They'd discussed everything the day before, but he wanted to be thorough.

"Yes."

He studied her. "You remember what we talked about? Offer nothing extra. Only answer the questions they ask. No need to elaborate. I'll jump in if they ask something I don't want you to answer."

"I have nothing to hide."

"I know, but they're looking for a killer, and you're the obvious suspect. You have to be smart and protect yourself."

She nodded. "Okay."

There was a knock on the office door, and Laura poked her head in. "You two okay? You need anything?" They were in Preston's home office, but Preston had gone into the city to work.

"Just great," said Madison, sighing. "Just enjoying my last moments of freedom."

"Stop it," said Laura. "You are not going to jail."

Madison couldn't help but chuckle. "You and I have seen plenty of true crime TV shows. Spouses, guilty or not, go to prison all the time."

"Would you tell her to stop worrying?" Laura asked Stephen. "That's why you're here."

"She's right," said Stephen. "Stop worrying. I know it's scary, but we'll get you through it."

"Biggles tries to take you to jail, and he'll have to deal with me," said Laura. "I'll make such a stink, he'll compare skunk spray to a blooming rose."

"It's not Biggles I'm worried about," said Madison. "It's the other two."

"You let me handle them," said Stephen.

"Just tell them the truth," said Laura. "They have no evidence against you."

Madison made eye contact with Stephen. She started to answer when the doorbell rang. Her body instantly reacted. A chill ran through her and her stomach clenched. "Here we go."

Laura put a hand on her shoulder. "Just relax. It will be fine. Stay here. I'll show them in." She nodded at Stephen and left the room.

Madison stood and shook out her hands. She heard Laura answer the door and the sound of male voices. Biggles' familiar baritone traveled and grew closer. The door pushed open and Madison turned to face Biggles and two men, both tall and lean with muscle, but one with sandy blonde hair and the other with long dark wavy hair. Their faces exhibited strong features; the blonde with sharp cheekbones and pointed jaw, the other with piercing eyes and a brooding expression, and they exuded a quiet confidence.

Biggles stepped inside. "Madison."

"Sheriff Biggles," she answered.

Stephen rose from his seat and held out his hand. "I'm Steve Webster, Madison's attorney."

Biggles shook his hand and introduced the two men. "This is Detective Gordon Daniels and Detective Aaron Remalla. They came in to help me with this case."

Madison shook their hands.

"Thank you for talking with us," said the blonde who was Detective Daniels. "We're sorry for your loss."

"Thank you," said Madison.

"We know this is a difficult time, but we appreciate you helping us out," said Remalla.

"Why don't we have a seat?" said Stephen, gesturing toward a round conference table in the corner with four chairs around it.

Biggles gestured toward a side chair by a small sofa. "I'll sit over here."

Laura walked in with a tray and five glasses. She placed it on the table. "I brought you all some water. Would anyone like some coffee?"

Biggles and Remalla both answered yes at the same time. Madison asked for some as well.

"Thank you," said Daniels, as Laura left and shut the door.

Madison sat at the table along with Stephen and the two detectives. She fiddled with the hem of her sleeve. Her heart pounded in her chest.

"Mrs. Vickers..." said Remalla.

"Madison is fine," she said. "We might as well be informal."

"Ok," said Remalla. "Madison." He paused. His astute eyes made her nervous. She felt like prey. "We'd like to talk to you about what happened the other night when your husband was murdered."

Madison breathed, seeing the scene again in her mind. "Okay."

"Before we get started, I want to remind you of your rights," said Daniels. "You obviously have an attorney. And you are not obligated to speak to us, but anything you say can be used against you in a court of law. Do you understand that?"

Madison clenched her hands. "I do."

Daniels nodded. "Good." He reached for a water glass. "Would you mind telling us what happened the night Donald was killed."

Madison looked at Stephen, who nodded at her. She took her time, gathered herself, and dove in, telling them everything that happened, up until the point that Biggles had arrived at the scene. There had been a brief pause when Laura had arrived with the coffee, but Madison finished once Laura left. She struggled through the telling at the mention of finding Donald's body but got through it.

Daniels and Remalla sipped their water and coffee as she spoke, but their body language revealed nothing of what they thought. She couldn't decide if that made her more or less nervous.

Finishing her story, she finally took a sip of her coffee, noticing that her fingers trembled.

There was a brief pause before Remalla finally spoke. "Did you touch the murder weapon?"

Madison held her breath. "Not when I saw it on the floor. But it's a knife from our kitchen. I'd used it earlier that day. I believe it was sitting in the drainer by the sink when we left for dinner."

"Your fingerprints will be on it?" asked Remalla.

"If it's the knife I used, then yes, probably," answered Madison.

"Can you tell us about the boat ride?" asked Daniels. "Why go out on the boat so late at night?"

"I told you we had an argument. I was upset. I wanted to get out of the house. Going out on the lake helps calm me."

"Did you have a lot of arguments with your husband?" asked Daniels. He casually took another sip of his water. Laura had brought in a cheese and fruit tray with the coffee and Remalla reached for a grape.

Madison glanced at Stephen, who nodded again. "We had our share of arguments."

"How many is that?" asked Remalla, eating the grape.

Madison put down her coffee. "I can't give you a solid number. Our marriage had its issues."

"What issues?"

"How about we keep these questions to the crime itself, gentleman?" asked Stephen.

"This will come out either way, Counselor. Better now than later," said Daniels.

Madison crossed her arms when Stephen didn't argue. "Donald and I hadn't been happy in a while. I'm a painter, and once I started to see some success, I think Donald felt uncomfortable with it."

"Was he threatened by it?" asked Remalla.

"Let's not put words in her mouth," said Stephen.

"Fine," said Remalla. "He didn't like you making more money. Is that it?"

Madison hesitated. "I think so, yes."

"Wasn't he successful?" asked Daniels.

"He was. I just think..." Madison stopped. She was trying hard not to elaborate, but she found it hard not to jump in and explain.

"You think what?" asked Remalla, leaning in. His eyes never left hers and she found it hard to concentrate.

"Donald envied my life. I didn't have a 9 to 5. I could do what I loved and make a good living, without needing anything from him."

"But you had money when you married him, plus an inheritance, didn't you?" asked Daniels. He helped himself to a piece of cheese.

"I did. Dad left me the cabin when he died, plus some money."

"How was your relationship with your dad?" asked Remalla.

"Don't answer that," said Stephen. "It's not relevant to the case."

"We'll know eventually," said Remalla.

"I'm fine with that," said Stephen.

Remalla took a sip of his coffee. "Did you have a prenup?"

"No," said Madison.

"So Donald could have made things nasty if you'd asked for a divorce?" asked Daniels.

"Yes. He could have."

Daniels nodded. He reached into his pocket and pulled out a small notepad and pen. He flipped the notepad open.

"You could have lost the cabin?" asked Remalla.

"Maybe," said Madison.

Remalla slid back in his seat, holding a piece of cheddar. He eyed Daniels. "Let me ask you something. These arguments with Donald. Did they ever get physical?"

Madison stilled in her seat. In her retelling of the events, she had not gotten specific about Donald's behavior toward her the night of his death. Stephen had said to leave that out unless specifically asked. Now she glanced over at him. His look told her to answer.

She played with her fingers. "Yes."

Daniels put the notepad down. "How so?"

Madison put her hands in her lap and swallowed. "He'd push me. Pull my hair. Yell in my face. Say things like he was sorry he'd met me, or married me. Or that my work was crap, and he didn't know why it sold. He'd lock me out of the bedroom and tell me to sleep in the guestroom. Told me I was ugly, and I was lucky I had him because no other man would want me."

"Did he physically strike you?" asked Remalla.

Madison bit her lip. "Yes. He slapped me a few times."

"What about the night of his death?" asked Daniels.

Madison took a breath. "He grabbed me by the throat."

Remalla's eyes darkened. "He tried to strangle you?"

"He squeezed, but then let go. His intention was to scare me, belittle me."

"What caused him to get so angry?" asked Remalla. "What were you arguing about?"

Daniels scribbled in his notepad.

Madison recalled that night. "He was angry I'd shown Laura my latest work and not him. I'd questioned him about going into work on a Saturday, and he got angry about that." She shook her head. "He also got mad that Laura mentioned how our cabin was haunted. He thought I made him look foolish in front of our friends." She rubbed her forehead. "Stupid stuff, but he was furious. I didn't help matters by telling him it was his own fault he was miserable."

Daniels wrote some more.

Remalla raised a brow. "Haunted? Is your cabin haunted?"

Daniels looked up at his partner and Remalla shrugged.

"It's an old cabin. The oldest on the lake. Strange things happen sometimes. No big deal. Donald hated it though. Didn't want to acknowledge it. Said it was all in my head."

"So Donald was verbally and physically abusive," said Daniels. "How long had that been going on?"

"About three years," answered Madison.

"Why didn't you leave him?" asked Remalla.

"Again, that has nothing to do with the case," said Stephen. "This is not psychoanalysis."

Daniels tapped his pen against the table. "Do you know of anyone else who might have a grudge against your husband?"

Madison considered that. "It's a good question. I don't know much about his work. It's possible he made some enemies there."

"Do you know of anyone who might have benefited from his death?" asked Remalla. "Any other relatives?"

"He has a mother he barely speaks to in Florida, but you'd have to talk with her. It's possible he sent her money."

"Any life insurance policies?" asked Daniels.

"None that I created," said Madison.

"What about Karl Scott?" asked Remalla. "What was his relationship with him?"

Madison took a sip of her coffee. Now that they were past the murder, she relaxed a little. Her stomach rumbled, and she reached for a grape. "Karl was a business owner and investor. He always had a deal going on and he shopped around for additional investors, most of whom lived on the lake. Donald was one of them. I don't know details because Donald didn't provide them."

"They had an argument not long before Karl died," said Daniels. "Any idea what it was about?"

Madison shook her head. "None. Donald never mentioned it. I just heard about it through the rumor mill."

"You think maybe Donald lost money because of Karl?" asked Daniels.

"I know he did. But it's hard to say how much. I mainly focused on my art," said Madison, reaching for some cheese. "And Donald never talked about his business deals with me."

"What was your relationship with Karl Scott?" asked Remalla.

Madison hesitated. "He was a friend." She put the cheese on her napkin.

"What kind of friend?" asked Daniels.

Stephen straightened. "Watch it."

"It's a legit question, counselor," said Remalla. "And very pertinent to this case."

Stephen relaxed. "Let's keep it that way. No need for insinuations."

Madison played with the handle of her mug. "It's no secret Karl was more affectionate than he should have been with some of the women around here."

"By affectionate, do you mean affairs?" asked Daniels.

"I can't be sure. You'd have to talk to his wife about that," said Madison.

"Did you have an affair with him?" asked Daniels.

"You don't have to answer that," said Stephen.

"It's a good question," said Daniels. "One we'd like an answer to."

"You're here to talk about Donald, not Karl Scott," said Stephen. "My client has nothing to do with his death."

"That's for us to determine, not you," said Remalla.

"Well then, do your job, but she does not have to answer," said Stephen.

"Does she have something to hide?" asked Remalla, his brow furrowed.

Madison observed the exchange, her stomach rumbling, but not from hunger. "He hit on me once," she said.

The men turned their attention back to her. Stephen squinted.

"Really?" asked Daniels. "What happened?"

Madison shifted in her seat. "It was last summer. It was at a party and he was drunk. I'd had a had a few myself and I'll admit, I might have flirted a bit with him. But it was harmless. I excused myself to go to the bathroom, and he followed. He cornered me outside the ladies' room and tried to kiss me. I told him no, and he told me I'd disappointed him. He thought we had a connection. I told him he was wrong, and I left."

"Nothing came of it?" asked Remalla. "Did he try again?"

"Things were different after that. I avoided him. I think he tried with others though. I wasn't the only one."

"You know anyone specifically?"

Madison recalled her friend's conversation she'd overheard. "My friend Lucy. They made out in the basement of Karl's house, but she stopped it. I overheard this though. Didn't hear more than that."

"Lucy?" asked Remalla.

"Lucy Angelo. Her husband is Thomas Angelo," said Madison. "They live on the lake."

Daniels scribbled again in his notepad. "Anyone else?" asked Daniels.

"Not that I know of," said Madison.

"You think Donald knew about Karl hitting on you?" asked Remalla.

"I never told him," said Madison.

"Would Karl have told him?" asked Remalla.

"I can't imagine why he would," said Madison.

"What about Donald? Did he have affairs?" asked Daniels.

Madison sighed. Stephen had asked her the same question the day before. "My gut tells me yes, although I don't know with whom. I wondered if that was the real reason he had to work on Saturdays, or why he came home late."

"Did you ever confront him on it?" asked Remalla.

"No. Never. To be honest, I wasn't sure I cared. Plus, I knew what would happen if I accused him. He'd fly into a rage."

Daniels and Remalla paused. Daniels took a swig of his drink, and Remalla sipped his coffee. Madison hoped the questions were over when there was a knock on the door. Laura stuck her head in. "Sorry to interrupt. Would anyone like a coffee refill?"

"Please," said Biggles, lifting his mug.

Laura entered with a pot. She refilled Biggles mug and Remalla's too. Madison waved her off. She'd barely touched her coffee. Laura winked at her as she left.

Stephen crossed his arms. "Are we done here, gentlemen?" he asked. "Any more questions?"

Daniels eyed Remalla, who tipped his head. A silent communication seemed to travel between the two.

Madison gripped her cup, hoping it was over when Remalla leaned in. "Just one." He put his elbows on the table. "Did you kill your husband, Madison?"

Madison clenched her jaw. "No. I didn't."

Remalla stared, his gaze challenging hers. "You admitted you two were unhappy, he abused you prior to and on the night he died, he may have been having an affair, he could have fought you for your home with a divorce, your fingerprints are probably on the murder weapon, you were the only one present at the time of the murder, you have no alibi, and you 'found' him," he used his fingers as quote marks, "in the bed with his throat slit. Not only that, but you have a connection to Karl Scott, who hit on you and argued with your husband a week before his death." He clasped his hands together. "It's a good thing you have an attorney with you, because if I was Biggles over there, I'm not sure I wouldn't arrest you right now."

Stephens smacked his hand on the table. "This interview is over."

Daniels closed his notepad. "It may be over today, but we're not done by a long shot."

Madison gripped the edge of the table. "I didn't kill him. I didn't kill anybody. I'm telling you the truth."

"Don't say another word, Madison. We're done talking. You have anything else you need from my client, you come through me first," said Stephen, standing.

Biggles rose from his chair. "You heard the man, detectives. Let's go."

Daniels and Remalla stood. Remalla stepped around the table. "Once we get the evidence back from the crime lab, we may serve an arrest warrant. Think about that Madison. Tell us the truth up front, and this will go a lot easier on you."

Madison sprung out of her seat. "I did nothing wrong. I didn't kill my husband." Her face flushed, and she broke out in a sweat.

"Madison..." said Stephen.

"Get your story straight then, because what you're telling us right now makes no sense," said Daniels, slipping the pad into his pocket.

"You had the means and the motive, and something tells me you might be leaving some details out," said Remalla. "Maybe you knew about that argument. Maybe you knew about an affair Donald was having and were a little more pissed about it than you let on. He got rough with you and you hit back. Understandable, only it went farther than you expected. My advice, tell that to the jury, and you might get out of prison in time to start a new life, raise a family. Don't let it be a life sentence, Madison."

Madison tried to breathe. Her mind raced, and her head pounded. Jail? For life? Everything started to spin. "I didn't do this," she said, but she barely heard herself. She reached out for the back of her chair, when something crashed to the floor.

Everyone jumped and Madison saw one of Laura's vases shattered on the ground in front of a small fireplace. Madison had seen it on the mantel earlier.

"What the...?" asked Biggles. He stepped over and squatted down, picking up one of the pieces.

The door opened. "Is everything okay?" asked Laura.

"No. The police were just leaving," said Stephen. "Would you mind showing them out?"

Madison sat as the room spun. She squeezed her temples.

"Think about what I said, Madison," said Remalla.

"We'll be in touch," said Daniels. "Madison. Counselor."

Madison looked away as the detectives and Biggles left the room. Stephen squatted next to her. "You okay?"

She wanted to put her head on his shoulder. "I'm screwed." She waited to hear him defend her, to tell her she would be okay, but when she heard nothing, the days of emotion surfaced, her eyes welled up, she dropped her head and cried.

SEVEN

....

Sharie Scott rearranged the angel figurine on a bureau, then stepped into the bathroom to check her face. Seeing her reflection, she patted her cheeks and reapplied some lipstick. She considered making another appointment with the plastic surgeon. Her nip and tuck from the previous year seemed to be losing its luster. Her eyelids drooped lower than she liked.

Sighing, she stepped away from the mirror. She would think about it later. Since Karl's death, everything seemed to droop.

Biggles and two detectives wanted to talk to her about Karl, and she'd arranged to meet them at the house. The doorbell rang, and she took one last look, smoothed her clothes, tucked her hair back, and went to answer the door.

Her and Karl's home had finally been cleaned after his death and she was ready to be home. People wondered how she could sleep in the house where Karl had died, but she had no problem with it. She'd always loved being on the lake, and it helped her feel closer to Karl.

After opening the door, she greeted Biggles, who introduced her to Detectives Remalla and Daniels. Meeting them, she couldn't help but wish she'd added more blush and worn something a little less modest. Most of the men around the lake were showing their age.

Marriage, kids, and financial worries took their toll, eventually. But these men showed no signs of that. She especially liked the blonde one.

"Can I get you gentlemen something to drink?" she asked, smiling.

Biggles followed her into the living room. "No, ma'am. We're fine."

"No, thank you," said the tall blonde one. His name was Daniels.

She waved a hand. "Oh, Sheriff. Call me Sharie. We should be on a first name basis, by now. You, too, Officer Daniels." She poked Daniels gently on the arm.

Daniels glanced at his partner, who grinned.

"You mind if we have a seat, ma'am?" asked the dark-haired one.

Sharie stared up at Daniels.

"Uh, ma'am?" he asked again.

Daniels pointed. "Do you mind if we sit, ma'am?"

Sharie giggled. "Of course. Please do."

Daniels, his cheeks red, sat along with his partner and Biggles.

"We'd like to ask you a few questions, Sharie, about Karl," said Biggles.

Sharie sat next to Daniels on the couch. "But you already know everything."

"Yes. But they're new to the case. We are re-interviewing everyone involved."

"Oh, I see." She shifted on the couch to face Daniels. "What would you like to know?"

Daniels cleared his throat and looked at his partner, who seemed to pick up on Daniels' discomfort. That grin returned, and Sharie could understand how women would like him. What was his name? Remalla. But she preferred blondes.

"Ma'am," asked Remalla, "could you tell us about the day Karl died, please?"

Sharie recalled that day, and it brought her back to stark reality. Her smile faded, and she stared off toward the backyard, feeling the heaviness in her chest. "There's not much to say. I'd been out of town. I'd talked to Karl that morning. He was fine. Said he had a slew of business meetings, but he'd be there to pick me up at the airport that afternoon. Then we'd go to dinner at Chez Lin. It's one of our favorites in town." She sighed and fiddled with her necklace. "I flew in that afternoon, but he wasn't there. I tried to contact him, but he never responded. I figured he'd gotten tied up in a business meeting and couldn't get away. It happened sometimes. I got a driver service to bring me home. When I arrived, the house was quiet. I looked for him and went into the office, and I found him."

Daniels leaned forward, his elbows on his knees. "What did you find? Sorry. I know this is hard."

She nodded, her mind still on that day. "There was blood everywhere. Karl was on the floor, face up, covered in blood." She paused. "I didn't know what to do. I was frozen." She clenched her hands together.

"Take your time, Sharie," said Biggles.

Sharie took a deep breath. "I'm sure it was just a second or two, but it felt like an eternity, when it hit me what I was seeing. Karl was dead. I wanted to scream but it wouldn't come. The only thing I could do was race for the phone, and I called Sheriff Biggles."

Remalla shifted in his seat. "Do you know of anyone who might want to hurt your husband?"

Sharie shook her head, pulling her thoughts from the past. "Oh, yes, detective. Plenty of people."

Daniels brows rose. He pulled a pad from his jacket pocket. "Why do you say that, ma'am?"

"Sharie. Ma'am is for my mother."

"Ok," said Daniels. "Sharie."

She stood and walked over to a small bar on the side of the room. After picking up a bottle, she poured herself a sliver of bourbon. "You sure you all don't want something?"

"No, thank you," said Daniels.

"Well, if you don't mind, I'm going to help myself." She sipped from the glass and the alcohol warmed her throat.

"You were saying about who would want to hurt your husband?" asked Daniels.

"Yes," she swirled her drink. "Let's see. His business partner, his investors, an ex-wife, a potential stepchild, although that's just my theory, oh, and the woman he was sleeping with, to name a few."

Daniels and Remalla's eyes widened.

"Excuse me?" asked Biggles. "How come you didn't mention this before? I asked you the same question."

Sharie picked up a magazine about interior design and fanned her face. "You asked me a few hours after finding Karl. I was a mess. I've slept since then, and I've had time to think. Now I have a clearer head. Karl had enemies. I can't deny that."

"Was his business in trouble?" asked Remalla. "Did he have money problems?"

Sharie returned to her seat next to Daniels. "Oh, heavens no. Karl always took care of himself first. That's why anyone involved in business with him might get screwed. Karl was good at spreading the wealth when there was plenty of it, which is what attracted investors, including a few people around this lake. But when the signs were there, and the sharks were swirling, Karl was the first one out, and he wasn't always as kind to his friends."

"We heard he had a fight with Donald Vickers not long before he died. Was it about that?" asked Daniels.

"Probably. Karl had a lot of fights in that room. It wasn't the first. But I suspect that fight was more about Madison." She sipped her bourbon and put it on the table, still fanning herself. It was either Daniels making her sweat or her hormones. Getting older sucked.

The men all made eye contact. "Why do you say that?" asked Daniels.

Sharie put the magazine in her lap. "Madison Vickers is a beautiful woman and the men around this lake noticed. Donald was an asshole, but very possessive. He caught any man looking at her, and he let them know about it."

"Did Karl look at Madison?" asked Daniels.

"All the time. He looked at many women all the time, but there was something about Madison..." She clenched the magazine.

The men paused. "You mentioned a woman Karl was sleeping with. Was it her?"

Sharie shook off her reverie. "I have no idea, but I always wondered. There was a night we had a party here. Everyone was drinking, lips were loose and so were bodies. I know Karl may have a hit on more than a few women. I made a few passes myself." She caught the look from the men. "Oh, gentlemen. Don't be such prudes. Karl and I were very open about our interests in the other sex. We weren't foolish enough to believe we would be faithful to only each other for the rest of our lives. How boring. Our only promise was not to fall in love with someone else. If that happened, then it could never work."

Daniels wrote in his notepad. "You were talking about the party?"

She nodded. "Yes, I was. Madison had disappeared for a bit. I guessed to throw up. Donald had been in the hot tub, talking about a recent business success, not the least worried about his wife's physical state. I'd been in the kitchen, supervising the staff, when I'd gone looking for Karl. He wasn't in his usual places. I was about to head into the bedroom, wondering if he'd passed out when I found him in the hallway. He told me he'd been lightheaded and had to wash his face. I asked if he wanted a protein shake and he said yes. He relied a lot on his supplements, you know, when he didn't feel well."

"His shakes are pretty good," said Biggles. "He gave me a sample once."

"Where was Madison?" asked Daniels.

"I went to the kitchen to make the drink. Karl went outside to get some air. Minutes later, Madison came into the kitchen. Her eyes were red and her hair disheveled. She looked upset. I asked her what was wrong and if she needed anything. She waved me off, told me she was fine, but she was leaving. She didn't even look for Donald. She just left."

"This was last summer?" asked Remalla.

"Yes."

"Did you ever find out what upset her?" asked Remalla.

"No. But if I remember correctly, she didn't touch alcohol afterward. Hasn't had a drop since, from what I hear."

Daniels scribbled in his pad. "But you're not sure if she had an affair with Karl?"

"I don't know. Karl didn't tell me, but I knew there was someone. He said it was nothing. Just a fling. I believed him. But it was someone on the lake. I'm sure of it. It would be too hard to hide if it wasn't."

"What about Lucy Angelo?" asked Remalla.

Sharie rolled her eyes. "It wouldn't surprise me if it was. She loves to have men look at her. She's usually missing half her clothes. I doubt her husband Thomas satisfies her. He strikes me as a limp fish."

"Anybody else?" asked Daniels.

"Their little group is all suspicious. Angela Desmond and her husband Samuel. Angela drinks like a fish, and her husband is as boring as a golf game. I wouldn't blame her if Karl caught her eye.

And that Laura Benoff. She's a lioness around her husband Preston. Defends him to the death." She paused. "If they only knew..."

Daniels bobbed his head up from his writing. "Knew what?"

Sharie played with the pages of the magazine. "I had a brief fling with...one of their husbands."

Biggles mouth dropped open. "You did? Which one?"

"Oh, Sheriff, a lady never kisses and tells. And stop acting so surprised. That's nothing. This lake is aptly named. The people around it have their secrets. It's nothing new. Most of the people here have too much money and time, and not much sense. I have to admit, I'm one of them."

"When did this happen?" asked Biggles.

"Oh. Not recent. Maybe two or three years now. It didn't last long."

"Did Karl know?" asked Daniels.

"Yes. Of course."

"What about the man's wife?" asked Remalla.

"Not that I know of. I suspect I would have heard if she'd figured it out. Everyone would have known."

"Would she have confronted you?" asked Remalla.

"Probably. I doubt he told her though, not if he wants to stay alive, or married."

"Are you saying she would get violent?" asked Daniels.

Sharie took another sip of her drink. "What wife wouldn't be angry if her husband was diddling the neighbor? But from what I see now, she loves her husband. They seem to be happy. Maybe he just strayed that one time."

"Do you think that could have some connection to Karl's death?" asked Daniels.

Sharie threw out a hand. "Don't be silly. It was years ago and water under the bridge. If I thought it did, though, you'd be the first to know."

Remalla nodded. "Anybody else we should know about, who might have been a threat to Karl?"

"You mean did I sleep with someone else?" She tipped her head. "No. At least no one around here. And not anyone married. I've learned that's too messy. Single men only please."

Daniels asked more questions about Karl's business deals and other potential investors and business issues, but she couldn't offer much in that area. She knew little about who would want Karl dead when it came to money. She only worked part time now with her interior design business because she'd wanted to spend more time with Karl. Sharie had no problem being the pampered wife, and Karl loved his role as the provider, although she'd always had plenty of money of her own. They'd had a happy life together. A lump in her throat swelled.

"What about his ex-wife?" asked Daniels.

"We talked to her," said Biggles. "She was cleared, as was the stepchild you mentioned, Sharie. There were issues, but we could find no evidence that they had anything to do with this. Nor did Karl's death benefit them."

Sharie shrugged. "You say one thing, I say another. They may not have held the knife, but they sucked the life out of him in their own way."

"Unfortunately, there's no arrest warrant for that," said Remalla.

"Good thing. The jails are overcrowded as it is," said Daniels. "Plus, we'd be working a lot of overtime."

Sharie smiled. "I suppose your girlfriend wouldn't like that."

Daniels hesitated. "No, she wouldn't."

"Especially with a newborn," said Remalla. "He's a new dad."

Sharie tried not to look deflated. "Girlfriend? Not wife?" Perhaps there was some hope.

"Not yet," said Daniels. He fiddled with the notepad in his hand.

"He's workin' on it," said Remalla.

Sharie placed the magazine on the coffee table. "Lucky lady."

"She is," said Remalla. "He's pretty lucky, too. I wonder how he did so well. He rarely comes out of his cave dwelling."

"It's called the bat signal, partner," said Daniels.

Sharie smiled, enjoying seeing the banter between the two. "I like you two. I'm glad you're working with Sheriff Biggles to find Karl's murderer."

"We have every intention of finding him, or her," said Daniels. "But we have to ask, did you have anything to do with your husband's murder?" His kind eyes turned serious.

Sharie held her hands in her lap. "It's a fair question. The sheriff asked the same thing. But no. I had nothing to do with his death. I loved Karl. We were happy. I'd planned to be with him for a long time. And I believe he felt the same about me." Her eyes filled, and she blinked unshed tears. "I miss him."

Remalla watched her as if studying a painting. "You think it was someone on the lake?"

She wiped a tear and composed herself. "If I had to bet this house on it, then I'd bet yes."

"What about Donald Vickers?" asked Daniels. "Who do you think killed him?"

Sharie sniffed. "Donald Vickers was a complicated man. He liked to act superior and hated it when Madison got more attention. He was rude to her, and I know Karl didn't care for him. Most of us only put up with him because he was with Madison. I always wondered why she didn't leave him." She sighed. "Maybe she killed him instead. He was a terrible husband. Why wouldn't she want him dead?"

"Do you think the same person killed Karl and Donald? Could Madison have killed them both?" asked Remalla.

Sharie had not considered that. "That's another good question, Detective. To be honest, I don't know. If there was more going on between Madison and Karl than I knew about, then it's a very good question indeed." She took a last sip of her bourbon, wondering, but then decided they'd had enough talk of murder. She patted Daniels on the knee, letting her fingers linger. "So tell me all about your new baby, Detective Daniels. Something tells me you're not afraid of diaper duty. Am I right?"

EIGHT

....

Madison's small boat floated gently along, the only evidence of its movement being the gentle waves lapping against the still water. Madison sat in a cushioned seat, sitting quietly. There was no noise and she could see only fog. It had rolled in out of nowhere, but Madison didn't move, unconcerned about the lack of visibility. The craft cut through the soupy mix, with no one behind the wheel. Madison didn't know where she was headed, but didn't think about it. She relaxed and enjoyed the peaceful quiet. After what seemed like a few minutes, the boat bumped gently against a hard surface and came to a stop. Curious, Madison stood and stepped closer, seeing a wooden dock. The boat softly rocking, she stepped onto the hard surface. The fog was too thick to see anything.

Taking a few steps, she squinted when she thought she saw a figure in the mist. The figure approached, only a silhouette, and Madison stopped. The figure became two; one a man and the other a woman.

Madison's heart thudded. Who were these people? Why was she here?

The woman came closer, holding out her hand as the man stayed back. Madison didn't feel afraid, only uncertain. The closer she got, the more interested Madison became. Madison took a step, and as the woman began to show herself, a new presence emerged from behind the man standing on the dock. The figure was tall with broad shoulders, walking at a rapid clip. A chill swept through Madison and goose bumps broke out on her skin. This person was not curious, he was angry, and as the woman reached out, the dark figure broke out into a run. The other man turned to face the running figure, but was shoved violently to the side, and Madison took a step back.

"No," said the woman, as she reached out, but the figure shoved her away and the woman disappeared into the fog.

Fear now cutting through her, Madison turned as the menacing figure raced toward her and she ran. The dock ended, and she fell face first into icy cold water.

Madison came awake with a start, breathless, and with a scream stuck in her throat. She blinked several times, trying to remember where she was and then recognized her bedroom in Laura's house. Throwing off the covers, she swung her legs out over the bed. Damp sweat made her skin slick, and she put her head in her hands. *What the hell was that?* It was such an odd dream, but more like a nightmare. Who were those people, and what did it mean? It made no sense.

Her throat sticking, Madison reached for the glass beside the bed, but it was empty. Standing on shaky legs, she took a moment to ensure her balance before leaving the room and going into the kitchen. The house was dark, illuminated only by a soft light from the refrigerator. Madison got some water from the sink and leaned against the counter, trying to clear her head. Looking out the windows, she saw Secret Lake. The water was calm, and the trees drooped in silent observation. The clock said it was four a.m. Without thinking, she put the glass in the sink and walked to the back door. She punched the alarm code Laura had given her into the keypad and the red light turned green.

Madison opened the door to the back patio and stepped outside. A cool breeze fanned her skin, and she immediately felt like she could breathe again. She grabbed a towel laying over a chair and wrapped it around her to help against the chill, walked to the stairs, and headed down. The sandy dirt brushed against her feet, and she tried to be careful where she walked to avoid rocks and debris. Reaching the edge of the lake, she stepped in up to her ankles and the cold water made her suck in a breath, but something inside her released. All the pent-up tension, anger and fear melted away and for the first time in days, Madison relaxed. Laura and Preston's small speedboat rocked gently on the pier and Madison wished she could take it out onto the water. She imagined the wind racing through her hair and the smell of the fresh air filling her lungs. But she knew she couldn't, so she made do with walking along the shoreline.

It took about fifteen minutes, but the hidden tension in her back and shoulders began to uncoil. After the stressful interview with the detectives, her talks with Stephen, finding her murdered husband, her lack of sleep, and now that weird dream, her stress levels were at dangerous levels. She knew Laura was worried about her. Madison was worried too. Life in prison was looking more and more possible, despite what Stephen said.

Running her fingers through her hair, Madison exhaled. If she'd had a lounge chair or a hammock, she would have stretched out right there by the water and gone back to sleep. She doubted she'd get much if she went back to bed. Wondering if there was a chair nearby she could pull to shore, she turned to check and heard a snap, as if a someone had stepped on a twig. The wind was light, so the trees didn't sway hard enough to crack a branch. Madison swiveled toward the sound, which seemed to come from the side of the house. It was dark though, and difficult to see. She kept still, but saw nothing. *You're paranoid, Madison,* she thought to herself. *Your brain is in overdrive.*

Seeing a lawn chair under the second-floor landing, she went to retrieve it when the sound came again. *Snap.* She spun toward the noise and saw the small rock path that led along the side of the cabin to the front. It cut through the grass and heavy shrubs and trees. Madison squinted but again saw nothing. A stronger gust of wind blew and a shrub swayed, and for a moment, Madison could see the outline of shoulders and a head standing there, watching her through the trees.

Her blood turned freezing cold, and her heart stopped. She wanted to speak, but her throat locked up, and nothing emerged. The shadow man stood there, and she knew that he could see her watching him. She could feel it in her bones. But he didn't flinch. It was as if her fear excited him.

The breeze blew again and another gust briefly obscured, then exposed him again. His face was in total shadow, but she sensed his need to be seen. They stared as if some strange thread connected them. Madison swallowed, still frozen in place, when she distinctly heard the whispered words "I did it for you." It wasn't audible. The man did not speak, but the sentence appeared in her head like a digital crawl across her brain. He had communicated, but not with words.

A few more seconds passed, and he moved, taking a step forward. The movement pulled her out of her trance, and her legs unlocked. Running, she took the stairs back up to the deck two at a time, too afraid to check behind her. Her voice still wouldn't work, but she made it to the back door, threw it open, and slammed it shut behind her, locking it. Her breathing coming in rapid gasps, she held her chest while her heart slammed against her ribs.

Peering out the window, she saw no one, only the gentle lapping of the lake against the shore and the swaying of the trees.

"Madison?"

Madison swung around, a small yelp finally escaping her throat. She reached out and grabbed the wall.

Laura stood there in her robe. "Are you okay? What are you doing?"

Madison clutched her stomach and tried to speak. "Out there," she pointed. "There's someone out there." She tried to catch her breath. "I saw him."

Laura's face dropped. "What? Someone's outside?" She walked to the window. "Where?"

Madison tried to slow her breathing. "Down by the water. By the side of the house. He was watching me."

"PRESTON!" yelled Laura, catching Madison off guard and making her jump. "Preston, get in here!" Her eyes surveyed the backyard. "Hurry."

Preston, his hair askew and in his boxers and t-shirt, came running out of his bedroom. "Jesus, what is it?"

Laura pointed. "There's someone outside. By the side of the house. Maddie saw him."

"What?" asked Preston, scratching his head. "What are you talking about? Who would be outside at this time of night?"

Laura strode to the phone hanging on the kitchen wall. "I'm calling Sheriff Biggles."

"Wait a minute. It's four o'clock in the morning," said Preston.

"I don't care what time it is," said Laura, dialing.

Preston walked to the window. "What did you see?" Madison told him what happened down by the water. "What are you doing outside at this time of night?"

"Preston, what the hell does that matter? She saw someone watching her." Laura held the phone to her ear. "He could still be out there."

Preston opened the back door. "Don't be silly. It's probably the neighbor." He stepped out onto the porch.

"Preston, what are you doing?" asked Laura. "And why would Billy be outside at this time of day? The man takes enough sleep aids to knock out a horse. He considers ten a.m. to be an early morning."

"I don't know," said Preston from outside, rubbing his arms against the chill. "Maybe this time he couldn't sleep. Like Maddie."

"Answer the damn pho...hello, Sheriff?" said Laura.

Madison watched as Preston walked to the rail and looked below, and listened as Laura talked to Biggles, but she knew neither mattered. The man who'd been there was gone. She knew he'd left the moment she'd reached the steps. His presence had been only for her and no one else. She didn't know how she knew, but the whispered voice and the shadow man in her dream surfaced in her mind. Closing her eyes, she hugged herself.

**

Remalla bit into his waffle laden with chocolate chips, and maple syrup dripped onto his cotton t-shirt. He wiped his face and took a sip of his coffee, dabbing at the stain with his napkin.

Daniels shook his head. "It's like I never left home." He took a bite of his scrambled eggs.

"Hey, at least you don't have to change my diapers." He grinned.

"Are you wearing diapers?"

Rem dampened his napkin in his water and rubbed his shirt, creating a watermark. "No. Not yet anyway. Did you know my grandpa had to wear diapers though? He had a terrible prostate."

Daniels put down his fork. "Could we talk about something else?"

Rem put the napkin aside, satisfied his shirt was clean. "You're the one who brought up diapers."

"Actually, it was you."

Rem paused. "Oh. I guess so. Since we're talking about 'em then, how's little JP? You talk to Marjorie this morning?"

"He's fine. Doing great. He slept a full six hours last night."

Rem poked his waffle with his fork. "Well, that's good news. Is Marjorie's mom able to stay and help?"

"Yes. She'll be there to help today. Told her I'd let her know tonight how much longer we might need to stay." He added coffee to his cup from a thermos on the table.

Rem stabbed some hash browns. "This is looking more and more complicated. I was hoping it would be an open and shut case."

"You don't think it's Madison Vickers? I thought you were convinced." He sipped his coffee.

"I'm not so sure anymore. I tried to push her buttons yesterday to see what she'd do. I was hoping she'd crack." He ate the hash browns.

"But she didn't. She kept to her story too. She seemed legitimately honest about what happened." He slathered butter on his bagel. "I can't decide if she's playing us or telling the truth."

Rem swallowed. "Maybe she killed her husband, but the Karl Scott murder is throwing me. Why would she kill him? Because of some supposed encounter with Scott last summer?"

"We don't know what that encounter was. Madison said all he did was hit on her, but Sharie's story sounded like it was more than that."

"Plus, Karl Scott had plenty of other people who wanted him dead. We can't let them off the hook just yet. The argument with Donald Vickers. The fact that Sharie thought Karl was sleeping with someone else. Sharie's fling with one of the husbands. This whole lake is nuts."

Daniels sipped his coffee. "I can't argue with that. I wonder if Lozano has any idea who his neighbors are."

Rem added more syrup to his waffle and didn't miss Daniels rolling his eyes. "Lozano only comes up here a few weeks a year. I doubt he knows most of his neighbors, other than Biggles."

Daniels grunted. "Marjorie and I were thinking of coming up for a weekend sometime soon. Maybe leave little JP with his grandparents. Now I might think twice."

Rem picked up more waffle with his fork. "Don't let the murderous neighbors stop you. God knows who you're living next to in the city." He popped the bite in his mouth.

"Good point," said Daniels. "What about you? I know you were thinking of coming up here with Jacobs. Have you talked to her?"

Rem finished chewing his food. "I did. Talked to her last week."

"How is she?"

"Doing better. She's seeing a shrink. Says it's helping. Her relationship with her dad is still a little rocky, but she says it's better than before." He added cream to his coffee and swirled it with his spoon, recalling his conversation with Jill.

"What is it?" asked Daniels.

Rem looked up. "What is what?"

"I recognize that faraway look. What's on your mind?"

Rem shrugged. "Nothing. Just thinking."

Daniels squinted. "About Jacobs? Did you talk about her visiting?"

"Yes. We did. We actually talked about coming to the cabin in a few weeks, depending on how things go here."

Daniels observed him, and Rem could almost hear the wheels turning. There was little he could hide from his partner. They knew each other too well.

"You thinking twice about that?"

Rem put his fork down and pushed his plate back. "No, to be honest. I'd like to spend a little time with her. After that crazy Makeup Artist case, and how it ended..."

"Don't remind me," said Daniels.

"We've never had any normalcy. This will be our first shot at it. Other than our phone calls."

"Does that make you nervous?" asked Daniels, wiping his fingers on his napkin.

"A little maybe. Her, too, I think. But to be honest, I don't think that's what's buggin' me."

Daniels paused. "Let me guess. You're worried it might go well. That you two might be a great fit, and you could be happy with her."

Rem's belly tightened, and he gripped his napkin. The reaction surprised him. "Anyone ever tell you you should be a shrink?"

"Once or twice. But then who would save your ass when you're hell-bent on chasing an armed perp down a dark alley?"

"I could have taken that guy," scoffed Rem.

"You tripped on a broken bottle and fell in glass. You needed fifteen stitches in your hand."

Rem pointed. "I could have still pulled the trigger."

"It's hard to pull a trigger when you're dead."

Rem shrugged. "Details."

"Uh-huh." Daniels sat back. "So, you're afraid this might work with Jacobs?"

Rem tapped on the table with his spoon.

"And you don't want to get hurt again."

Rem sighed. "Maybe."

Daniels studied him. "You know, what happened with Jennie doesn't mean it will happen again."

Rem scratched his head. "I know that. Logically, I know that. But she's also trying to get her life together. She may decide to stay put, to build her life elsewhere..."

"Without you," added Daniels.

"Maybe," whispered Rem.

Daniels nodded. "Well, you have a dilemma. On the one hand, you could pursue a beautiful woman who whom you've started something rather promising. She actually likes you, which is a miracle in itself. She's getting her life together, and in some ways, so are you. You two are a good match. Maybe it will work and maybe it won't. It's a risk." He sat forward and clenched his fingers together. "Or you can stop it dead in its tracks. Protect yourself. Sleep with women with whom you have no emotional attachment. Go through the motions. Have no meaningful relationships, other than me of course, but let's be honest, there's only so much I can do, and you can end up changing your diapers all by yourself when your prostate goes out." He picked up his coffee cup. "Hmm. Which would I choose?"

Rem couldn't help but smile. "Point taken."

His partner smiled back. "Everything's a risk, partner. You know that. You do it every day at work. Marjorie could leave me tomorrow and take JP with her. You might love Jacobs to death, and then she leaves. There's nothing we can do about it. But that doesn't mean we stop living. That's even worse."

Rem nodded. "Could this maybe have something to with why you're hesitating to pop the question to Marjorie?"

His partner stilled. "I thought we were talking about you."

Rem refilled his coffee cup. "Goes both ways, partner."

Daniels rubbed his face. "I know it does."

"Good." Rem was about to take another sip when he stopped. "Oh, boy. That whole risk-taking thing?"

Daniels picked up his bagel. "What about it?"

"We're about to get some practice."

Daniels turned to look. "Is that...?"

Rem watched three women head in their direction. "Yup. Laura Benoff. And she's got two friends with her."

"Wonderful," said Daniels.

"Took the words out of my mouth."

**

Laura Benoff strode into the restaurant, Angela and Lucy behind her. After the early morning events at her home, she was pissed. Biggles had arrived and found no one in her bushes, Madison had curled up on the couch with a blanket because she wouldn't go back to her room, and Preston, thinking Madison was ready for the looney bin, got dressed and headed into work early.

Laura had called Stephen to tell him what had happened, and he'd agreed to stop by later to talk to Maddie. The whole thing was crazy, and Laura needed to do something. Her best friend might go to jail and she needed help. Laura had never been the kind of woman to sit back and wring her hands. Once everything had settled down, she'd called Angela and Lucy and they'd met for coffee at Angela's. They talked about the case and Maddie's situation, and that's when Laura thought of the two detectives helping Biggles. Biggles might be an idiot, but maybe those two weren't. Someone needed to talk to them about this case other than Biggles.

After a few phone calls, Laura had tracked them down. Angela and Lucy were initially reluctant, but Laura didn't care. She'd left, and they'd followed. Now, entering the restaurant and seeing the two men eating in a booth, she approached.

Seeing them coming, the long-haired one wiped his face with a napkin which he apparently needed because he had a stain on his shirt, and the blonde one shifted in his seat as they neared.

85

"Detectives," she said.

"Mrs. Benoff," said the blonde one. "How can we help you?"

"You're up early," said the long-haired one. "You here for breakfast?"

Laura crossed her arms. "Please stop blowing smoke up my ass, gentlemen. I don't have the time for it."

"Excuse me?" asked the blonde.

"Ladies, grab a seat." Laura slid into the booth next to the blonde. Angela hesitated, but then slid in next to the brunette. Lucy grabbed a chair, pulled it up and sat. There was silence as the detectives moved further in and stared at each other, not knowing what to say.

"Cat got your tongue?" asked Laura. "Fine. I'll start. This is Angie and Lucy. We are Maddie's friends. Ladies, this is..." she pointed but paused.

"Detective Remalla," said the long-haired one.

"Detective Daniels," offered the blonde.

"Thank you. I couldn't remember your names. No offense."

"None taken," said Remalla.

Laura crossed her arms. "I'll get to the point. While you two are here enjoying your nice meal, Biggles is investigating a stranger on my property watching Maddie. She saw him this morning."

The men's faces frowned. "Somebody was watching Madison? When?" asked Daniels.

"I told you. This morning. Maddie went outside around four a.m. She saw a man watching her in the dark. She ran inside, and I called Biggles."

"He find anyone?" asked Remalla.

Laura rolled her eyes. "No. By the time he got there, the guy could have had tea and a Danish. He was long gone."

"What did he look like?" asked Remalla.

"Maddie couldn't see him. He was in the dark. But he was there." She waited as the two detectives made eye contact. "What? You think she's lying?" She sat forward. "This guy could be our killer."

Daniels put his napkin on the table. "We're not saying she didn't see anybody, but she goes outside at four o'clock in the morning and someone, who she can't describe and who no one else sees, is watching her? This person then disappears, well..."

"It's not very helpful," added Remalla. "Maybe she should stay inside, because this going outdoors in the middle of the night business is not helping her."

"Maddie wouldn't lie about this," said Lucy.

"She's always going outside," said Angela. "Especially if she can't sleep. I prefer to take a Xanax. Works like a charm."

Laura ignored Angela and smacked her hand on the table. "I hope to hell you two know what you're doing because if you're thinking my friend did what you are accusing her of, you're dead wrong."

Daniels cleared his throat. "No one's accusing anyone of anything."

"That's not what I heard."

Remalla sat back, his elbow on the booth. "Well, since we're all here, why don't you tell us what you think happened."

"You should talk to Sharie," said Laura. "Karl's wife. She had plenty of motive to kill him. He had affairs. She had affairs. God knows what his finances were like. I'd check his books if I were you. Lord knows he was cheating people, and they lost money."

"Your husbands included?" asked Daniels.

Laura dropped her jaw.

"Yes, our husbands included," said Angela. Her puffy eyes told Laura she'd been drinking the night before. "Karl probably stole from everyone on the lake, Donald Vickers included. Maybe

Donald figured out what Karl was doing and threatened Sharie, and she killed him too."

"Sharie seems to be in everyone's crosshairs. Is there a reason for that?" asked Remalla. "You said she was having affairs? Who was she sleeping with? Anyone you know?" He glanced at his partner before looking back.

Laura opened her mouth to speak, but Lucy answered first. "You might check in town. I heard she's been hooking up with a younger man. She told me she'd sworn off married men."

Daniels opened his jacket and pulled out a small notepad and pencil. "Any idea who this younger man is?"

"No idea," said Lucy. "Sharie didn't elaborate."

Daniels scribbled. "And she didn't sleep with any of your husbands?"

Laura gasped. "Excuse me?"

Angela snorted. "Good luck sleeping with Sam. I can barely get him to move off the couch, much less move over me." She reached over Remalla and picked up an unused coffee cup on the table. "You don't mind, do you?"

"Help yourself," said Remalla.

"Thanks," she answered, filling the mug with coffee.

"Thomas wouldn't sleep with her. He's a rule follower. And if he did, he'd tell me. He's a terrible liar," said Lucy. The spaghetti strap on her fitted top slipped down, and she pulled it up. Shifting sideways, she crossed her long legs barely covered by her short denim shorts.

"I can't believe we're having this discussion," said Laura. "How are we suddenly defending ourselves?" She leaned forward. "We came here to defend Maddie."

"Well, if Maddie didn't kill Donald or Karl, then somebody else did, and my guess it was somebody they knew. And they knew people around the lake." Remalla eyed each of them. "And you all live on the lake. So put two and two together..."

Laura's heart thumped and she could almost feel her blood pressure spike. "How dare you. None of us here would kill anyone, nor would our husbands. We may have our issues, but murder isn't one of them. Maddie either. You two schmoozers need to do your job and stop wasting time. I don't know where Biggles found you, but I'm not impressed."

The detectives made eye contact.

"Schmoozers?" asked Daniels. "Are we schmoozers? I don't think so. Are you a schmoozer, Rem?"

"Are you kidding? I got my degree in it. Just call me Dr. Schmooze."

Daniels nodded. "Good to know. That'll come in handy on this case."

Lucy smiled and Angela added two sugars to her coffee.

Laura didn't know what to say.

"Speaking of schmoozing, let's get back to Karl. You said he had affairs," said Rem. He paused. "Any of you sleep with him?" He raised his coffee and sipped it.

Laura rubbed her temples "Oh my God. Are you serious?"

"It's a good question, Dr. Schmooze," said Daniels.

"Thank you," said Remalla.

The men waited for them to answer, and Laura sighed.

"I almost did," said Lucy, in a whisper. "We made out once in his basement but I stopped it before anything happened." She gave the details of her incident with Karl.

Daniels scribbled in his pad. "Anybody else?"

"Certainly not," said Laura. "Personally, I thought he was a little creepy. I mean, with all those sexual partners, God knows what he was exposed to."

"I didn't sleep with him," said Angela. "Although who knows what would have happened if he'd tried. He might have gotten lucky."

"Angela..." said Laura. "Really?"

Angela shrugged. "Just sayin..." Her fingers trembled slightly as she drank her coffee.

Remalla tapped his finger on the table. "Maddie didn't sleep with him?"

"Of course not," said Laura. "Maddie would never sleep with Karl."

"You sure?" asked Daniels, looking up from his notepad. "We heard about an incident at a party last summer where Madison left early, looking disheveled. Karl had been MIA right before that." He waited.

"Any idea what might have happened?" asked Remalla.

Laura couldn't believe her ears. "That's what you have to go on? Maddie left early from a party at the same time that Karl reappeared? Is that according to Sharie? Where you'd get your degree from Dr. Schmooze? Bermuda? Please. She probably had too much to drink, got sick, and went home. God knows what Karl was up to. Probably snorting drugs or sleeping with someone else. Is this what you call good detective work?"

"Did Karl do drugs?" asked Remalla.

Laura threw up her hands. "I don't know. I'm just saying there's a million reasons why he was absent. It doesn't mean he was sleeping with Maddie."

"We heard about Donald Vickers arguing with Karl not long before Karl's death. Any of you know what that was about?" asked Daniels.

"Everyone heard about that fight," said Lucy. "I assumed it was money. Thomas lost money, too."

"So did Sam. I told him not to trust Karl, but he did it anyway," said Angela. She fidgeted. "Anybody here got a cigarette?"

"Angela," said Laura. "I thought you quit."

"Sorry, but murder makes me nervous, and this talk isn't helping. I need a smoke."

"No cigarettes here," said Remalla.

"You can't smoke in here anyway, Ang.," said Lucy.

"What about your husband, Mrs. Benoff. Did he lose money?" asked Remalla.

Laura hesitated. "Yes, he did."

"A lot?" asked Daniels.

All eyes flicked toward her. "Let's just say Christmas might be thin this year."

"No trip to Vail?" asked Angela.

Laura squinted. "You want to go there, Angela? Should we talk about how much Sam lost?"

Angela waved her off. "Whatever. We all lost money. Doesn't mean we killed Karl. I think we'd all rather be in the poorhouse instead of jail."

"Besides, killing him doesn't bring the money back," said Lucy.

"Nor does it explain Donald's death," said Laura. "Which is why we came here in the first place. Maddie didn't kill anybody."

"We can appreciate your defense of your friend, Mrs. Benoff. But she was home that night, and her only alibi is that she was out on the boat when Donald was murdered. There are no witnesses to that. And he was murdered with a knife from their kitchen. Plus, from her account, Donald was abusive to her." Daniels tapped his pencil on the table. "Did you know about that?"

Laura took a breath and wondered how to answer.

"Mrs. Benoff?" asked Remalla.

Laura debated what to say. "I knew. She mentioned a few things, but I don't think she told me everything."

"I always wondered," said Lucy. "How come you never told us?"

"Because Maddie made we swear. I told her to leave him, but she couldn't bring herself to do it. That asshole father of hers did a number on her, and his voice is always in her head."

"I wouldn't blame her if she killed him," said Angela. "I'd have shot Thomas dead if he ever laid a hand on me. In anger, of course."

"Angie..." said Laura. "You're not helping."

"I always suspected he was an asshole," said Lucy. "He made a pass at me once. Got angry when I turned him down."

"What?" asked Laura.

"Really?" asked Angela, putting her coffee down.

"You want to tell us more about that?" asked Daniels "When did this happen?"

"Last August. I came over to deliver some wine Maddie had ordered from a party at my house. It was in the trunk of my car. Maddie wasn't home, but Donald was. He came out with me and I leaned in to get the box and he grabbed my ass. I think he'd been drinking. I shoved him off, but he got pushy, so I kneed him in the balls. He sobered up fast after that. I left the wine next to him and got in the car to leave. He yelled at me not to tell Maddie, or he'd blame me for the whole encounter."

"You said nothing to Maddie?" asked Laura.

Lucy scratched her bare shoulder. "I almost did. But that was the time Maddie sort of holed up for a while. I didn't see her for maybe six weeks after. By then, it didn't seem that big of a deal. Donald acted like nothing ever happened and so did I. Now I'm wondering if I should have told her."

"You think?" asked Laura. "Christ."

"You guys are her friends?" asked Remalla.

Laura eyed him. "We are, detective."

"Not very good ones," muttered Angela. She drained the remains of her coffee, and Laura flicked an angry gaze at her. Angela sighed and rubbed her neck. "Crap, I could use a smoke."

NINE

....

Stephen threw a file in his briefcase and closed it with a slam. Frustrated, he walked to the window and stared out, his hands on his hips. This day was going from bad to worse. He'd just gotten off the phone with his ex, who'd told him she wouldn't be back in time to bring his son, Byron, to Stephen for the weekend. It was Stephen's weekend to have him, and now it looked like his ex would prevent that. It wasn't the first time she'd pulled this. He'd have to contact his attorney to deal with it because if he didn't, she'd continue to pull this crap.

Then Laura Benoff had called and told him what had happened with Maddie at her house in the early morning. Someone had been outside watching Madison, but Madison couldn't say what he looked like, and the man had disappeared.

Stephen didn't know what to think about that. He wanted to believe her, but some small part of him wondered. Was Madison telling him everything?

He turned from the window and walked to the mantel, seeing his law degree on display on the wall. He'd busted his butt through law school, determined to graduate at the top if his class, and he'd succeeded. It's where he'd met his wife, whom he'd divorced a little over a year ago. Their son would turn two next month.

Sighing, he thought back to high school, and seeing a book on the shelf, he picked it up and flipped through it, finding the picture he sought. It was a picture of Madison from their senior yearbook. Smiling at the camera, her blonde hair shimmered in the sunlight, and her blue satin shirt brought out her blue eyes. Touching the photo, he remembered his crush on her. His heart had thumped at the mere mention of her name, and when she'd sat next to him in math class, he'd thought he'd died and gone to heaven. She was the most beautiful girl in school, and most of the boys vied for her attention. She'd dated the football quarterback for a while, but then had dumped him before graduating. It had been the talk of the school, and Stephen had entertained the crazy thought that maybe she'd liked Stephen until the day came when school had ended and she'd gone one way and he another.

Once he was in college, he'd thought of her less and less until the day came when Laura Benoff had called him and mentioned Madison's name, and strangely enough, his heart hammered once again.

But there was little he could do about it, because she was now his client, and he couldn't touch her, no matter how much he might dwell on doing just that.

Sitting at his desk, he pondered his next move. If the forensic evidence came back and Madison's fingerprints were on the weapon, he had to plan on Biggles arresting her for murder. Spying a file on his desk, he picked it up and flipped it open. Reviewing Madison's file once again, he wondered how to defend her. The evidence didn't help. He had to figure out who else would want Donald Vickers dead. Donald wasn't a nice man. Not to Madison or anyone else. From what he could gather, the man had no friends. He hung out with people along the lake, but only because of his relationship to Madison. Without her, Vickers would have been an outcast.

Checking his watch, he had fifteen minutes before leaving. Thinking about his options, he picked up the phone and dialed a number. Maybe someone could get some answers for him.

**

Madison sat on a porch chair and drank some iced tea. It was quiet. Preston had gone into work and Laura had left earlier that morning, telling Madison to get some rest. After the pre-dawn visitor though, Madison had been wide awake. She kept remembering him staring at her through the trees, and that eerie voice in her head. *I did it for you.* Had he been the person who'd killed Donald? Had he killed Karl too? Would he kill her next? Maybe the police had it wrong and all of this had to do with Madison. Was someone stalking her? Tired and weary, she'd been on the verge of tears all morning, but couldn't bring herself to cry. It took too much energy.

She poured herself more iced tea as a boat sped past on the lake, pulling a water skier. A man drove, and a woman sat in the back, laughing and watching the skier who appeared to be a teenager. Madison envied their existence and carefree fun. It had been a long time since she'd felt that way.

"Madison?"

Maddie jumped in her chair, almost spilling her iced tea. Stephen stepped up onto the deck, holding his briefcase.

"I'm sorry," he said, holding out a hand. "I didn't mean to scare you."

Madison held her chest. "It's okay. I'm just a little jumpy today." She noticed his more casual attire. Instead of the formal suit, he wore brown slacks and a navy short-sleeved shirt, revealing his muscular arms. His tan skin and light hair made her think of the old photos of the Kennedys sitting in the sun at their beach house in Hyannis Port. Stephen could have fit right in.

"I knocked, but nobody answered, so I thought I'd check around back. That okay?" he asked.

Madison held her head. She'd had no alcohol, but she might as well have had a hangover. "I'm sorry. I didn't hear. Yes, it's fine. Have a seat."

He took the seat beside her, putting his briefcase down. "I heard about your intruder this morning."

"It wasn't exactly an intruder. He never entered the house. Just sat and watched me down by the water."

"Still, he's on the property where he shouldn't be. You didn't get a look at him?"

"No. It was still dark. I mainly just saw a silhouette." Madison rubbed her arms. "It was creepy."

"He didn't do anything? Just watched?" he asked.

Madison thought back. "He started to take a step forward, but that's when I started to run. He didn't follow. I don't know what he would have done if I hadn't moved."

"He wasn't a neighbor? Someone else along the lake?"

Madison shook her head. "No. It wasn't. But..."

"But what?"

"I don't know. For some odd reason, I feel as if he knows me."

"Maybe from the past?"

"Maybe." Madison sighed. "I can't be sure. It was just so weird. But he disappeared and nobody else saw him. Biggles came by and found nothing. Not even footprints, so I'm sure everybody thinks I'm hallucinating."

"Nobody thinks that."

"Maybe I shouldn't have said anything. I'm afraid I've added fuel to the fire. I'll be the crazy lady who killed her husband because she sees people that aren't there. The press will have a field day with that."

Stephen put his hand on her arm. "Madison, that's not the case. Nobody thinks you're crazy."

Madison put her tea on the side table. "I'm not so sure about that." She put her hand over his. "But thanks for trying." His hand under hers was warm, and she briefly made eye contact with him before he pulled his hand back and she thought she detected a shy blush on his cheeks. Something inside her fluttered, and she chastised herself. The last thing she needed was male attention or attraction. It had never ended well for her, and it certainly wouldn't help now.

Stephen grabbed his briefcase, seeming to be a bit flustered himself. "I contacted a private investigator."

"You did? Why?"

"We need to know more information on Donald. Considering his behavior, I think he may have kept a few things from you. And if he did, we need to know what. It could help our case."

Madison considered that. "Probably not a bad idea." She wondered if this PI would investigate more than just Donald. "What about me? Will he be looking into my background too?"

Stephen popped the briefcase open, but paused. "Does he need to? Is there something I need to know?"

Madison gripped the armrest. "No, I was just wondering."

They stared for a moment before Stephen broke the contact. "Good." He pulled a file out of the briefcase. "I want to go over a few things with you. Ask you a few questions about..."

The sliding glass door opened and Madison turned to see Laura step out. Biggles was behind her. "Madison?"

Madison stood. "Hey, Laura. Sheriff? You're back? Did you learn something?" Biggles shuffled on his feet, and Madison sensed his discomfort. "What's wrong?"

Laura frowned. "I'd like to know the same thing. He pulled up to the cabin at the same time as me. Said he needed to talk to you."

"Sheriff?" asked Stephen. "What can we help you with?"

Biggles hesitated, and Maddie tensed, sensing it wasn't good news.

"We got the forensics back from the crime scene, Madison. The fingerprints on the knife are yours and the skin under your nails matched Donald's. There is no other evidence that anyone else was in the house." Biggles grasped his belt buckle. "I'm sorry, but the D.A. has issued a warrant for your arrest for the murder of your husband. I'm here to bring you in."

The air became thick and hard to breathe. Madison held her stomach. Laura went into bulldog mode and immediately began tearing into Biggles, accusing him of idiocy and stupidity, and adding in a few well-placed curse words, but Maddie barely heard it. Everything went dull and flat, and a white noise muffled the sound. She couldn't move, and it was only when someone took her arm did she actually snap back, and she heard Stephen's voice.

"Madison, listen to me. Do as he says, but don't say a word until I'm with you. Okay? I'll get you through this I promise."

Laura's face went redder. "You're going to let this happen? What the hell is happening here?"

"I'm sorry, Laura. I don't have a choice," said Biggles. "Come with me, Madison. I won't use the handcuffs."

"The handcuffs? You wouldn't dare use handcuffs on her. How could you?" Laura roared with anger. "You are so going to regret this. When she's found innocent, we will sue you for everything you have. This county won't be able to afford the annual summer picnic when we're done with you."

"Laura, please. Just let me do my job." Biggles raised a hand toward the door. "Let's go, Madison."

The white noise softened as Biggles' voice penetrated. Looking to Stephen for reassurance, she nodded, but couldn't take the step. Her entire world was crumbling around her. But then she felt a hand on her back and Stephen spoke into her ear. "It's okay. I got you. I'll be right behind and I promise, you won't be alone."

Something inside her broke and Madison bit back the tears. She wouldn't let them see her cry, so she took a deep breath and took that first step. Biggles moved back, and by the strained look on his face, Madison thought he might cry too. Laura continued to rage, but Madison kept going, telling herself to just put one foot in front of the other. It was all she could do.

After walking through the house, they left out the front and Madison saw the sheriff's car waiting, like an empty cell ready for its next occupant. Biggles opened the back door. Madison paused and finally spoke.

"I didn't do this, Sheriff." It was all she could muster.

Biggles set his jaw, as if wanting to say something but knowing he couldn't. "You'll have your day in court, Madison." Then he put a hand on her shoulder and guided her into the back seat.

Stephen leaned over. "Remember. Don't say anything. I'll be there as soon as I can."

Laura yelled from behind him. "Don't worry. Maddie. We'll get you out. I promise. These guys don't know their ass from their ear-lobe. Hang in there."

Madison barely nodded before Biggles closed the door, got into the driver's seat, started up the engine, and drove off.

TEN

....

The next few hours only added to Madison's misery. Biggles drove her to the county courthouse where she was booked and processed. They took her fingerprints and her clothes, giving her an orange jumpsuit to wear. The process yanked any sense of hope from Madison, and she began to see her life in black and white. All color had been rendered obsolete. Despair made her shoulders ache and her head throb. When they took her to a holding cell, she wondered if this would be her home for the rest of her days. Maybe not this cell, but something similar. No more cabin, no more lake, no more art. The thought of it was almost too much to bear.

She'd sat there, staring at the walls, for what felt like hours, when she heard a door open, and footsteps on the hard floor. A guard appeared and told her she had a visitor. He opened the door and led her to a small cell with a table. Stephen sat, still in his navy shirt and brown pants. He stood as they led her in, and the guard closed the door behind her.

Madison could barely think, and she almost walked into Stephen's arms, just to be held, but thought better of it and sat at the table instead.

Stephen sat beside her. "How are you?"

Madison bit her lip, and a tear escaped and slid down her cheek. "How do you think I am?" Another tear spilled over.

Stephen pulled out a handkerchief and handed it to her. She took it and dabbed her eyes, trying not to dissolve into tears, but not succeeding.

Stephen gave her a minute to compose herself. "I'm sorry about this, but I was afraid this would happen. This is not entirely unexpected."

Madison nodded. "Speak for yourself," she said with a shaky voice.

"But I don't want you to panic. We've got a long way to go on this. All is not lost."

Madison sniffed. "It's not feeling that way right now. Everyone thinks I did it."

"The only opinion that matters is a jury's. Nobody else."

"Biggles said there's no evidence that anyone else was there. Donald was abusive and mean. My fingerprints are on the knife. Plus, I scratched Donald that night when he grabbed my neck. I don't have an alibi. I know how it looks."

He put his hand on her arm much like he did on the porch earlier that morning. "Madison, I don't want you to get caught up on how it looks. There are plenty of ways to show reasonable doubt in this case. There is Karl's murder to consider, and Donald's vices. I doubt you're the only one who may have wanted him dead."

Madison wiped her eyes. "They will try to pin Karl's murder on me. You know that don't you? If they can get me for both, then it's a win-win for them."

"They have no evidence to suggest that you killed Karl. That works to our advantage."

"I think you're being optimistic. If they want to accuse me, they'll find a way."

Stephen squeezed her arm. "You let me deal with that, okay? That's my job. I just want you to focus on being strong through all of this. It won't be easy, but I promise, we'll figure it out."

Madison blinked back tears, unable to think past the next day. "What happens next?"

"They'll arraign you tomorrow. We'll go before the judge with the D.A. I'll ask him to set bail, and hope he says yes."

Madison closed her eyes, considering what would happen if she did not get bail. She could be in a cell for a long time. "Dear God, Stephen. I don't know if I can stay in this place until a trial."

Stephen moved his hand down to hers, and she took it and held onto it like a lifeline. "I'm going to do whatever I can to be sure that doesn't happen."

Madison breathed deeply, trying to gain some sense of control, but her mind was reeling. How was this happening? "So, I'm sleeping in here tonight?" She thought of her small cell with the cot and toilet and cringed.

"You are. I know. It's not pretty. But if we can get bail for you, hopefully tomorrow, we can get you home."

Madison thought of her home. The cabin. The big open windows that looked out onto the lake, the fireplace, the soft sandy lakeside beach. "If I get out of here, that's where I want to go. Home." She didn't care that Donald had died there. It had been her father's house and now it was hers. Her family's roots grew down from that house. She'd sleep in the guest room for now. "I want to go back to my cabin. Can I do that?"

Stephen furrowed his brow. "You want to go back there?"

"Yes. I do."

"I'd have to check with the sheriff to see if the crime scene is cleared to be released. And it would have to be cleaned."

"Ask Laura to find a cleaning company. I'll pay her back."

Stephen started to say something, but then just said, "Okay. I'll check."

"Thank you." She put her other hand over his. "I need you to make this happen, Stephen. Please. I just want to go home. Whatever happens after that, I'll deal with it."

Stephen held her gaze, and she wondered what he was thinking. "I'll do my best. Try not to worry."

**

Remalla rapped on Biggles' office door and heard a 'come in.' Rem opened the door and he and Daniels entered. "Sheriff," he said.

"Detectives," said Biggles. "How are you? Have a seat. You want some coffee? I just made it."

Rem and Daniels sat across from Biggles. "Please," said Rem.

"No thanks," said Daniels.

Biggles grabbed a mug and filled it with coffee. "Cream and sugar, right?"

"Does a bear poop in the woods?" asked Rem, with a smile.

Biggles grinned.

"Rem takes cream and sugar on his vegetables," said Daniels.

Rem scowled. "Not on my broccoli. Cheese sauce is better with broccoli."

Daniels rolled his eyes.

Biggles handed the doctored coffee to Rem, who sipped on it.

"We heard you arrested Madison Vickers this morning," said Daniels.

Biggles sat back at his desk. "Yeah. I hated doing it. I've known her a long time. About broke my heart. But the evidence is what it is."

"You think she did it?" asked Daniels.

Biggles grunted. "That's not for me to decide. It'll be up to a jury now. But it doesn't look good."

"Based on our interviews though, isn't there a hint of doubt? Could someone else have wanted Vickers dead? And what about Karl Scott? His killer is still out there," said Rem.

Biggles rubbed his jaw. "The D.A.'s consensus is she killed 'em both. We just can't prove it yet with Karl Scott. But with a little more digging, maybe we'll find the smoking gun."

Rem shifted in his seat and glanced at Daniels. "Is that what you're hanging your hat on? Sounds like you've decided she's the one and now you have to find the evidence. Shouldn't it be the other way around?"

"Where there's smoke, there's fire, gentlemen. Don't you think?" asked Biggles.

Daniels pulled out his notebook and flipped through it. "There are a lot of reasons to think Karl Scott's murderer could be someone else. Maybe even Donald Vickers. These men had enemies. Madison could be an easy mark as the abused wife. We think it's worth a little more investigating."

Biggles leaned back and hooked his thumbs around his belt buckle. "Listen. I can appreciate what you two have done. You've talked to several people and you've been a big help. I don't disagree we have some oddballs around here. We're not perfect. We all have our secrets. But that doesn't make everyone a killer. But we have to follow where the evidence takes us. You even said you thought she did it." He cocked his head at Rem. "Going around making more people nervous and scaring the locals is unnecessary."

Rem sipped his coffee and placed his mug on Biggles' desk. "So basically, you've got your man, so it's easier to pile more shit on her rather than get off your ass and do some legwork? I thought she was your friend."

Daniels tapped on his notepad with his finger. "There's more to this story, Sheriff. I think you know that."

Biggles scowled. "Listen, Detectives." He leaned forward. "I get it. You're from the big city where murderers and rapists run amok, and you're used to liars and cheats and not trusting anyone. Everyone's a suspect in your book. But it's not like that around here. When it comes to murder, once you shake a few trees, the bad apple usually falls out. It doesn't take much."

"Problem is, Sheriff, there's more than one bad apple around here. Doesn't that concern you?" asked Daniels.

Biggles clasped his hands together. "No, not really."

"Sheriff..." started Rem.

Biggles stood. "I want to thank you two for coming up to help, but I think we've got it from here. Tell Lozano I appreciate it. He's a good friend."

Rem stared for a moment before putting his hands on his knees. Looking over at Daniels, who cocked an eyebrow at him, he stood. "Okay. I think we take the hint."

"That wasn't much of a hint," said Daniels. "He's kicking us out." Standing, he closed the notebook and put it back in his pocket.

"Nothing personal," said Biggles. "I like you two. We just don't need your help anymore. We found our killer."

Rem sighed, frustrated. "Whatever you say, Sheriff. I hope you know what you're doing, because if it was me, I wouldn't be able to sleep at night. You may have an innocent woman in jail and a murderer still on the loose."

Biggles stood, his face impassive. "Take care, gentlemen. If I need anything, I'll let you know."

Daniels eyed Rem who shook his head, and they opened the office door and left. Exiting the police station, they stepped out into the warm sunlight.

"Well, what do you want to do?" asked Daniels. "We're officially off this case."

Rem kicked at the dirt, and a stone skittered across the ground. "It's ridiculous. We're just starting to get somewhere, and they yank this out from under us."

Daniels leaned against the car. "It wasn't ours to begin with. He could be right. Madison could be our killer."

Rem crossed his arms. "If you really thought that, you'd be the first guy in the car, ready to get back to Marjorie and JP. But you're thinking exactly what I'm thinking. Something else is going on here. I can't put my finger on it. And I can't sit back in my seat on the drive back, listening to good music, and pretend to forget this case. It doesn't sit right with me."

Daniels nodded. "Lozano will expect us back."

Rem thought about it. "We've both got plenty of vacation days. Feel like spending a little time at the lake?" He held out his arms. "Plenty of sunshine and nature. Maybe enjoy a few beers."

Daniels pulled out his cell. "Somehow I don't think we'll be doing any of those things."

"Who you calling?"

"Marjorie. Telling her I'm gonna be a few days longer."

ELEVEN

....

Madison sat wearily at the table in front of the judge's bench. Stephen sat beside her, dressed in a handsome brown suit with a white shirt and yellow tie, looking every inch the high-paid attorney she'd hired. Madison struggled to stay focused. Her night before had been nothing but tossing and turning in the uncomfortable cot, and when she slept, she dreamed of the man on the dock who'd chased her before. But now he was the same man from the shadows behind Laura's house who'd watched her.

In the dream, she still couldn't see his face and that same whispered voice had echoed in her ear. *I did it for you.* She couldn't escape it. The other man and woman had been there too, but in the distance, too far away to touch. But she sensed their worry and concern and Madison tried to run toward them, but each time they faded, and she could never reach them.

Madison rubbed her temples, remembering the dream, trying to understand it all, but her mind was a fog.

"All rise," said the bailiff, and Madison popped her head up. An older man with white hair, a broad face and a serious expression wearing a black robe entered and sat in the judge's seat. Stephen had told her his name was Judge Thomas McCarthy. He had a good reputation, was well-respected and thought to be fair, although tough.

Madison stood. Laura had brought some clothes for Madison to wear so she would look presentable. Madison turned to see Laura, Lucy and Angie, sitting in the front row. They gave her nods of encouragement. The rest of the courtroom was empty, save for one older woman in the back. She had dark hair with gray roots and wore a bright loose dress with sunflowers on it and large chunky jewelry. Madison didn't recognize her.

Judge McCarthy took his seat and told them all to do the same. Then the talking started. She and Stephen stood, and Madison stated her plea as not guilty. Then she sat and listened as the D.A. tried to pin her as a flight risk and how she should remain in jail. Madison clenched her hands as Stephen argued the opposite and tried to attain bail.

Madison breathed deeply as the men argued her fate. All she could do was pray that she could go home today. Finally, the judge decided. He granted her bail and set it at one million dollars. He slammed the gavel, and everyone stood, and then he disappeared. Madison's head spun. She'd gotten her wish, but her heart sank.

Stephen took her arm. "Madison, you okay?" Madison shook her head. "What's the matter? We got bail. We can get you out of here."

Madison bit her lip. "Stephen, I don't have that kind of money."

Stephen's face fell. "It's okay. You only need ten percent. A hundred thousand. Can you do that?"

A hundred thousand sounded better than a million. "That's still a lot of money. I don't have that lying around."

"What about the cabin? You can use it as collateral."

"The cabin is old and needs work. Plus, I still have to pay you. Donald pilfered most of our savings. My art can't bring in that kind of money. I could maybe raise thirty thousand but the rest, well, I don't know."

"Your friends can help..."

"No. Don't you dare ask them. They have their own money problems to deal with and I can't expect them to do that."

"Madison...you can't stay in here. You know they'll want to help."

Madison wanted to cry but stopped herself. There had to be another way. Her father had left her with other investments, but she would need to contact the right people and go through the red tape to access those funds. "We'll think of something. Just please don't ask them."

The bailiff returned to bring her back to her cell, and she had a moment to wave at her friends, who waved back and gave her the thumbs up sign, before they took her away. Madison didn't know if she could feel more tortured. She'd gotten her wish, but her hope had been short lived. Being led out of the courtroom, Madison saw the woman in the sunflower dress watch her with a somber expression. It was the last face she saw before returning to her cell.

**

Two hours later, Madison lay on her cot, staring up at the ceiling. She was numb. Stephen had left thirty minutes earlier, promising her he'd help figure out how to raise the bail money without asking her friends. A hundred thousand dollars. She wondered about her father's assets and how quickly she could access them. Would it be enough? The emotion rose and her chest tightened, but she refused to cry. She'd done enough crying, and it wasn't helping.

Footsteps returned, and she heard her name. Looking up, she saw the guard.

"You have a visitor."

Madison assumed it was Stephen. Maybe he would have good news. She could use some right now.

Following him, she returned to the same cell as before, but stopped when she saw her visitor. It was the woman in the sunflower dress.

The woman smiled. "Hello, dear."

Madison, perplexed, walked closer to the woman as the guard closed the door behind her with a clang. "Do I know you?" she asked.

The woman patted the tabletop. "Not really. No. Come and sit. Take a load off, dear. You've had a rough week."

Madison slowly moved forward and sat at the table across from her. "Who are you?"

The woman fiddled with a large green-stoned necklace which had become entangled with a smaller red one. "My name is Sonia Vandermere. I've been watching your case with great interest."

"My case? Are you an attorney?"

"Oh, heavens no. I could never be a lawyer. Don't have the stomach for it. I dabble in lotions and creams. Make my own as a matter of fact. I'd give you a sample, but they wouldn't let me bring my purse in with me. Such a shame. You could use a little chamomile and lavender."

Madison knitted her brow. "I'm sorry. I don't understand. Why are you here?"

Sonia stopped fiddling with her necklace. "To help you dear. I think you need it, don't you?"

"How are you going to help me? Do you have a hundred grand?"

Sonia fanned herself with her fingers. "Oh, no, dear. I wish I did. I could make a lot of lotion with that, now couldn't I?"

Madison dropped her jaw, unsure of what to say.

"I just feel you need a little encouraging. You've been through a lot, and I thought maybe I could help."

Madison scoffed. "I wish you could. But I don't think you have the help I need."

Sonia paused. "And what exactly is it you think you need?"

"Money. Right about now, money would be great."

"And once you get the money, then what? What happens after that?"

Madison picked at the metal table. "Then I get out of here. I can go home. Then figure out what to do next. How to defend myself. How to prove I'm innocent."

"And how do you plan to do that?" Sonia rubbed her hands together.

"I have no idea." Madison scratched her head. "I thought you were here to help."

"I am, dear. Just not the way you think." Sonia reached over and put her fingers on Madison's forearm.

Tingles ran up Madison's skin, and Madison held her breath. The tingles traveled up to her shoulder and a soothing warmth spread through her chest. It was the oddest sensation, but a welcome one. The warmth spread through her body and it was the calmest she'd felt since this ordeal had begun. "What are you doing?"

"Exactly what I do with my lotions and creams. Infuse a little love into them."

Madison wondered about this strange woman. How was she doing this? "You're here to make me feel better?"

"Among other things."

Madison relaxed even more and almost yawned. The thought of taking a nap was appealing. She sighed, and Sonia removed her hand.

"Better?" she asked.

Madison studied her. "Are you sure I don't know you?"

"I'm pretty certain."

"Then why do you feel so familiar to me?"

"Ah, now we're getting somewhere."

Madison cocked her head. "I'm sorry. What?"

"You're starting to feel, instead of think. That's what I'm hoping for. It will aid you immeasurably."

"I don't know what you're talking about."

Sonia leaned close, her arms on the table. A piece of her chunky bracelet banged against the table. "My dear. You have no sense of who you are or what you're capable of. There are signs and symbols all around you and you have no awareness of them. Your power lies dormant but now it's time to discover it. You can no longer linger on the sidelines. You've waited too long and doubted yourself and allowed others to control you. First your father, then Donald. You can't do that anymore, my dear. If you don't stop it now, it will destroy you, and you'll spend the rest of your life in prison, whether this one or one of your own making. The timing is critical, and it's why I am here to remind you of who you are."

Madison sat frozen, uncertain of what she'd just heard. This woman, whom she'd never met, was telling her things that made no sense. Madison started to object, but hesitated.

"Good. Don't respond just yet. Just take a moment to absorb it. You know what I'm saying is true."

Madison swallowed. This small, round woman in a sunflower dress with gray-haired roots was suddenly in her head, and Madison had no clue how she'd gotten there.

Sonia removed one of her bracelets with several purplish stones, and she placed it on the table. "Now, let's make sure that nice guard, Officer Potter over there, doesn't notice, but this will only take a moment." She slid the bracelet closer. "Take this. Hold it in your hand."

Madison stared at it.

"It's fluorite. It will help you with balance and clarity. You need it right now."

Madison wanted to tell her she was crazy, but something made her reach for the stones. They were cool to the touch, and she wrapped her fingers around them.

"Now close your mind and relax. Take a deep breath."

Madison did what Sonia asked. She released a deeply held breath and allowed her shoulders to drop and the tension to fall from her body.

"Good. Forget about where you are and what you've been through. Let everything go quiet." She paused. "Tell me. What do you see?" asked Sonia.

Madison squinted. Her jumbled mind slowly began to clear and the darkness behind her eyes took shape into a figure. "My father." She clenched the stones.

"Don't tense up. Stay relaxed."

Madison released the tension that tried to creep in at the thought of her dad. "Donald. I see Donald too."

"Mmhmm. Anyone else?"

Donald's face swirled and morphed. "Stephen."

"Your attorney?"

"Yes."

"Nice looking man. Very Paul Newman."

Madison focused on Stephen's face and he smiled at her.

"Sorry," said Sonia. "Didn't mean to get off track. Anybody else?"

Stephen's smile faded and his face drifted as two other men appeared. Madison frowned.

"Who is it, dear?"

"Those two detectives. They questioned me. I don't remember their names."

"Oh, yes. Detectives Daniels and Remalla. Interesting."

Madison moved her head, but kept her eyes closed. "I think they're trying to tell me something."

"Just be still and listen."

Madison strained to hear, but the muffled words were hard to make out. She had a strange feeling it was a warning. "I can't hear them." Their faces began to fade like the others and another face began to emerge. Madison tensed. "It's him. He's here."

"Who, dear?"

"The man in the shadows. He was watching me. I see him."

"What does he look like?"

Madison willed him to come into view. "He's older than me. His face is harsh, stern. He's strong and muscled. His hair light brown, almost blonde, a little long and wild."

"Sort of like a young Rutger Hauer?"

Madison tried to make the comparison but realized he wasn't alone. "The other two are here as well. Another man and a woman. I've seen them before in my dreams." Rutger moved closer in her vision, almost as if to block the other two. "His eyes...his eyes...I can see his eyes."

"What about his eyes?"

Madison opened hers with a start. Blinking, Sonia came into view and Madison held her stomach. She pushed the bracelet back toward Sonia.

"What is it, dear? What did you see?"

Madison collected herself, uncertain of what had happened. She spoke carefully. "They were my eyes. It felt like I was looking into a mirror."

Sonia took her bracelet and put it back on. "Interesting."

Madison cocked her head. "Who is he? Do I know him? Does he know me?"

"That's not for me to say, dear."

Madison sat back, trying to understand what had just happened. "Who are you?"

"Like I said, I'm here to help. It's time you started to see things more clearly. This is just the first step. There will be others."

Madison threw out her hands. "I'm stuck in here. What steps can I possibly take from jail?"

"You just took a big one sitting in this cell. Don't be surprised at what can happen in the strangest of places. Knowledge and revelation are not wary of location. You only need to trust yourself and others. Your vision can help guide you."

Madison scrunched her face and threw out her hands. "I don't understand any of this. I don't know you. I don't know this strange man who haunts my dreams, although now I think he knows me. How is it I hold a few rocks and all these people appear?"

"Why is that, do you think? And you said people, but it was all men, save for one woman at the end, but she doesn't count. Not yet, anyway."

"Oh, Sonia. I don't know. I'm so confused. I just want to go home."

"Madison, my apologies, but please stop whining. It doesn't become you."

Madison straightened.

"You've played the victim for too long. Somebody needs to tell you that. Now think about it. Your father, Donald, Stephen, the detectives, the unknown man. Why did they show up? What are they trying to tell you? We don't have much time left, so make it quick."

Madison's emotions stirred. Anger rose, and she wanted to lash out, but not at Sonia. "The men in my life have not always been the best influences on me. They've mostly only cared about themselves, and I've allowed myself to fall victim, wanting only their approval and love."

"All of them? Did they all feel that way to you?"

"No. Stephen is trying to help."

"And the detectives?"

Madison shook her head. "I don't know."

"Yes. You do."

Madison sighed. "I think they're trying to help too. I sense no malice in them."

"And the man?"

Madison squirmed. "He's curious, but dangerous. I think he thinks what he is doing is justified, but for all the wrong reasons. And he doesn't want me to meet the other two. The man and the woman. That scares him."

"Much better, dear. Much better. It's amazing what a little intention can do and getting in touch with your feelings. You've avoided that for too long, and it's cost you greatly."

Madison drooped, feeling all the energy drain from her. "I'm exhausted."

"That's because you let it drain you. You'll learn how to fix that. Your energetic resources are vaster than you realize."

Madison made a sad chuckle. This situation was bizarre. "Sonia, forgive me, but you are saying some strange things. I wish I knew what was going on here. And why I was seeing these people."

"Oh, poo, dear. You'll figure it all out. No need to fret. This is only the beginning. Just wait till you figure out what else you can do." Sonia started to stand. "I think my time is up. Officer Potter will head over soon. Plus, you'll have other visitors coming, and I need to be gone before they arrive. It could make for an awkward situation."

Madison sat up. "What? Wait. You can't leave now. What else can I do? What other visitors?"

Sonia patted her hand. "Just trust your feelings, dear. They'll help you. You are safe and always have been. It's time you knew that."

"But Sonia..." Madison took her hand, and a light flashed in her head. In a split second, Madison saw the vase flying off the mantel at Laura's home, the mirror breaking at her cabin, the various other objects falling from their perches from the time she was a child, until now. It was like a strobe light in her head.

Sonia stopped and withdrew her hand. "I told you it was just the beginning. And just because I like you, as an added insight, ghosts do not haunt your house. They never did." She patted Madison's shoulder. "Until we meet again."

Sonia walked away as the guard named Potter encroached. "Time's up, ma'am." He swung the door open.

"Yes. I know. Thank you, Officer Potter." The guard stopped momentarily, looking confused. Sonia smiled. "Did anyone ever tell you that you look like Danny Glover?" The guard didn't answer. "No matter. I'm off to get my things. Have a nice day."

The guard closed the door but stared after Sonia. Madison stood, expecting the guard to take her away. A second passed, and the guard mumbled. "How did she know my name?"

Madison scanned his shirt and saw no name tag. Had someone told her Potter's name when she'd checked in?

The guard shook off whatever held him and swung the door open. "Let's go."

TWELVE

....

D aniels opened the car door and got out. Rem followed and joined him on the sidewalk. Daniels eyed the jailhouse's façade. "You sure you want to do this? Technically, we shouldn't be here."

"Since when has that ever stopped us?" asked Rem. "We're not on this case, so we're just two friends visiting a prisoner."

"I don't think her attorney will see it that way."

The door opened and three people exited; a man and a woman in professional attire, and a woman in a sunflower dress. Daniels and Rem held the door and entered as the others left. Once inside, Rem paused for a moment before returning to the door and peering out the glass.

"Forget something?" asked Daniels.

Rem stared. "Did you...?"

Daniels raised a brow. "Did I what?"

"I swear she was familiar."

"Who?"

He glanced at Daniels. "That lady. The woman in the yellow dress. I swear I know her from somewhere." He looked outside again, peering each way. "She's gone. Where the hell did she go that fast?"

"Maybe you dated her, and she had to make a quick exit. It wouldn't be the first time."

"Huh. That's strange." He scratched his head.

"Not really. Come on, Romeo. Let's go. Time's a wastin'."

Rem shook his head, and with one last look, he turned to follow Daniels.

They signed in, showing their badges and checking in their weapons, and then were escorted into a small cell where they waited. After a few minutes, a guard appeared with Madison Vickers. She wore an orange jumpsuit and sat at the small table with them as the guard closed the door but stayed within view.

"I get more visitors here than I ever did at home," said Madison, her eyes weary.

"Did someone else come to see you?" asked Daniels.

Madison waved a hand. "It doesn't matter. What can I help you two with? Did you come to take another swing at me? Get me to confess?"

Rem cleared his throat. "First of all, no. We're not here to take any swings at you. In fact, we're off the case. Biggles told us to go home. He thinks he has his killer."

Madison straightened. "Then why are you here?"

Daniels faced her. "We're not exactly sure this case is as cut and dry as Biggles thinks it is. We think there's more to this story. Now, we don't know if you killed your husband or not, or if you killed Karl Scott, but we think it's worth a little more investigating. The sheriff doesn't know we've stayed, and neither does your attorney. And he won't like this meeting once he hears about it, so you can tell us to leave and we will. But the fact is, we want more information, and if you didn't do it, we'd like to help."

"Just be warned. If you did it, we'll nail your ass to the wall," added Rem.

Madison held still, eying them both. "How do I know you're not here to find more reasons to bury me to prove Biggles right? How do I know you're telling the truth?"

Rem stuck his feet out and crossed his arms. "That depends on what your bullshit meter is telling you right now. Who you gonna trust?" He glanced at Daniels. "We don't have to be here. I'd be happy to go home, pick up a few Taco del Fuegos, and knock back a beer. And I'm sure he'd like to go home and see his kid." He shot a thumb at Daniels.

They waited while Madison played with her fingers. She closed her eyes for a moment and took a breath, appearing to calm herself. "I didn't do it," she said, opening her eyes. "I didn't kill either of them."

Daniels tapped on the tabletop. "We heard you saw someone watching you, at your friend Laura's house."

"Yes. I did."

"Can you describe him?" asked Rem.

She paused for a moment. "It was dark, and he was hard to see, but he was tall and looked like a big guy. Had sort of wild hair. I can't be sure, but I think it was blonde. He was very serious, just staring at me." She hesitated. "If I had to compare him to someone, he was sort of like a young Rutger Hauer."

"Rutger Hauer?" asked Daniels.

Rem raised a brow. "The actor. He was in *Blade Runner*. I think he was in a Batman movie, too." said Rem. "He died, but he was in several films." Daniels shrugged. "Seriously? I loved *Ladyhawke* myself. Michelle Pfeiffer is gorgeous in that movie. But I guess she's gorgeous in every movie." He pointed. "Matthew Broderick is in it, too. Huh. I may have to watch that again."

Daniels stared blankly at his partner. "Anyway, Mrs. Vickers..."

"Call me Madison."

"For someone who couldn't see somebody in the dark, that's a pretty good description."

"I've had some time to sit and think in this place. It helps with the memory."

"Did he say anything to you?" asked Rem. "Make any threats?"

Madison shook her head. "No. He didn't speak, although..."

"What?" asked Daniels.

"It's silly."

"Nothing's silly if it might help your case. If you think it's important, tell us," said Rem.

Madison stared at her hands. "He...um...he spoke in my head. I heard him."

"He spoke in your head?" asked Daniels.

"Yes. I know it sounds weird, but I swear I heard him. It wasn't audible, but I heard it."

Rem glanced at Daniels. "What did he say?"

Madison swallowed. "He said 'I did it for you.'"

Rem cocked a brow and Daniels sat forward, frowning. "He said what?" A strange chill ran up his back.

"He said 'I did it for you.'"

Rem made eye contact with Daniels, and Daniels felt certain the same chill was running up his partner's back. Neither of them said anything.

"Is that bad? You both look like you ate something off for lunch," said Madison.

Rem tucked his feet up under his chair. "Are you familiar with the Makeup Artist case?"

Madison's brow furrowed. "The serial killer? Yes. Of course. Who hasn't heard about it? It was horrible, and not that far away from here."

"You know anyone who worked that case? Maybe a cop, or someone familiar with the crimes?" asked Rem.

"No. Why?"

Rem shrugged. "No reason. Just curious."

"Your friends came to see us," said Daniels. "They were quite adamant about your innocence."

"My friends? Who?"

"Laura Benoff. Angela Desmond, and Lucy—" Daniels snapped his fingers, trying to remember.

"Angelo," said Rem.

"Right," said Daniels. "You have any reason to suspect them?"

Madison scowled. "My friends? Why would I suspect my friends? Those women have been with me through thick and thin. And how can you possibly suspect them? They may have their issues, but it doesn't make them murderers. How can you say that?"

Daniels shifted in his seat. "It's our job. We suspect everyone. And how sure are you they have your back?"

Showing a spark of anger, Madison rose out of her seat. "Would you suspect him if someone accused you of murder?" She cocked her head at Rem. "You know nothing about my friends. They are the strongest women I know." She put her hands on her hips. "Did you know Lucy had a miscarriage four months ago? Her third one. She and Thomas have tried to get pregnant for years and almost adopted, but it fell through. And Angela? Her mother is a nutcase, and she has a brother who's tried to commit suicide twice, plus a teenaged stepson who hates her, so if she drinks a little, there's a reason. And Laura? Her family lived on food stamps when she was a child. She worked her ass off to put herself through college and law school. Her first husband divorced her when he met someone else. Laura worked eighty-hour weeks to help pay for her mother's home and her dad's medical bills. She paid for her father's funeral, despite having two siblings who contributed nothing. When she married Preston and finally had a little money saved, she left the law firm and has taken time for herself which she deserves. And now this whole Karl Scott money fiasco happened, which may force her back to work. Laura is my best friend and biggest protector. She'd give me the shirt off her back if it would help." Madison took a breath and shook her head. "So, no. I don't suspect my friends. Not at all." She sat back down.

Daniels relaxed his stance. "Okay. Point taken. But you have to look at this from our point of view. If you didn't kill your husband or Karl Scott, then somebody else did. And in our experience, the likelihood that it is someone random off the street is slim to none. Which means it's probably someone along the lake, probably someone you know."

"What about Sharie Scott? She could have killed her husband. Maybe she could have killed Donald," said Madison.

"She has an alibi for her husband's death, and we've found no evidence that Karl's murder was a hit. Way too messy. Whoever killed Karl was angry," said Rem. "And why would she kill Donald?"

"Donald and Karl argued not long before Karl's death. Maybe Sharie knows more than she's saying. Maybe Donald knew something she didn't want him to know," said Madison.

"Could Sharie have been sleeping with Donald?" asked Rem.

Madison's eyes widened and Daniels thought she was about to laugh. "Donald? Sleep with Sharie? God, no. He hated her. Called her a cow."

"Nice guy," said Rem.

"Which is why I shouldn't be the only suspect," said Madison.

"But you think he was sleeping with somebody," said Daniels.

"Yes. I thought he was. I don't know who, though, and I didn't really care."

Daniels sighed and cocked a brow at Rem. "You have any more questions?"

Rem rubbed his jaw. "Yeah, I do. Sharie Scott says you left a party at their house last summer looking disheveled and upset. Can you tell us what that was about? She said Karl had disappeared and reappeared around the same time. Did something happen between you two?"

Madison paled and her shoulders dropped. "I was drunk. I got sick in the bathroom. Karl tried to help me, but I almost got sick on him. I left, feeling embarrassed. I haven't touched alcohol since."

Rem waited. "And that's it?"

Madison studied her fingers. "That's it."

Rem looked at Daniels, narrowing his eyes. Daniels could only shrug. "Okay," he said. "Anything else?" he asked Rem.

"That's it for me," said Rem, standing. "We'll be in touch. I assume you'll be posting bail soon."

Madison sighed sadly. "We'll see. A million dollars is steep."

"I'm sure your friends will help," said Daniels.

Madison nodded. "I'm sure they would." She stood as Officer Potter approached the cell door. "You're going to stay on this?"

Daniels met Rem's gaze. "I think so."

Potter swung the door open, and Madison headed toward him. "Thank you."

"You can thank us once we solve this thing. It's not over yet," said Rem.

"Let's go," said Potter, and Madison followed him out and disappeared behind the wall.

Daniels hit a buzzer and the door on their side opened. "What do you think?" he asked Rem.

"I think it's time we got more info on Donald and Karl, and I sure as hell want more info on that party last summer."

"You don't believe her either?"

"Nope. She's hiding something. Plus, that man in the woods? I want to find him too." They walked out of the cell and down the corridor, picking up their weapons on the way out. "'I did it for you.' You think that's a coincidence?" Rem holstered his gun.

"I don't know," said Daniels. "A man in the woods watching Madison uses the exact same phrase the Makeup Artist used for one of his crimes? It's a hell of a big one if it is. Although I'm not sure what to think of her 'hearing' it in her head."

"Maybe that's how she interpreted it. Fear can do that." He groaned. "Something tells me we'll be spending a little more time on the lake. You like to eat fish?"

"You know I do."

"Good. Cause you'll be eating all of them. I got to find myself a pizza joint, or maybe a taco place."

"I could cook you up something. How about some delicious fish tacos?"

"Ugh."

"I'll throw some pepperoni on them."

"Take out the fish and add some hot sauce and you're on."

Daniels grunted in disgust.

**

Two hours later, Madison sat in her cell, holding her head. The conversations with Sonia and the two detectives bounced in her head. She questioned everything. All the decisions she'd made, the mistakes, the arguments, the doubts and fears. The men in her life. Everything had led up to sitting in a jail cell accused of murdering her husband.

She decided that if she ever got out of here, she would change everything. If this wasn't a wake-up call, she didn't know what was. Sonia's voice echoed in her mind. *It was time to discover her power. Trust her feelings. She'd played the victim for too long. And ghosts didn't haunt her house.* She had no idea what that last one meant.

Sighing, she went to lie down when a door clanged; she heard footsteps and Officer Potter came into view.

Second Slice

"Madison Vickers."

Madison sat up, wondering if she had another visitor.

He shot out a thumb. "Your bail's been posted. Let's go."

THIRTEEN

···

Laura pulled up to the Vickers' cabin and parked in the driveway. "You sure you want to do this? My guest room is perfectly comfortable and available."

Madison stared out the window and she took a deep breath. The familiar front entry with the heavy trunked trees and low-hanging branches put her at ease, despite what had happened here. She hadn't been back since that early morning horror show when Biggles had arrived, and they'd taken Donald's body away. "It's my home. I can't leave it." Despite her need to be back, the memory of Donald's lifeless eyes, the blood and the fear bubbled up, and for a moment, she questioned her decision. Could she stay here? But in that same moment, she thought of what Sonia had said. This is where she belonged, and even if she never entered the master bedroom again, she wouldn't let fear decide for her anymore.

"It's also where your husband was murdered."

"You said it was cleaned."

Laura gripped the steering wheel. "Oh, it's clean. I made sure of it. You could eat off the floor. I had them take the bed away so you wouldn't have to see it. The guest room is clean, too, so you can sleep there."

"That's fine. It's where I usually slept anyway."

"What?"

Madison shook her head, her memories surfacing. "Nothing. It doesn't matter anymore." She opened the door and got out. "Thanks again for picking me up."

Laura exited the car. "Of course. Stephen said he'd be here a little later. He had a client meeting."

Madison faced her. "Are you telling me the truth? Are sure you didn't post my bail?"

Laura walked over to Madison's side of the car. "I wish I had. I was working on getting the money together, despite what you told Stephen. But someone beat me to it."

"I didn't want that burden on you or Preston, or anyone else."

"Honey, you're my best friend. I wasn't going to let you sit in jail for the next six to nine months. That's ludicrous."

Madison paused, enjoying the breeze and late afternoon sunshine on her face. "Well, thank you, and thank you for getting this placed cleaned up. Just tell me what I owe you."

"We can worry about that later. Let's just go inside and sit for a second. It's been a long couple of days. We could use a drink."

"You don't have to stay. I'll be fine."

Laura took her arm. "You are walking into the place where you found your husband dead. I'm not going to let you do it alone, and neither are Lucy and Ang. They're inside, and probably sweating it out as we speak."

"They're inside? Why?" asked Madison, as Laura led her to the door.

"Because we are your friends, and we want to be here for you, and because I told them to." Laura opened the front door and they walked inside.

The house looked the same. The kitchen, dining and living areas all looked pristine. The big windows showcasing the lake revealed Lucy and Angie on the porch. Seeing Laura and Madison arrive, they opened the sliding glass door and came in, greeting Madison with hugs.

"You okay?" asked Lucy. She wore a yellow slim sundress that showed off her tanned legs and arms.

"Now that I'm out, I'm better," said Madison.

"I can't believe this bullshit," said Angie. "What are they thinking? You wouldn't kill anyone."

"Biggles is an idiot," said Laura. "He has the thought processes of a sixteen-year-old on a weed and alcohol binge. Stephen will tear him apart in court."

"Will he?" asked Madison. Her body felt heavy and she wanted to sit. The stress of the last few days was catching up to her. "The evidence doesn't look good."

Laura frowned. "Don't you start with that attitude. You need to be positive about this. There are plenty of other suspects."

"Who?" asked Angie.

Laura sighed. "We are not talking about this right now. It's the last thing you need," she said, pointing at Madison. "Go sit on the couch. I'm getting you a drink."

"I don't drink," said Madison. Listening to Laura's advice, she sat on the sofa, slipped off her shoes, and put her feet on the coffee table. She avoided looking down the hall toward the bedrooms. Her heart picked up speed when she remembered running into this room, terrified, and calling 911.

Laura put her bag down and walked into the kitchen. "You listen to me, my dear. I know you stopped drinking last summer because you made some poor decisions because of it. I get it, and I commend you for it. But you've been to hell and back, and you've got a long road ahead of you, so I made us a batch of Vodka Martinis, and you are going to have one whether you like it or not. If there's ever been a time to have a drink, it's now."

"Hell, yeah," said Angie.

"Get some glasses," Laura said to Angie.

Madison didn't have the strength or desire to argue, and to be honest, a martini sounded great. Sighing, she laid her head back. "Okay. I'll take one."

Lucy sat next to her. "You're really going to stay here?"

"Yes, I am."

"You won't be freaking out when you go to bed?"

Madison raised her head, trying not to think about Donald's wide eyes and his slashed throat. "It's my home. I'm not leaving it. I won't go into the master bedroom. I'm staying in the guest room for now. I'll be okay. It will be a little weird at first, but I can't live in fear."

"Aren't you worried someone might come after you?"

Laura carried a drink over and put it in front of Madison. "Lucy, really?"

"That's what I'd be thinking. If someone broke in here to kill Donald, why couldn't it happen again?"

"Nobody wants to kill me," said Madison.

"You sure about that?" asked Angie as she took the seat on the other side of Madison, holding a martini in her hand.

"Yes. I'm the scapegoat, remember? Kill me, and then they need to find another murderer. I need to stay alive."

"This talk is ridiculous," said Laura, walking over with two drinks in her hand. She gave one to Lucy and kept one for herself. "Madison will be fine. You have an alarm system. You need to use it." She sat in an armchair across from Madison.

"I don't know if I even remember the code," said Madison, rubbing her face.

"It's Jackson Pollack's birthday," said Lucy. "I remember it from when I came to check the house when you and Donald went to Europe a while back."

Madison raised a brow. "That was over three years ago. You still remember that?"

"The Pollack thing is easy to remember. He still your favorite artist?"

"One of them," said Madison. "God. I miss my painting. It feels like years since I created something."

"Well, you can pick up the brush now. You'll have the place to yourself. You can immerse yourself in your work. Let out all these frustrations on your canvas. Should make for some interesting pieces." Laura held out her drink. "Cheers ladies. To friendship and Madison. May they both be protected."

Madison eyed her drink and picked it up. She clinked her glass with the others and took a sip. The liquid soothed her, and she sighed audibly. "That's delicious. I missed a good martini."

"I know they were your favorite," said Laura.

Madison took another sip and began to relax. The alcohol hit her blood stream and since she hadn't touched it in so long, she could feel the effects. "I think I'm going to sleep like a rock tonight."

"I hope so. You sure you don't want one of us to stay with you?" asked Laura.

"Uh, excuse me?" asked Angie. "I love you, Madison, but I am not sleeping here." She took a healthy sip of her martini. "It would creep me out."

"Me, too," said Lucy. "Unless you want me plastered up against you, because I wouldn't be sleeping alone."

"You two are silly," said Laura. "This is probably the safest place in the neighborhood. I'll stay with you if you want."

"A murder happened here, plus it has a reputation for being haunted. That's a 'nope' for me," said Angie, draining her drink.

Madison thought back to Sonia's comment. *Your house isn't haunted* and wondered again what she meant. "Nobody needs to stay with me. I'll be fine. I'm looking forward to having a little quiet time. And I'm certainly not worried about Donald's ghost."

"Why not?" asked Lucy. "If anybody was going to haunt you, it would be him."

Madison groaned. "He can't do any worse to me than what he did when he was alive. That was the true nightmare."

"You should have told us what was happening," said Laura, swirling her martini. "We could have helped."

"It wasn't something I wanted to talk about. I was embarrassed. Plus, I knew you'd tell me to leave him, and I didn't think I could. I wasn't strong enough." Madison chuckled sadly. "I wish I knew then what I know now." She held her head.

The women were silent as they sipped their drinks, and Madison wondered what they were thinking. Angie took a last gulp, finished her drink and stood to get more. "Anyone need a refill?"

"Just bring the pitcher over," said Lucy. "We're gonna need it." She took a sip and put her glass down. "What happens now? Does your attorney feel confident he has a good defense?"

"He told me he'd hired a P.I. to dig into Donald's and Karl's affairs. Hopefully, he'll find something that will point to someone else," said Laura. "Ang, there's a fruit and cheese tray in there, too, if you want to bring it over."

"Sure," said Angie, carrying a pitcher and placing it on the coffee table. Lucy picked it up and added more martini to everyone's glass.

Madison sat back on the couch. "Those two detectives are still on the case. They came to see me in jail."

"What?" asked Laura. "You didn't talk to them, did you? Was Stephen there?"

Angie brought the tray over, and Madison reached for a piece of cheese. The alcohol was going to hit her hard if she didn't eat something. "I did talk to them, and no, Stephen wasn't there."

Laura leaned in. "Madison, you can't do that. They can use what you say against you. You can't talk to them without your attorney present. You know that."

Madison took another sip of her drink. "I know, but they're not even supposed to be on this case. They're staying because they don't believe I killed anyone, and they want to find out who did. They think Biggles is rushing to judgement."

"Can you trust them?" asked Lucy.

"Cops will say whatever they want to entice you to say something you shouldn't," said Angie, returning to her seat with a re-filled glass. "You need to be careful."

"Exactly," said Laura. "What did they ask you about?"

"Who else I thought might be the killer. I mentioned Sharie. And they wanted to know more about Donald, and if I thought he was having affairs. I told them I was sure he was; I just didn't know with who."

"You think Donald was sleeping around on you?" asked Lucy.

"Of course. Don't you?" asked Madison.

The women looked at each other. "Absofuckinlutely," said Angie. "The guy was an asshole."

Lucy stared at the carpet. "I never told you this, but he made a pass at me once. Last summer. Outside by the driveway. I'm sorry I didn't say anything."

"When he grabbed your ass?" asked Madison. "He told me. Said it was a lot firmer than mine. I told him that since he was telling me, that you obviously walked away, probably because you sus-pected, correctly, that his dick was just as flaccid."

"No. You didn't," said Lucy, her hand over her mouth.

"I did. Our marriage was pretty much over by then. But I did get shoved into a wall for that comment. Banged the shit out of my head." Madison rubbed her scalp, remembering the encounter.

"Jesus," said Laura. "This whole thing just pisses me off." She pointed. "But you still have to be smart, Madison. I hope these cops really want to help, but you still need to have Stephen present when you speak with them. You have to protect yourself."

Madison took another sip of her drink. "I know you're right, but I felt like it was the right thing to do. If they can dig up some more information on Karl and Donald, or maybe find out who they were sleeping with, then maybe they can catch the real killer, and I can get back to my life." She took a bite of her cheese.

"Your attorney hired a P.I.," said Lucy. "He should be able to get the same info, don't you think?" asked Lucy.

Madison nodded. "Maybe, but two heads are better than one, and I can use all the help I can get."

"I hope you're right," said Laura. "And I hope you know what you're doing. Does Stephen know you talked to them?"

"No," said Madison.

"He's going to be furious," said Laura.

"Probably, but he doesn't have to know." Madison finished her cheese and reached for a cracker.

"You can't lie to him. That sort of defeats the purpose of having an attorney," said Laura.

"You're such a stickler for perfection," said Angie, who took another healthy swig of her second drink. "Madison's not stupid."

"I didn't say she was," said Laura, frowning at Angie. "But she should tell Stephen what happened. I did go to law school you know. I know what I'm talking about."

"I know," said Madison. "I'm not discounting your advice. I guess I'm just tired of people telling me what to do. It's not personal." She swirled her drink, staring into her glass.

Laura paused. "It's okay. No offense taken. Just know that I only have the best intentions. I want to get you out of this mess. And I don't want you to trust two cops who end up turning on you. Stephen is your last line of defense. You have to trust him."

Madison's heart sank with guilt. "Sorry. I didn't mean to sound harsh. I guess me having to answer to yet another man got my hackles up, but I know you mean well."

"Speaking of Stephen, has anyone else noticed how hot he is," said Angie. She was close to finishing her second drink, and she waved it toward Madison. "You should sleep with him."

"Angie," said Laura and Lucy at the same time. Madison had taken a drink and almost choked on it.

"What?" asked Angie, throwing out a hand. "Don't tell me you haven't thought about it. Please. It would be good for you."

"That's the last thing I need. More complications," said Madison, wiping her chin.

"What complications? It's a fling. Once you're free, and this is over, he can go one way and you can go the other. It's a win-win. I suspect he's thought about it. He is a man, after all." Angie stood. "We need some crackers."

Madison's mouth hung open, as did Lucy and Laura's. They watched Angie walk into the kitchen and search the kitchen cabinets.

"She's nuts," said Lucy. "Don't listen to her." She picked up some brie from the tray. "Unless you think it might help."

"Lucy, not you too," said Laura.

Lucy's brows rose. "Come on. We've all been there. Sometimes we just need to take the edge off. And I suspect he would be a great weed whacker."

Madison held her stomach as Laura stared with wide eyes. Angie walked over with a box of crackers and stopped as Laura and Madison made eye contact and started to giggle. "What?"

Lucy joined in and giggled as well. Madison's giggling turned into full-on laughter. Laura put her glass down and held her chest as the laughing became contagious, and Lucy joined them.

"What did I miss?" asked Angie.

Madison wiped her watery eyes. "Stephen's a weed whacker." She almost couldn't get the words out.

Angie dug through the box for a cracker. "Oh, I bet he whacks a whole lot more than weeds," said Angie, returning to her seat.

Lucy doubled over, and Laura almost spit out a piece of cheese. Madison tried to pull it together, but the more she tried, the harder she laughed. Tears ran down her cheeks, and she wiped them away. It had been a long time since she'd laughed this hard. "Oh, my gosh. I can't breathe," said Madison through a labored breath.

"I have a weed whacker in my garage. You think Stephen would want it?" asked Angie.

"Don't you dare," said Madison.

"You could ask him for help. Then give him the sexy look." Angie put the cracker box down, crossed her legs, cocked her head, flung her hair back, and narrowed her eyes. She spoke breathlessly. "I want you to, Stephen..." She paused. "...to whack my weeds."

The women laughed more. "You want him to sleep with Madison or call a gardener?" asked Lucy, wiping her eyes.

"Hey," said Angie, returning to the crackers. "There's nothing wrong with a threesome. Martin cuts our grass. He'd be a fantastic addition to this escapade."

Madison shook her head, her laughter slowly subsiding. "I'm sure a jury would love to hear all about that." She held up her hands. "Murder suspect caught in a sexual tryst with her lawyer and gardener. All three suspected in murder of her husband."

"That would be a helluva story," said Angie. "You might consider it. Give 'em something really juicy to talk about, instead of all this boring stuff."

Madison sighed, her thoughts returning to her current situation. "I'll consider it."

"The threesome, or just sleeping with Stephen?" asked Angie. She munched on a cracker, but her look suggested her question was serious.

Her friends watched her, and Madison wondered how to answer. "I don't plan on doing anything stupid. Trust me." She reached for her drink and sipped on it, wondering if she was telling the truth.

**

An hour later, Madison shut the front door after saying goodbye to her friends. Leaning against the back of it, she surveyed the house. It was quiet. The sun was almost down, and the lake was still. All the boaters had gone in for the night. She debated taking the pontoon out on the water, but Stephen would be by soon, and taking a hot shower was higher on her priority list.

Pushing off the door, she swayed slightly. She'd stopped at two martinis, knowing that the third one would tip her over into the badlands, where poor choices were made, and regrets were born. She needed to be clearheaded when she met with Stephen. Making her way into the bedroom, she paused outside the closed door of the master. She had no desire to open it. Pushing aside the thoughts that surfaced, she entered the guest room, stripped down, and jumped into a hot shower, letting the water shed all the stress and tension, plus the jail smell, down the drain.

She emerged feeling much better, and more sober, and threw on a pair of jogging pants, and a loose fitting, soft, long-sleeved t-shirt. It wasn't glamorous, but she was comfortable.

Her hair still wet, she went back to the living room, opened the back door, and sat on a lounge chair on the patio, letting her hair dry. Thoughts of Stephen intruded, and she smiled when she recalled the earlier conversation, picturing him holding a weed whacker. She wondered why he wanted to meet so late when they could have planned to meet in the morning. Laura had told her that Stephen said it was important and it couldn't wait. Yawning, Madison laid her head back, and she wondered if she'd be able to stay awake.

A noise startled her, and she opened her eyes. It was almost dark, and Madison realized she must have dozed off. Checking the time, she saw it had been only twenty minutes since she'd been outside. The noise came again, and Madison sat up. It sounded like wood against wood. Remembering the man who'd watched her at Laura's, her skin prickled. She stood, and determined not to be afraid, she walked further out onto the porch, checking the area. Hearing it again, she turned, and saw her neighbor two doors down, throwing wood onto a wood pile. Sighing, she hugged herself, relieved that no one was stalking her.

For a moment, she remained there, enjoying the peace, when she again thought of the man in the woods at Laura's. Could he be out there now, watching her? Her mind raced, and she imagined him hiding in the trees. It wouldn't be hard. He could easily use the thick shrubs and woods as cover. Her belly tightened, and although she told herself she was overreacting, she turned, left the patio, and went back inside the house, closing and locking the door behind her. Taking deep breaths to calm herself, she stared outside, seeing no one, but having that odd feeling that maybe someone was out there.

The doorbell rang, and she jumped. Cursing herself for being foolish, she pulled it together and went to the door. Through the peephole, she saw Stephen and opened the door. "Hey," she said.

"Hi," he said. His posture was tense and his face stern. "Can I come in?"

Madison frowned, wondering what was bothering him. "Of course." She pulled the door wider.

He strode in. He wore a suit, but his tie was loose and on the way in, he undid the collar button on his shirt. After dropping his briefcase in a seat at the dining table, he slid off his tie and jacket and tossed them on the back of a chair.

Madison closed the door and walked over. "Something wrong?"

Putting his hands on his hips, he faced her. "You want to tell me why you spoke to those two cops without me?" His eyes narrowed in anger.

Madison's heart fell, but her own anger sparked. "They wanted to ask me some questions."

"And you answered them?"

"Yes. I did."

"Damn it, Madison. What are you thinking? What are you trying to do? Do you want to go to jail?"

Madison crossed her arms. "Wait just a second here. I did nothing wrong. I have nothing to hide. They wanted to do more investigating because they thought there was more going on here. Why wouldn't I want their help?"

His voice rose. "Because you don't know what they're really doing. They can construe whatever the hell they want from your conversation. All they need you to do is say something stupid and you're screwed. You should know better."

Madison dropped her jaw. "Know better? What am I, a teenager? And why would I say something stupid? *I didn't kill anyone.*"

"You don't get it do you?" He pounded his chest. "I'm trying to help you. I can't do that if you go behind my back and talk to the police. They have ways of saying and doing things to implicate you. You walk into that and I might not be able to get you out of it. I have to be there."

"I said nothing incriminating. They merely wanted to know about who else could want Karl and Donald dead. It seemed like a logical question to me. Everybody else out there wants an easy fall guy. At least someone is trying to get to the truth. Biggles sure as hell isn't going to do it."

His face darkened. "You talked about Karl? Jesus, what is the matter with you? You want them to make it a double homicide charge?"

"You're not hearing me, Stephen. I didn't implicate myself. I answered what I thought were perfectly logical questions. I said nothing about Karl other than maybe they should look at Sharie...and that stupid party last summer." The words were out too quick before she could pull them back.

Stephen's eyes narrowed. "Party? What party?"

Madison groaned. "Nothing. It was dumb. I got drunk and sick at Karl and Sharie's party last summer. I disappeared into the bathroom for a while. Karl tried to help, but I ended up leaving. No big deal."

"No big deal?" His voice rose again. "How come I'm just now hearing about this?"

Madison's almost yelled. "Because I didn't remember it. It was last summer for God's sake. Apparently Sharie mentioned it to the detectives, and they were following up. What is the problem?"

Stephen threw out his hands. "It puts you with Karl at a time when no one else can explain your whereabouts. It sheds doubt on your story and makes it look like you're hiding something. It could look like you're having an affair with Karl."

Madison froze. Stephen's face was red with fury, and he gripped the back of a dining chair. Madison tried to speak calmly. "I simply explained what happened after I drank too much at a party. I can't help what anyone thinks."

He whirled on her. "You better start, or you're gonna end up in a jail cell for the rest of your life." His face was as cold as her tile floors, he stepped closer and Madison flinched, turning away. Memories surfaced of Donald's anger and her muscle memory kicked in, preparing for the blow.

Stephen immediately pulled back, as she deflected and stepped away. "Madison..." he said, his voice quieting.

Realizing he would not hit her, Madison held her stomach, amazed at how her body had reacted. She knew then that Donald would have a lasting impact on her psyche.

"I'm sorry," said Stephen. His face had fallen; the anger stripped away. "I..."

"It's okay," said Madison. A cold sweat broke out on her skin, and she pulled out a chair and sat down.

"The hell it is. I lost my temper." He paused and sat next to her. "I'm sorry I scared you."

She rubbed her temples. "I guess Donald's ghost will always haunt me."

"I would never hurt you. I hope you know that."

"My heart may know it, but you'll have to tell my body and mind. They haven't quite caught up yet." She sighed and realized her hands were shaking.

He reached over and took one. His warm skin against hers brought a rush of endorphins, helping to ease her anxiety. "You need anything? I feel like such an idiot right now."

"I'm better. Don't worry about it. You were right to be angry. I shouldn't have talked to them. They just sounded so sincere. I believed them."

He expelled a deep breath. "I hope they were, but I have to put your interests first, and I have to protect you. It's my job to think the worst. I've seen way too many cops take advantage of a person's trust, and I don't want that to happen to you. The last thing I need or want is for you to go to jail for something you didn't do."

Her jumbled mind wouldn't settle, and her hand in his distracted her. "I understand that. But you have to know I'm not stupid."

"I know that, but you're under a lot of strain and that can lead to poor decision making. Let me take the lead here. I know what I'm doing."

Madison tried to pull her thoughts together, but it wasn't working. She'd gone from yelling at this man to wanting him to pull her closer, and she couldn't reconcile the two. "The men in my life have never been very good at taking care of me, or anyone else for that matter. I'm not used to it."

Pensive, he nodded. "I get it." He continued to hold her hand, and his thumb stroked her skin. "Promise me no more talking to the police without my presence, okay?"

"Okay." Madison thought of the weed whacker conversation.

"It's time to trust me. Can you do that?"

His eyes had softened, and she imagined moving from her chair into his, sitting in his lap and kissing him. The urge was so strong, she had to force herself to remain in her seat. It had been ages since a loving man had held her. Warnings flared that starting something with her attorney would be a bad move, and she tried to heed them. "I recall sitting next to you in math class in high school. Do you remember that?"

He chuckled. "I was a seventeen-year-old kid sitting next to the prettiest girl in school. Yes. I remember that. I had a huge crush on you."

She smiled. "I cheated off your math tests. I used to look over your shoulders to get the answers."

"And I used to let you. I could smell your perfume every time you leaned in."

Her heart swelled, thinking of the smart, dorky kid who'd barely spoken to her. "I passed math class because of you."

"And you will be exonerated because of me too. There's nothing I want more. I can't have the prettiest girl in school go to jail. I helped you before, and I will help you again. Only this time there are no video games and I'm not that shy kid too scared to talk to you. This time I'm playing for keeps."

Her heart fluttered, and she held his gaze. Squeezing his fingers, she spoke honestly. "And I'm not that silly girl in high school. I've made choices I regret. I've done things I shouldn't have, but I've always been so afraid. I stayed with a man who didn't love me, and I've been a people pleaser. But I don't want to do that anymore. When I get through this, I'm going to embrace my life. Do the things I've always wanted to do. Be a woman who loves her life, who takes the bull by the horns and acts, despite the consequences. I want to take risks based on my choices and no one else's. And if I screw up, I'll do better. I'll surround myself with people who love me, care for me, and who would never hurt me. And I'll find a man who worships me and my body."

Taking in an almost imperceptible breath, Stephen's face colored. Madison's body bloomed with heat, and she did what she'd imagined. Standing, she loomed over him.

"Madison...," he whispered heavily.

Sliding into his lap, she put her arms around his neck. He leaned back against the chair, but his eyes roamed over her face, and his hand came up and rested against her cheek. "You're more beautiful now than you were in high school."

Running her hands through his hair, she leaned close enough to smell his aftershave. Her breathing deepened, and she spoke softly into his ear. "We probably shouldn't do this."

He groaned against her cheek. "I know we shouldn't."

"But we're going to do it, anyway." She stood and turned, shifting one leg over to straddle him. His hands encircled her waist, and she brought her lips to his and grazed softly against them.

He sucked in a breath. "God help me," he said, capturing her lips and pulling her against him.

Madison moaned and kissed him back, not being delicate. Now that she was kissing him, her entire body rocketed into fifth gear. She wanted and needed to be touched, tasted and ravished, and based on Stephen's reaction, he had every intention of doing all those things and more.

His hands stroked her back, and he straightened, bringing his body closer to hers. Madison slanted her lips over his, devouring him, loving the feel of his body pressed up to hers. The kiss deepened further, their tongues sliding back and forth. His hands found her buttocks, and he squeezed them and pulled her in.

Groaning with pleasure, Madison arched against him, and he kissed her neck and collarbone, his tongue teasing her skin. His hands found the edge of her shirt and he slid them under and caressed her belly and ribcage, eventually finding her breasts.

Madison sighed with pleasure, and she pulled her shirt off, allowing him more access. He slid her bra straps down and exposed her breasts, peppering them with soft kisses and delicate nibbles, making her writhe and gasp.

"My God. I want you," said Stephen, nipping at her skin.

Madison tried to gain control of her senses. "I want you too. Come on."

She forced herself to stand, her legs wobbly from desire. He stood next to her, but pulled her back in, kissing her neck and shoulders.

She yanked up his shirttail, pulling it out of his pants, and then tried to unbutton his shirt, but it was taking too long. Stephen pulled away to help but, impatient, he yanked on the shirt, ripping the buttons off. "I've got plenty more."

His chest exposed, Madison kissed his torso and abs, dragging her tongue over the hard ridges. Her belly flipped and gripping his back, she dropped lower to find his waistband when he stopped her and pulled her up. "The bedroom," he said lustily. "I want to make you scream my name."

She bit her lip in anticipation. Her heart was thumping hard, and she could barely control her breathing. All she could do was picture him looming over her, his naked body over hers, as he rocked against her. She squealed as he grabbed her by the waist and held her, her feet off the ground, as he walked her toward the guest room.

"We're gonna make new memories here," he said into her ear. "And let tomorrow take care of itself."

Madison wrapped her arms around him. "I want you to scream my name too."

He chuckled. "I'm counting on it." Kissing her, he carried her into the bedroom.

FOURTEEN

....

Rem studied the laptop. The information they'd requested from Captain Lozano had arrived in their email earlier that afternoon. After talking to Madison, they'd spent the rest of the day talking to the locals about the lake and the murders, gleaning whatever information they could about the Vickers and the Scotts, plus anyone else who might be of interest.

So far, all they'd discovered is that Madison was well-liked, but her husband wasn't, and her art was too expensive. Sharie and Karl liked to flaunt their wealth, although no one minded because the Scotts liked to spend it on lavish parties and lots of alcohol. Karl was a flirt and so was Sharie. The rumor mill seemed to think the Scotts were swingers, although no one could provide proof. Everyone had theories on who killed Karl and Donald, ranging from the spouses to alien visitors.

They'd picked up burgers after a long day, and Rem ate a fry. "Anything of interest?" he asked, looking over Daniels' shoulder.

Daniels picked up a pickle. "Not yet. Just trying to decipher the numbers."

They'd requested the financial information on both the Scotts and the Vickers, hoping it might provide more insight into both couples.

Rem rubbed his tired eyes. "I hope there's something in there, otherwise we're at a loss. We didn't get a lot of help today."

Daniels bit into his pickle and took a sip of his water. "Oh, I wouldn't say that. We learned how sweet Madison was and about her poor senile dad, and how grouchy Donald was, plus Karl was a sex addict and Sharie didn't care because she liked the money."

Rem sat back in his chair. "Oh, and they loved the Fourth of July parties the Scotts threw. The fireworks show over the lake was as good as any city show." He smacked Daniels' shoulder. "Oh, and what about that Anne and Bob couple...what was their last name?"

"Hell if I know."

"Well, apparently Anne makes a great lasagna and Bob's a maniac behind a speed boat. Almost threw some chick he was pulling on a raft out of the lake on a tight turn."

Daniels chuckled, put down his pickle and grabbed a napkin. "And nobody likes Madison's artwork. They don't get it."

Rem nodded. "And Biggles does a shitty job of enforcing the 'clean up after your dog' rule, and can we arrest someone for that?"

Daniels shook his head. "You shouldn't have advised that woman to pick the shit up and put it in the neighbor's mailbox."

"Why not? It's what I would do."

"Biggles is gonna love that," said Daniels.

"It'll give him something to stay busy. Dog shit issues are more up his alley."

"Murder certainly isn't," mumbled Daniels, picking up his chicken sandwich.

"Nope."

Rem picked up his double patty with cheese and took a big bite. "Wha bout Dona one?" he asked through a mouthful.

Daniels raised a brow. "What about Donald's phone?"

Rem made a nod and pointed.

"Amazing. After all these years, I'm finally learning to speak Rem," said Daniels. He punched up another email.

Rem chewed and swallowed. "I'd think you'd be fluent by now."

"You'd think," said Daniels, studying the laptop. "Nothing of importance on the phone that they could find. A few heated text exchanges with his wife, some fishing and lake photos, and some uneventful voicemails. They are going to send us transcripts. But no smoking gun."

"Really? The man who supposedly is sleeping around has nothing incriminating on his phone? Hard to believe."

"If he was smart, he'd have another phone. Use that one to talk to his mistress." Daniels reached over and stole one of Rem's fries.

"They didn't find one."

"Were they looking for one? Maybe they weren't checking the right places. He probably kept it hidden. He wouldn't want Madison to find it."

"Good point. We should ask her to look around. Since she made bail, she could check the house." He picked up a napkin. "I wonder who posted her bail?" asked Rem, wiping his mouth.

"Probably one of her friends."

"Considering what we've learned about Karl and the money he lost, that may not have been so easy."

"Maybe she has a mysterious benefactor," said Daniels.

"Maybe," said Rem.

Daniels flipped back to the financials and read the screen while he picked at his sandwich. Rem took another large bite of his burger.

"This is interesting," said Daniels.

"What?" Rem leaned in.

"Two large sums of money were taken out of the Vickers' account about six months ago. Twenty grand and ten grand."

"Where'd they go?"

"Don't know. Wait. Here." He pointed at the screen. "He wrote a check for 20k to Karl Scott's investment group. The 10k was a cash withdrawal."

"Cash? Why cash?" asked Rem. "Why not write another check?"

"Because he doesn't want anyone to know who he gave the money to, most likely. Why else keep it secret?"

"Maybe it went to a woman that's not his wife?"

"Could be."

"We're gonna have to talk to Madison again."

"Her lawyer will love that." Daniels took a bite of his chicken.

"He should. We're trying to help."

Daniels paused to chew. "He may not see it that way. This could be a motive. If Madison discovered what Donald was doing, it gives her a reason to kill him."

"None of this should be a shock to him. He's likely got someone doing some investigating as well. He can learn this stuff just as easily as we can."

"Maybe not as fast though."

Rem grabbed three fries, slathered them in ketchup and ate them. "I'd love to see his face. Would he be happy or sad?"

"Should be happy. It gives him someone else to look for."

"Depends. Maybe Donny Boy gave the cash to his mother. All we have are assumptions that he was sleeping with someone."

Daniels, eyeing the screen, knitted his brow. "Wait a minute. Maybe not." He tapped on the screen. "Look at this."

Rem leaned over. "What am I looking at?"

"One of Donald's credit card statements." His finger scanned down the screen. "Do you see that?"

Rem squinted. "Twenty bucks at Condom Sense?"

"No, you bonehead. Here."

Rem noticed a seventy-dollar charge at Lou's Inn. It was dated two months ago.

"And here." The same charge was noted two weeks earlier. "And here."

Rem followed Daniels' finger. Donald had five charges for Lou's Inn over two months. "Lou must have comfy beds. Maybe Donnie slept better there."

"Sleeping being the immediate question."

"Maybe he and Madison had a fight."

"Madison slept in the guest room, remember? Donald threw her out of the master. He didn't feel the need to defer their bedroom to his wife."

Rem pulled his cell out of his pocket. "Lou's Inn?"

"Yup."

Rem hit some buttons. "Huh. Well, I doubt he went there on a whim. It's a good forty-five-minute drive from here."

"Good place to go if you don't want to be recognized," Daniels.

Rem nodded. "You make an excellent point."

"Thank you."

"Anytime." Rem put the phone down. "Care to make a trip to see Lou tomorrow? Check out his fine establishment."

"Would love to. Hopefully Lou's a talker."

"If we're lucky, we'll find out who this mystery woman is."

"We could use some luck right now," said Daniels.

"I hear you." Rem stretched and stifled a yawn. "I'm beat."

"We have Karl Scotts' financials too. You want to look at those?" Daniels accessed another email.

"Can't wait. This is almost as exciting as that movie you dragged me to last month."

"You loved that documentary. It was all about the war."

"Of 1812. You didn't specify that."

Daniels smirked. "Minor detail."

"Sure it was."

"A little education never hurt anybody."

Rem snorted. "It pained the hell out of me. The only good thing that came from it was the thirty-minute nap I got in the middle of it."

"You snored by the way."

"Who would have noticed? We were the only ones in the theatre. Next time, I'm picking the movie."

Daniels frowned. "I don't think so. I refuse to see anything with flying sharks and tornadoes. Talk about pained. I almost stabbed myself with a fork."

"You didn't though. Secretly, I think you were hooked."

"Hooked on sanity. I'm surprised I kept mine. It explains a lot about yours though."

Rem picked up another fry. "My sanity is, for the most part, fairly stable."

"That's one way of putting it." Daniels clicked at the mouse and opened the next set of files. "Ok, let's see what we—"

A loud bang on the wall interrupted, and Rem jumped in his seat. "What the hell was that?"

They listened to the silence for a second before Daniels stood. "It sounded like it came from outside."

Rem took a quick swig of his beer before standing as well. "Maybe it's that mystery animal from the other night?"

"Maybe." Daniels walked away from the table and toward the front door. His gun and holster hung from a chair and he picked up his weapon.

Rem followed. "We're out in the middle of nowhere. Whatever it is, it's big."

"It's probably nothing, but we are two cops hanging around to solve a murder, and if Madison isn't our gal, then somebody else is. And if that somebody is still hanging around..." Daniels walked to the window to the side of the door and peered out.

Rem picked up his holster and gun from the sofa and slid it on, buckling it on the side. "Don't forget Rutger Hauer."

"Who?"

"Madison's man in the shrubs."

"Oh, yeah. Him, too."

Daniels looked outside. "All I see is blackness. We need to turn off the lights."

"The hell we do," said Rem. He went to the side window and peered out.

"Then we need to go outside." Daniels opened the front door.

"Wait a minute," said Rem. He struggled to secure his holster to his belt as Daniels walked out onto the porch. Rem finally got it attached at the same time as something hit the roof, and Daniels yelled "Freeze!" from the porch and took off in a run.

"Shit," Rem ran after his partner. He pushed the door open and sprinted out onto the porch with just enough time to see Daniels jump over the side rail and disappear into the woods, chasing something or someone. Rem took off after him, trying to keep up. He was fast and could normally beat Daniels in a foot race, but the woods were foreign to him, and it was dark. He did his best to avoid low-hanging branches and the roots that sprung from the ground, but he almost tripped twice, and his face stung with the sharp sting of the branches that smacked his face. He could still make out Daniels ahead of him though, and he ran faster, determined to keep Daniels in his sights.

Still running, Rem sensed a shift in the air and heard Daniels yell, "Don't move," and then silence. The footfalls of his partner stopped, and Rem expected to run up on him. Then there was a thump and Rem entered a small clearing. Breathing hard, he saw Daniels lying sideways on the ground beside a large tree, unmoving. Rem started toward him when he saw the figure in the trees.

He stopped short and raised his weapon. "Stay right there. Don't move."

Sweating, Rem's heart thumped, and he slowly moved forward. The figure was shrouded in darkness. A crescent moon provided little light, but Rem could see he wore a dark hoodie which obscured his face. The man stood and stared, seemingly unconcerned that Rem held his gun on him.

Trying not to worry about his partner who still hadn't moved, Rem cocked his gun. "Get down on your knees, hands in the air. Now."

The figure stayed still.

"I said get down on your knees, hands up." He took a step forward. "I don't want to shoot you, it's too much paperwork, so do me and you a favor and do as I say."

In the low light, Rem could detect a slight smile on the man's face. And then he spoke in a low whisper. "I did it for her."

Rem strained to listen; unsure he'd heard correctly. Aiming the weapon, he spoke louder. "I said get down on—" Something hard hit his head, and he grunted and went down.

FIFTEEN

....

Madison rolled into Stephen's midsection, putting her head against his chest. He pulled her close, and she snuggled against him. "What are you thinking?" she asked, playing with his chest hair.

She heard him sigh. "That I'm getting into deep waters here. I just had the most incredible sex, and I'm holding my high school crush in my arms, and my mind is whirling about how to defend you, when what I would rather do is just enjoy this moment."

She looked up at him. "Could you get into trouble for this?"

"It's not exactly recommended. It's considered unethical."

"Could you be disbarred?"

"I suppose if you complained, I could be."

Madison smiled. "I'm not complaining."

He stroked her skin. "Neither am I. But it opens a host of potential issues. If it comes out that we have a relationship, and I lose and you go to jail, you could say that this relationship affected my ability to be your counsel. It could even be construed that I extorted sexual favors from you to provide you representation."

"That's silly."

"Maybe. But there's a long road ahead. A lot can happen between now and then."

Madison sighed. "Are you saying we shouldn't do this again?"

He studied her in the darkness. "God, I hope not. But it's something to consider."

Madison pushed up on her elbow. "Stephen, I know this is probably ill-timed, but I also have to think that maybe it's not such a bad thing either. We're both under a lot of stress. We're attracted to each other. Why not enjoy this time that we have together?"

"Because emotions get involved. And when the stress hits the fan, and it will, we need to keep our feelings for each other out of it, or we could both get hurt."

"You think that might happen? We could do that to each other?"

"It's hard to imagine in the glow of our lovemaking, but yes, it could happen."

She rested her head in her hand. "I just had the most amazing night of my life in the arms of a man who worshipped me, instead of degraded me, and now you're saying this is a bad idea."

His hand slid down her back and glided over her skin. "I don't want to stop, believe me. It's just in my experience, it doesn't end well, and I don't want that to happen to us."

Madison frowned. "You've done this before? Sleep with a client?"

Stephen paused. "Once. Early in my career. It was a disaster. But I was stupid. I let my lust get the better of me, and it didn't end well."

Madison's heart sank. "Is that what this is? Lust?"

His face fell. "God, no. I think that's why I'm conflicted. I told myself I would never do that again. Get involved with a client, but here I am, in bed with you. And the only way I can reconcile it is because you're not just a client. I think I've been secretly in love with you since tenth grade, and the more I'm with you, the more I want to be with you. And how any man can treat you the way Donald treated you is beyond my understanding."

Madison traced one of his ribs with her finger, and she heard him inhale. "I don't want you to take pity on me."

He sat up, taking her face in his hand. "You don't get it. I've been dreaming about this moment. You're in my arms in this bed, and naked against me. This isn't about pity. This is about getting a grip on reality. I'm with the woman of my dreams, but I'm tasked with keeping her out of jail. Can I handle both at the same time? And what if I lose?" He stroked her cheek. "It would mean losing you too."

Her heart skipped, and Madison questioned her own motives. Was this just a distraction to get her mind off the case? Did she just need this man to put his body against hers to make her feel alive again? Or was she falling for him? How would she handle being found guilty and having to say goodbye? She put her hand over his. "Listen, Stephen. I don't know where this will lead. Maybe it is a bad idea. Maybe we're both operating from lust. I must admit, it's been a long time since I've felt this good with someone. Is that because I had such a shitty life with Donald? Probably. Does it mean I want to spend the rest of my life with you? No. I think I've got a lot to figure out just like you do. But I'm okay with that. I'm not expecting love. With everything happening, we can just take it a day at a time. I need you focused on exonerating me, and if you can't do that and this then I respect that. Just know that I will wish you might jump my bones, anyway."

He chuckled. "You're saying you can control yourself around me?"

His nearness made her blush, and she brought her face closer and brushed her lips against his. "Absolutely. I'm tougher than I look." She peppered his cheek with kisses, making a trail with her tongue down to his neck, where she nipped at his earlobe.

His arms encircled her waist, and he moaned. "You're a strong lady."

Madison slid her hand down his stomach to his leg, where she stroked his inner thigh.

He moaned, and his hands traveled to her hips and he gripped them. "I wish I could say I was that strong with you, Madison. But you take my breath away."

She pushed against him and he fell back against the mattress with her astride him. Sliding her hands down, she smiled as he squirmed against her. "Don't worry. I'll be strong for both us." She kissed his sternum, moving slowly downward to his belly and beyond. She spoke against his skin. "As I recall, I wanted you to scream my name."

He laid his head back. "Oh God, Madison."

Traveling lower, she grazed her mouth over his hipbone. "I think I'm going for something louder." She slid her tongue over his skin.

He sucked in a sharp breath. "Oh, Madison."

She smiled. "Now we're getting there."

**

Rem blinked his eyes, trying to see. His head pounded, and he reached to touch it, feeling the warm liquid trickle down his skin. What the hell had knocked him out, a boulder? His mind did a quick rewind, and he recalled the man in the woods. Rem sat up quick, looking for his gun, which he saw was still in his hand. He groaned as the pain in his head flared. Despite the discomfort, he did a quick check of the area, looking for his assailant. He saw no one. The man in the hoodie was gone, but next to Rem was a decent-sized rock, and Rem wondered if that was what hit him, and if it was, where did it come from?

A moan made him turn, and he saw Daniels struggling to get up on his knees with a grimace while holding his chest. Rem, seeing there was no imminent threat, slid his weapon into his holster and crawled over to him. "Daniels, you okay?"

Daniels groaned, holding his side, and got up far enough to lean back against a tree. "I'm alive."

Rem did a quick once over of his partner. He didn't see any blood, but Daniels was obviously in pain. "What happened?" Thinking of Daniels' gun, he looked around. "Where's your weapon?"

Daniels looked pale in the low light. "I don't know." He held his head as if dizzy. "He took it."

"What?" asked Rem. "How?" Rem knew it would take a feat of strength for anyone to take his partner's gun without getting a serious beating.

Daniels held his ribs and shifted uncomfortably. "I don't know. He just took it."

"You're not making any sense." A trickle of blood ran down his neck and he wiped it away. His head ached, but he started to check the area. "Where'd he get you?" he asked, looking around. He didn't need the hooded man to come up on them while his partner was down.

"My ribs," said Daniels. "He threw me against the tree."

Rem raised a brow. When he'd come onto the scene, the hooded man had only been standing there, appearing calm. There would not have been enough time for him to engage in a fight with his partner before Rem entered the scene. "Just stay put. I'm gonna look for your gun."

Daniels laid his head back and Rem slowly stood. He weaved a bit when his head swam, and he grabbed onto a branch for balance. After a second, his head cleared, and he scanned the clearing, looking for Daniels' weapon. It was dark, but he hoped the moonlight would reflect against the metal, otherwise they'd have to wait until morning to find it. As attractive as it was to Rem to get them the hell out of these dark woods, the thought of his partner's gun being in the wrong hands was far worse. He walked further into the trees, near where the man had stood, and pushed back shrubs and kicked the dirt, when he saw it. The handle poked out from a fallen log, and Rem picked it up, confirming it was Daniels' weapon. Relieved, he tucked it into his waistband.

After walking back to his partner, he squatted next to him. "Can you walk?"

Daniels cracked an eye open. "You're bleeding."

Rem touched his temple, pulled his fingers back and saw the blood. It had run down in rivulets from his scalp to the side of his face and neck and onto his shirt. "I'll live, although this shirt won't. Which is a shame 'cause it's one of my favorites."

"I guess you'll have to choose another one from your 1980's shirt collection."

"They're comfortable."

"That's one way of describing them." He tried to get up but grimaced and grabbed his side.

"That's what you get for making fun of my shirts." Rem reached around Daniels' back and helped pull him up. "Come on, partner." He got Daniels' to a standing position with Daniels' arm over his shoulder as Rem supported him. "One step at a time."

They ambled back to the cabin. Daniels stumbled a few times, but Rem caught him, and despite his throbbing and bleeding head, Rem got them back to the house. They took the stairs slowly, walked through the open door, and Rem carefully lowered Daniels to the couch. After getting him situated, he closed and locked the door, and pulled out his cell.

"Who are you calling?" asked Daniels.

"An ambulance. You need to go to a hospital."

"Put the phone down. I'm fine."

"You can barely walk."

"I just got my ass thrown into a tree. I cracked a few ribs. All they're gonna tell me is to go home and rest. There's nothing else they can do."

"You could have a punctured lung."

"Does my breathing sound labored to you?"

Rem had to acknowledge that Daniels sounded fine.

"Besides, if anyone needs a doctor, it's you. You look like something that walked out of The Night of the Living Dead. Are you sure you're okay? You could have a concussion. Plus, you're still recovering from the Artist. How's your injury?"

"My belly is fine. It's a little sore, but not bad." Rem looked down at himself and saw the ruin of his shirt. Blood had dripped down his shirtfront and stained it a dark red. He checked his reflection in the living room window, and he could see the blood smeared on his neck and face. He would have scared himself if he hadn't been prepared. "It looks worse than it is."

"You sure about that? You might need stitches."

"I'm fine."

Daniels held his side. "Well, if you're fine, then I'm fine."

Rem held his phone, deciding what to do. "If you cough up blood or do anything weird, I'll take you to the hospital myself. You got that?"

"Same goes for you, partner."

"There's a local doc here in town. If we make it through tonight, maybe we can check in with him tomorrow. Sound good?"

"Sounds good."

Rem pulled out Daniels' gun and put it on the table. "I found it in the shrubs." He sat next to Daniels. "You want to tell me what happened out there? How the hell did he get your gun? I was right behind you and didn't see a thing."

Daniels stared ahead, not saying anything. He shifted on the couch and grimaced. "I wish I could explain it. It doesn't make sense."

Rem grabbed a throw pillow. "Here. Put this behind you." He shoved the pillow behind Daniels' back. "Better?"

Daniels groaned. "A little."

"It's gonna hurt for a while."

"I know." He glanced at Rem. "You're getting blood on the couch. You need to do something about that cut."

Rem touched his head and felt the warm stickiness again. "Shit. Hold that thought." He stood and wobbled slightly.

"Woah. You sure you're okay?" asked Daniels. "Don't faint on me. I'm in no condition to catch you."

Rem regained his balance. "Don't worry. If I fall, just leave me there. Maybe I can get some rest."

"Get a wet towel. There's one in the bathroom."

Rem headed into the bathroom, ran the sink, and threw a hand towel into it. He pulled his shirt off and tossed it in the trash. After wringing out the towel, he wiped off the blood on his arm and torso and cleaned his face. He needed to take a shower, but this would have to do for now. He threw on another shirt and went back into the front room.

"Better?" he asked, holding the towel against his head. "I'm going to have to buy Lozano new linens."

"He'd like that," said Daniels. There was more color in his face now. "Maybe something with butterflies."

"Or daisies," said Rem, with a grin. He sat. "You were saying?"

Daniels went still again. "I was chasing him. I was getting closer, gaining on him, when he stopped, and..."

"And what?"

Daniels shook his head. "I don't know. I raised my weapon. I think I yelled 'Don't move.'"

"You did. I heard it."

"Then...then...the gun flew out of my hand. Before I could even react, I was shoved backward and into the tree."

Rem scowled. "Did he attack you? How did he push you against the tree?"

Daniels raised a hand, his eyes wide. "That's just it, Rem. He never touched me."

Rem studied his partner, wondering if Daniels also had a head injury. "You're saying he took the gun away from you?"

"No. The gun flew out of my hand. Like that scene in *Star Wars*, where Vader pulls Han Solo's gun away from him. It was like that."

"You mean *The Empire Strikes Back*."

"Whatever. You get the point."

Rem shifted to face Daniels. "You're saying he used the force to pull the gun away from you?"

Daniels gestured in frustration. "I didn't say he used the force. But the gun flew out of my hand. And then I flew into the tree."

"And he never touched you?"

"He never touched me." Daniels sucked in a breath when he moved on the couch. "Damn that hurts."

Rem held the towel against his head. "You're sure? Could there have been another assailant?"

"There was no one else. You were right behind me. Did you see anyone else?"

Rem recalled running into the scene, seeing Daniels on the ground. "No. I didn't."

"How did you get hit on the head?"

Rem pictured the hooded man. "I saw him in the woods, just standing there, looking cocky as hell. I told him to get down on the ground, but he ignored me. I yelled again, and that's when I got hit in the head. I think it was a rock."

"You didn't see anyone?"

"No. Doesn't mean someone wasn't there."

"Did you sense there was someone else?"

Rem thought back. Cops were known to have a sixth sense about things, but he'd felt no other presence in the woods. He felt certain the man in the woods had been alone. "No."

"So, who threw the rock?"

Rem tried to think. Where had the rock come from? "I don't know." He paused. "There was something else. He spoke to me."

"He what?" Daniels gripped his ribs. "What did he say?"

Rem held his throbbing head, thinking he needed to take some aspirin. "He whispered 'I did it for her' right before I got knocked in the head."

Daniels frowned. "Well, that's interesting."

"I thought so, plus I could kinda sorta could see him in the moonlight, despite the hoodie."

"And?"

He cocked an eyebrow at Daniels. "I swear he bore a slight resemblance to Rutger Hauer."

Daniels squinted and sighed. "This case makes me want to fly to Mexico, open a bar, and drink margaritas until I die."

Rem pressed the towel against his head. "Care if I join you?"

SIXTEEN

....

Maddie stretched and rolled in the bed. Remembering Stephen's touch, she smiled. It had been an enjoyable night, and she found it hard to believe that her first hours back in the house where she'd found her husband's murdered body had been so amazing. She hadn't thought once about Donald or that she was out on bail. Stephen had successfully distracted her from all of it and it had been a welcome respite.

Now that she was awake, reality set in. Stephen had left fifteen minutes earlier after awakening in a rush. He had an early morning meeting, and he would need another shirt. Not wanting to be late, he'd jumped in the shower, quickly dressed in his slacks and an old t-shirt she gave him, gave her a kiss goodbye with a promise to call soon, and had left. Maddie wondered if his car being out front all night might have drawn the neighbors' attention, but she decided she didn't care. They already thought she was a murderer. How much worse could it get?

Wanting some coffee, she got up out of bed and put on a robe from the closet. Stepping out of the room, she glanced at the closed door to the master and the memories rushed back. Seeing the blood in the bathroom, running to find Donald, and seeing his lifeless body, and his cold dead eyes.

The bile rose, and she put a hand on the wall to steady herself. She closed her eyes, trying to regain her composure as the images flashed through her mind. After a few seconds, she began to feel better, and she forced herself to think of something else. She thought of Stephen and sighed, wishing he were there. Straightening, she took a breath and walked down the hall away from the master. One day, she would have the courage to enter that room, but it wouldn't be today.

After walking into the front area, she stopped. The dining room was quiet. Stephen's tie and jacket were gone, and she guessed he'd grabbed them on his way out. She knew he hadn't lingered because she'd heard the door open and shut right after he'd left the bedroom. But looking into the kitchen, she could see something on the floor. Stepping closer, she could see it was a lemon rind.

When Laura had been in the kitchen making drinks the previous day, she'd cut up a lemon. She had left a few rinds on the counter, along with the cutting board, a knife, and a half-filled bottle of vodka. Maddie had left it to clean up later, but walking into the kitchen, she saw all of it, except the vodka bottle, on the floor, including a dish towel that had been hanging from the refrigerator door. The vodka bottle was lying on its side. The lid was on, but not tightly and vodka slowly dripped down the counter.

Maddie had lived in the cabin long enough to know that strange sounds and odd movements were not uncommon. Her father had remarked on it when Maddie was a child and Donald had noticed too after he'd moved in. Over the years, the rumor that the home was haunted took hold and now it was part of the allure of the house. Maddie had never felt unsafe though. This home was her haven, and ghosts and murders would not throw her out.

Maddie thought of Sonia Vandermere. There are no ghosts and *your house isn't haunted.* Madison studied the mess. How had these items been thrown off the counter, and why? Stephen wouldn't have done it. And this wasn't the first time Maddie had found something odd like this, but it was the strangest.

Grabbing the towel, she began to mop up the spilled vodka, wondering how it might have happened. Nobody had snuck into the house to make a mess of her kitchen. She and Stephen had been in the bedroom all night, enjoying the pleasure of being together. They'd both made good on their promises to scream each other's—

Maddie went still as a strange chill ran up her back. She recalled gripping the bedsheets, writhing while Stephen teased her with his tongue and rocked her into oblivion as she'd screamed his name. In her mind's eye, she could see the items flung from the counter as the energy swirled through the house. An unbelievable realization occurred to her. Had she done this? Had she made this mess in the throes of passion?

She thought back to the other times she could recall other strange things occurring in the home. Mirrors breaking, pictures falling from their perches, paint spilling in her studio, canvases falling from her easel. She'd always attributed it to the house, but now she had to think twice. She and her father and she and Donald had experienced many arguments and heated exchanges between these walls. Had her anger and the energy she'd exuded somehow moved the items? Had she caused this since she was a child?

It's just the beginning. You don't know what you're capable of. Sonia's words echoed in Madison's head, and she had to just sit on the kitchen floor as her mind swirled. My God. It was the only coherent thought she could muster. Was it possible? All this time, she'd been throwing things around with the power of her thoughts, and not even known it?

Madison couldn't bring herself to believe it. It was too far-fetched and outrageous. She'd heard of such abilities through various TV shows and books, but she'd never considered herself to have the same potential. That was crazy.

Madison stared at the rind on the floor. If she had the ability to move objects with her mind, then she should be able to move the rind. Feeling silly, but curious, she focused on the rind, willing it to move. Squinting, she imagined the rind sliding over the floor without being touched. When the rind didn't move, she tried harder, pushing with whatever mental strength she could find and focusing it on the lemon. Nothing happened. The rind remained where it was. Madison chuckled, glad that no one was there to witness her brief fling with stupidity. Did she really think she could move things without touching them? Stephen and Laura would think she was certifiable, and she didn't feel much different.

It had been a long and stressful week, and that strange visit with Sonia had her thinking all sorts of crazy things. Madison didn't have an explanation for the strange happenings in her house, and probably never would, but what she knew was that she wasn't the cause. She didn't have paranormal abilities. There were definitely strange things going on, but they had to do with murder, not ghosts, and if she wanted to prove her innocence, that was what she needed to focus on. Not spilled vodka or fallen lemon rinds. Laughing at herself for her moment of insanity, she picked up the towel and resumed her cleaning.

**

Stephen walked to his car in the parking lot. It had been a long three-hour meeting. He'd agreed to do some pro bono work for the justice center in town and they had quarterly meetings which he'd needed to attend this quarter. The meeting had gone on far longer than he'd planned, and his stomach growled. He'd had no breakfast, and only a couple of cups of coffee. Looking at his watch, he thought of what and where to eat when his phone rang. Checking the number, he saw it was Desmond, the private investigator he'd hired for Madison's case. It was his third call in the past hour.

Loosening his tie, he answered. "Desmond?"

"Steve. Where you been?"

"Meetings. What's up? You got something?"

"You could say that. You got some time for lunch? We need to talk."

**

Remalla pulled into the parking space in front of Lou's Inn. It was small with a long row of rooms on two floors extending from an older building with wood siding and brick exterior. A big sign with neon lights flashed "Lou's Inn" and below it the word "Vacancy"

"Nothing fancy," said Remalla, killing the engine.

Daniels shifted with a grunt and held his side. "Do you need fancy when you're just here to have sex?"

"Maybe not fancy, but hopefully it's clean."

"It's seventy bucks a night. It can't be that dirty."

"True. How's your ribs? The pills helping any?" They'd stopped by the local doctor's office on their way to Lou's. Remalla had ended up with eight stitches in his head and Daniels had been correct. X-rays showed he had two broken ribs and there was little to do except rest. The doctor had told him to take ibuprofen and sent them both home.

"Oh, yeah. I feel great. Like I just got out of the ring with Andre the Giant."

Rem rubbed the bandage on his head. The injury ached, but his headache was better and his side felt fine. "Great wrestler, although he'd have broken more than two of your ribs."

"He'd have taken my head off." He popped the door open. "How's yours by the way?"

"Still there. You ready?"

Daniels braced himself and then slowly exited the car, holding the frame for support.

Remalla walked to the front as Daniels joined him. "You sure you're up for this? I can handle it if you want to wait in the car."

"I'm fine. It's just getting up and down that hurts. Asking a few questions won't kill me."

Rem opened the door, and they walked into a sparse but clean lobby area. Beyond it were a few tables and chairs with a coffee machine and cups along the wall. No one was at the front desk, but Rem rang the bell.

A young man who looked to be around twenty-five with thin hair and round glasses came out from the back. He was thin but not muscled. Rem thought he looked like someone who watched a lot of TV or played video games all day.

"Can I help you?" he asked. He looked between the two of them. "Need a room?"

"No, thanks," said Daniels. He held out his badge. "I'm Detective Gordon Daniels and this is my partner, Detective Aaron Remalla." Rem held out his badge. "We'd like to ask a few questions if that's ok."

The man studied their badges. "What's this about? Something wrong? We had some other dude in here earlier."

"Really?" asked Rem. "Do you know who he was?"

"Some P. I. Asking questions about a murder on some lake."

Rem glanced at Daniels. "Probably working for Madison's attorney."

"Guy doesn't waste time," said Daniels.

"Who?" asked the man.

"Nothing," said Rem. "You mind if I ask you your name?"

"Billy."

"Billy," said Rem. "We're wondering if you've seen this man before? He's checked in here several times in the last six months." Rem held up a picture of Donald Vickers.

Billy stared at it. "I don't think so, but I've only been working here the last few weeks, and only on weekends."

"Today's Thursday," said Daniels.

"I took Donna's shift. She wants to hang out with that loser boyfriend of hers." Billy rolled his eyes.

"How long has Donna worked here?" asked Daniels.

"I don't know. Maybe a year?"

"When will Donna be back?" asked Rem.

Billy pushed his glasses up on his nose. "Next Monday, I think."

"What about this woman?" asked Daniels, holding up his cell. Rem could see Madison's face.

Billy squinted. "She's pretty."

"You seen her around here?"

"No, but again, I haven't worked here that long, but Donna might."

Rem sighed and looked around the lobby. "Those work?" he asked, pointing at a camera in the corner.

"Coffee machine works fine," said Billy.

"No. I mean the cameras," said Rem.

"As far as I know."

"You mind if we look at the footage?" asked Daniels.

"What about the other guy?"

"What other guy?" asked Rem. "The P.I.?"

"No. Not the P.I. The other guy in the picture."

Daniels frowned. "The other guy in the picture?" He glanced at the picture of Donald. "This guy?"

"No. The other man, the P.I. He had a picture of another man. You gonna ask about him, too?"

Rem squinted at Daniels. "Wait. You mean this guy?" Rem scrolled through some pictures on his phone until he found a picture of Karl Scott. "Him?"

"Yeah. That's him."

"Have you seen him?" asked Daniels.

"No, I haven't."

Daniels scowled.

"I was just wondering if you were gonna ask about him. He's rich, isn't he?"

"Yes. He is. Or was," said Rem.

"That pretty girl hooking up? Is she a prostitute?"

The pounding in Rem's head resumed. "No. She's not a prostitute."

Billy's eyes rounded. "Drugs? Are they drug dealers?"

Daniels stared at Billy with a look of impatience that Rem was familiar with. "Billy...listen. We just—"

"You think she killed him?" asked Billy.

Daniels sighed. "That's what we're trying to figure out."

"Is she the wife? Isn't it usually the spouse? Or is she the other guy's wife? Or is she the mistress?" He pointed at Madison. "What's her deal?"

Rem shook his head, which he regretted. "Billy. The cameras. Do they work?"

"I think so, but you'd have to ask Lou to be sure."

"Lou?" asked Daniels. "The owner's here?"

Billy shot out a thumb. "Sure. In the back. How did you know it was the owner?"

Daniels paused. "Um. It's called Lou's Inn. I made an assumption."

Billy chuckled. "Oh, my gosh. That makes sense. You want to talk to Lou?"

Daniels held his ribs. Rem wasn't sure if Daniels was hurting from his injury or this conversation. "Please," said Daniels.

Billy disappeared behind a door.

"I hope Lou does a better job running this place than he does with hiring people," said Rem.

"Of course, we pick the day Donna decides to hang out with her loser boyfriend," said Daniels.

"Of course."

The door opened, and Billy stepped out with a woman behind him. She was short of stature with blue silver hair and a wrinkled face. Glasses hung around her neck and she put them on. "What can I help you with, gentlemen?" Her voice was raspy and Rem guessed she was a smoker.

"You're Lou?" he asked.

"I am. Who's asking?"

They flashed their badges and introduced themselves.

"Listen. I'll tell you what I told that other fella. I can't show you any video without a court order. You bring that, and I'll set you up in the back and bring you some drinks and peanuts, but without it, you don't get squat."

"You recognize any of these people?" Rem flashed the pictures of Donald and Karl and Daniels held out Madison's photo.

"I seen 'em on the news. That's about all I can tell you."

"This man has been here several times. Any chance we can talk to Donna?" asked Daniels.

"She'll be here on Monday. Feel free."

"Any chance we can call her?" asked Rem.

"On her day off? You'll be lucky if she answers. And I'm not giving out any personal information."

Daniels straightened and groaned. "Ma'am, we don't want to inconvenience anyone but we are trying to solve a murder here. We'd appreciate any help you can offer."

Lou pulled her glasses down. "Detectives, I get it. We've all got jobs to do. You're trying to find out who's sleeping with whom, and I'm sure with those good lucks of yours and those nice smiles, you usually get what you want. But I'm old now. Maybe in my younger days..." She winked at Daniels, who raised a brow. "Believe me, I don't doubt that man has been here with his mistress many times. It's how I stay in business. But I can't give you information I don't have and I won't compromise my employee's privacy. So come back on Monday with a court order, and I'll give you a corner with a TV and Donna can sit with you and give you a play-by-play, but until then..." she checked her watch "...times a wastin' and I'm missing my soap opera."

Rem scratched his head, trying to avoid his stitches. "Okay. Thanks for your time. Enjoy your show."

Lou started to turn for the door, but paused. "You know, you boys should consider something."

"What's that?" asked Daniels.

Lou raised a brow. "I was young once. I had my hell raisin' years and been to a few hotels myself. But as I recall, we never just went to one. We moved around a bit. Didn't want to be too obvious. If he came here a few times, he probably went somewhere else around here too. Just a thought."

Daniels nodded. "You make a good point."

"You gentlemen have a nice day," said Lou, and she disappeared behind the door.

Billy stood there with his mouth open. "Sorry. She's a stickler for rules."

"I can see that," said Daniels. He looked at Rem. "Well, you want to hit a few other hotels around here? We might get lucky."

"Nothing else was on the credit card statement."

"Doesn't mean they didn't pay cash."

Rem shrugged. "Can't hurt."

"You want me to call Donna for you?" asked Billy. He pulled out his phone.

Rem checked that the door to Lou's office was closed. "You sure about that? Your boss didn't seem too keen on it."

"She didn't say no. She just said Donna probably wouldn't answer."

The slight blush to Billy's cheeks made Rem suspect that Billy might have a crush on his coworker and was looking for a reason to call her. "That would be a big help."

Billy dialed and put the phone to his ear. "So we need to know if that woman slept with those two men?" His eyes widened and his face flushed a deeper red. "I'll find out."

"Why don't you let us ask the questions, okay?" asked Daniels.

"You sure?"

"Absolutely," said Rem.

Billy listened as the phone rang, but Donna didn't answer. Billy slowly deflated. "She must be busy with that dumb boyfriend."

"Don't worry about it. Just tell her we'll plan to be here on Monday. We'll talk to her then," said Daniels.

"I'll keep trying," said Billy.

"Thanks," said Rem. "You ready?" he asked Daniels.

"As I'll ever be." He waved a hand. "Thanks, Billy."

Billy tried to dial again. "If she slept with those two, I'll find out."

Rem didn't bother to correct him. "That's great. See ya, Billy."

They left Billy behind the counter still trying to phone Donna and stepped outside.

"I think that was more painful than my last root canal," said Rem.

"And I thought my ribs hurt," said Daniels. "But at least we know we have nice smiles." He opened the passenger side door and slid in carefully.

Rem sat behind the wheel. "What do you want to do now?"

"We could call Lozano. Get that court order."

Rem checked his watch. "He'll probably be at lunch. I'll call him in an hour." He looked up and down the street. "There's a few hotels in the area. You want to go ask some questions?"

"You know, we never looked at Karl Scott's statement. We got interrupted by Rutger Hauer. Maybe he has a few interesting entries."

"Maybe. Can you pull it up on your phone?"

"Should be able to." Daniels shifted and grimaced. "You mind if we get a quick bite? I could use some food."

Rem noticed Daniels' pale pallor. "You all right? I can leave you somewhere to rest. I can do the questioning."

"Nonsense. I'm fine. Just need to sit somewhere other than a car. Besides, you got your brains knocked around. You need the help."

Rem rubbed his scalp. "That conversation didn't help my headache any."

"I saw a diner on the way in. It's just a few minutes from here. Let's go there."

Rem started up the car. "Sounds good." He put the car in reverse when Billy shot out of the lobby and rushed to Daniels' side of the car.

"Wait." He yelled, his hands waving as he held his phone.

Rem hit the brakes. Daniels rolled down his window. "Billy? What?"

Billy was breathless as if he'd run a marathon. "I got her. I got Donna. She's on the phone. She wants to talk to you." He held out his cell.

Daniels glanced at Rem, who shrugged. Daniels took the phone. "Hello? Donna?"

Rem listened to one side of the conversation.

"Yes. This is Detective Daniels. I wanted to ask..."

Daniels paused as he listened. "What?" His face darkened. "Yes. We came to ask about them. Yes. They were on the news." He listened again, his face serious. "You're sure?"

Curious, Rem turned to face Daniels.

"When?" asked Daniels. "You know it was them? You'd testify to that? Have you told this to anyone else?"

Daniels held the phone on his shoulder and pulled out his pad and paper from his pocket. Rem noticed he wrote a phone number and Donna's name.

"Thank you, Donna. We'll be in touch." He hung up the phone and handed it back to Billy. "Thanks, Billy. Donna's a smart lady. You should fight for her."

Billy's jaw dropped as Daniels rolled the window back up. "Have a nice day." He glanced at Rem. "Let's go."

"What did she say?"

"Oh, nothing much. Just that she remembers Donald Vickers vividly. Saw him on the news when he was murdered. He hit on her once when he checked in. Doesn't know who he was here with though. The lady never came in the lobby."

"Really? That's too bad." Rem pulled the car out and headed down the street, leaving Billy in the parking lot. "At least we tried."

"Oh, but that's not all, Tonto. She knew who Karl Scott was too. He came in last summer and he tipped her big time. Plus, he was on some infomercial around then, so she recognized him. She couldn't believe it when he was killed."

"Did he come with someone?"

"Sure did."

Rem waited. "Well, don't leave me in suspense. Did Donna see her or did this mystery lady stay in the car, too?"

"Nope. She came in. Helped herself to some coffee."

Rem's heart thudded. "Donna recognized her?"

"Did she ever. Said it was Madison Vickers. Saw her on the news when Donald died."

Rem almost braked in the middle of the road. "You're kidding."

"That's what she said. Said she'd swear to it."

"Shit."

"I know. Hold up. There's the diner."

"You still want to eat?" asked Rem.

"Yes. We're gonna need our strength. Madison's got some explaining to do."

SEVENTEEN

....

Madison perused the books on Laura's bookshelf. Laura had asked her to lunch, but was stuck on the phone in the office. She told Madison to wait a few minutes but would be out soon.

Madison saw a yearbook, and out of curiosity, she pulled it out and opened it. She smiled when she saw a picture of Laura from her college days, standing with a group of women, sticking her tongue out and holding up a peace sign.

"Hey, Maddie. How are you?"

Maddie jumped and turned. "Preston. Hey. I didn't realize you were home."

"Yes. I worked late last night so I'm going in a little later today. Laura told me what's been going on. I can't believe it all."

Madison closed the book. "It's been crazy. The last few days have been tough."

Preston sat on the couch. "I hope you already know this, but we're here if you need anything. This whole thing about you killing Donald is crazy. We know you didn't do anything and never would. It thrilled Laura when you made bail. She was planning on pulling out all the cash we had to help you."

Madison sighed. "I didn't want that. I'm glad you didn't have to use your money, although I appreciate your willingness to help."

"You know we'd do it for you. Besides, we weren't worried. You're not a flight risk. Unless you were preparing to flee to South America or Europe."

Madison smiled and sat next to him on the couch. "Well, I hear Bolivia is nice this time of year."

He chuckled. "Spain, too. I've always wanted to go there."

"Well, maybe once I get through this, we can all take a trip somewhere. Get the hell out of town for a while."

He nodded. "We'll make margaritas, eat lousy food, get sunburned, and sleep late."

"And come back only if we feel like it."

They chuckled at the same time a door opened and Laura stepped out. "Sorry about that. I got tied up. Give me a couple more minutes, and I'll be ready. You headed out, hon?"

Preston stood. "Yeah. Duty calls. It's good to see you, Maddie. Let's have dinner soon, before we head to Spain."

Maddie laughed softly. "That would be great. Good to see you Preston."

Preston gave Laura a quick kiss and headed to the back door. "Bye, hon."

"See you tonight." Laura waved, and Preston left.

Madison noticed Laura stare off after he'd left. "Everything okay?"

Laura shook her head. "Yes. It's fine. He's just been working long hours. And I'm not working right now. It's been stressful. But listen to me complaining, considering all you've been through. Just ignore me."

Maddie stood. "Laura. You can talk to me. Just because I'm dealing with a lot doesn't mean you aren't. I can be here for you like you're here for me. It goes both ways. You can still talk to me."

Laura reached out and took Maddie's wrist. "I know that. I just don't want to burden you with anything else. It's not that big a deal. I worry too much anyway. Preston tells me to stop, but I do it anyway." Laura sat in a chair. "So enough about me. How did your meeting with Stephen go last evening? How's he feeling about everything? Any news about who posted your bail?"

Madison held the yearbook to her chest, unsure of what to say.

Laura tipped her head. "Maddie? What is it? Is it bad?"

Maddie sat back on the couch. "No. It wasn't bad."

"It was good?"

Madison felt her skin warm. "It was very good."

Laura narrowed her eyes. "Why do I have the feeling we're not talking about the same thing?"

Madison bit her bottom lip. "We didn't talk much about my case."

Laura scooted forward on her seat. "What did you do?"

Madison cleared her throat, unsure of what to tell her friend.

Laura's eyes widened. "You didn't. Did you sleep with him?"

Maddie could feel herself blush. "It just sort of happened."

"I don't believe it."

Maddie nodded.

"What are you thinking?"

Madison's face fell. "What do you mean?"

"He's your attorney. He should know better."

"You didn't seem to think it was a bad idea yesterday."

"Yesterday, we were drinking and joking around. I didn't think you were seriously considering it."

Maddie didn't know what to think. "Are you saying I made a mistake?"

"Maddie, he's supposed to defend you during a very difficult time. How can he do that if he's emotionally involved? Plus, you just lost your husband. Do you think now is the time to have an affair?"

Maddie gripped the book. "I'm not saying I'm in love with him. You know what I put up with while married to Donald. It was a loveless marriage. Stephen is..."

"Stephen is what? Kind, compassionate, supportive? That's his job."

Madison sucked in a breath. "Are you saying he's just taking pity on me?"

"Not at all. I'm sure he's smitten with you. Most men are. You're the girl who got away in his mind. He's got a crush. But he should be professional here. Ethically, this could get him into trouble. Once the trial is over, and you two want to pursue a relationship, that's fine. But wait until then. This will only lead to trouble."

Madison didn't know what to say. Logically, Laura had a point. But did that mean she was right? Staring at the floor, Madison felt childish, but that small voice inside her told her she was a big girl and could make her own decisions.

Laura's cell rang. She picked it up and groaned. "Hold that thought. Give me a few more minutes." She stood and went back into her office.

Madison sat, holding the book, thinking. Had she screwed up? Her night with Stephen had been magical, and she'd felt better that morning than she had in a long time. Sighing, she fell back against the seat. Could she get Stephen into trouble? Would he be able to defend her properly if he was sleeping with her?

Her weariness returning after Laura's comments, she opened the yearbook and flipped through it. She sighed as she flipped through the pictures and stopped dead at a photo. Sitting up, she studied the picture, not sure she was seeing it correctly.

It was Laura and a man, arms entwined, standing under a tree. Laura smiled up at him while he smiled at the camera, his boyish features emanating an impish mood. They looked happy together. Madison studied the man, recognizing the classic good lucks. Sonia was right. He looked very Paul Newman.

Everything went cold; her body went rigid. Laura and Stephen together in a yearbook photo? They'd known each other? My God. Madison touched the photo. What was happening here? Had they had a relationship? By the looks of it, they were much more than friends.

She flipped through more photos, coming to a stop at Laura's individual photo along with several more of her classmates. Written in the margin was a note.

To my lovely Laura. You are the best and the brightest. Thanks for making my days (and nights) so much better. Love, Stephen.

Madison closed the book with a snap. Shit. How could Laura not have told her? Her mind raced. Even worse, how could Stephen not have told her? He'd slept with her best friend?

She stood, prepared to leave, when the office door opened, and Laura stepped out. "Sorry about that. That should be the last of the interruptions."

Madison didn't move, but held the book against her chest.

Laura put her cell down. "Maddie, don't be mad at me. It's just I don't want you to get hurt. Getting involved with Stephen is just a bad idea. Especially right now."

Madison frowned. "I'm sure you don't approve. It can't be easy for you."

Laura paused. "It has nothing to do with me. But I am an attorney. I know how this can happen between two people during an emotional time, but it never turns out well."

"Did it turn out well for you? With Stephen?"

Laura cocked her head. "Excuse me?"

Madison dropped the yearbook on the coffee table. "Thanks for making my days and nights better. I believe that was the quote. From Stephen to you. Or should I jog your memory?"

Laura stared at the book, and her eyes rounded. "Oh, shit."

"Oh, shit? That's your contribution to this conversation? How could you not tell me?"

Laura held out a hand. "It was ten years ago, Maddie. I didn't think it mattered."

"Didn't think it mattered? You recommended your old boyfriend to defend me?"

"Come on. It wasn't like that. Yes. We dated. But that's how I knew him. We went to law school together. He's a great attorney. We haven't seen each other since school. He went one way, and I went another. We married other people. It's not like we're still involved. But when you needed help, I went to the best, and he is the best."

"How could you not have said anything?"

"Because I didn't think it mattered. Did he ever say anything to you?"

Maddie tried to rein in her anger. "Never. But it sure would have been nice to know before I slept with him."

Laura threw out her hands. "I didn't think you would sleep with him. Come on. That's the last thing I expected."

"We talked about it last night. Did you hear Angela? She even suggested it."

"It's Angela, for God's sake. She'd suggest sleeping with Ronald McDonald if it would get you a free Big Mac. I didn't think you would take her seriously. I thought you were smarter than that."

"Now I'm the stupid one? You're blaming me?"

"I'm not blaming anybody. I'm just trying to explain—"

"—why you didn't tell me you'd slept with Stephen. I'm still not clear on that one. That should have been the first thing out of your mouth."

"Why? What did you expect me to say? Here's your attorney. Oh, and we've had sex."

"It would have been nice."

"Oh, come on, Maddie. Use your head. You're just mad because he didn't tell you, and you're taking it out on me. And I think you know you shouldn't have slept with him. But I know why you did. You needed someone who treated you better than Donald, and you knew Stephen wanted you, and I can't blame you for that. I can't say I would have done any different. But don't blame me for your mistake."

Madison dropped her jaw. "I can't believe this. You both lied to me, and instead of having the decency of being honest up front, you both kept it a secret, and now you're trying to put it on me? If nothing else, a good friend would apologize. You should have told me."

Laura put her hands on her hips. "Maybe I just don't feel like being a good friend right now. To be honest, I'm exhausted. This friendship has worn me out."

Madison went still. The words stung, and she took a second to collect herself. "I think maybe we're not going to have lunch today. I'm going home." She picked up her purse from the table and headed to the back door.

"Suit yourself," said Laura.

Madison left, slamming the door behind her.

**

Sharie Scott pulled down the purple suede pants from the hanger, and held them, smelling the familiar scent. A tear escaped, and she wiped it away. She had made up her mind that she needed to clean out Karl's side of the closet. She couldn't do it all at once though. It was too hard and the memories surfaced. Deciding to take it slow, she chose one item per day to fold and pack. Today it was the suede pants. He didn't wear them often, but when he'd wanted to stand out, they were a unique choice. Karl didn't like to blend in and clothing was his way of expressing himself.

Taking one last whiff, she folded the pants and put them in the box. Looking up at the rest of the items in the closet, she realized at the rate she was going, she wouldn't get the closet clean for at least a year. Perhaps she could bump it up to two items per day. Spying a leather jacket he'd worn sporadically, she took it off the hanger, and held it. It retained fewer memories than the others since she couldn't remember him wearing it that often with her. She did recall he looked good in it, but then, he looked good in most things.

Hugging the jacket and smelling the leather, Sharie caught sight of herself in the large full-length mirror. Sniffing, she wiped her face when she saw her mascara was running. Her eyes were red and her skin dull. She hadn't slept well and it showed. Plus, she wasn't the ageless beauty she'd hoped to be. Although she took care of herself, maintained a trim physique, and was still wearing the clothes she'd worn when she'd first met Karl, she felt old. The laugh lines were showing. Karl had never stopped telling her though how beautiful she was, but now that he was gone, so were the reminders, and sadness and depression had crept in.

Sharie thought of Madison Vickers and her friends, and how the men watched them. Especially Madison. She'd always been the one everyone gravitated to. Sharie wished now that someone would gravitate to her. Yes. There would always be men in her life. Sharie knew that, but there would never be another Karl. Despite his wandering eye, he always came back to her. And she always came back to him.

Sighing, she looked away from the mirror and began to fold the jacket. Checking the pockets, she felt something and reached in and took it out. She half expected to see one of Karl's expensive cufflinks; the man was forever misplacing them. But it was a different piece of jewelry - a beautiful blue stone; Sharie thought it was turquoise; encircled by small diamonds with a pin on the back. She didn't know if the diamonds were real or not, but a memory flickered. She'd seen it at a party last summer and Sharie had commented on how beautiful it was and where could she get one?

Holding the pin, she thought back, and recalled clearly who'd been wearing it. Madison Vickers.

**

Madison stomped through the woods, furious. She'd walked to Laura's for the fresh air, and now she was returning the same way, glad that she was alone on the trail. Hot tears streamed down her face, and she swiped them away. How could she be so stupid? They'd lied to her, and worse, she'd done the very thing she'd told herself she wouldn't do. Get caught up with yet another man who'd promised to take care of her. When would she learn? Sitting in jail had apparently not been a big enough wake up call. The only person capable of taking care of her was her, and maybe one day she would figure that out.

Her nose running, and her eyes filling, she held back a sob. All she wanted to do was fall into bed and hide. The world felt far too cruel right now.

Stopping on the trail, she reached for a tissue in her purse. Wiping her face, she heard a rustling in the woods. The trail was normally busy on the weekends with joggers and bikers, but since it was the middle of a weekday, she was alone. Checking the area, she saw no one, but a chill crept up her back, and she remembered the man in Laura's backyard, watching her.

The noise came again, and she whirled to look behind her, but saw nothing. An odd feeling ran through her, and she remembered the strange dreams. The man and the woman nearing her, and the other man, menacing, trying to prevent that from occurring. Listening intently, she waited. She no longer felt alone. There was a definite sense of being watched.

"Who are you?" she yelled. "What do you want?" Turning in circles, she hoped for a response. Her heart thumped, and her skin prickled, but she wanted to know who this man was and what he wanted from her. Taking a steadying breath, she asked the big question. "Did you kill Donald?"

Nothing. Not even the birds were singing. Her fear rising, she decided that maybe she didn't want the answer as much as she thought. A twig snapped, a bird cawed, and Madison took off in a sprint.

EIGHTEEN

···

M adison made it to the back of the cabin, unlocked the door and ran inside, closing and locking it. Breathless, she stared out the back window, but it all looked quiet. She'd seen no one on the trail, but that odd feeling wouldn't leave her. Someone had been out there.

Telling herself to calm down, her mind replayed her argument with Laura, and her anger returned. How had her best friend decided not to tell her about her relationship with Stephen, and why had Stephen also stayed silent? Did they really think it was no big deal?

Madison sighed and turned away from the window, wondering what to do next. How would this affect her relationship with Stephen and his ability to defend her? There was no way she couldn't confront him about this. She was furious, and he needed to explain himself. Angry, Madison strode toward the kitchen, tossing her purse in a nearby chair, when the doorbell rang.

Startled, Madison jumped, still a little rattled by her walk on the trail. Refusing to give in to her fear, she went to the door and checked the peephole, seeing a delivery driver outside. She opened the door.

"Delivery," said the scrawny driver. He wore a baseball cap and chewed his gum. He held a paper-sized brown bulky envelope.

Madison took the envelope and signed for it, closing the door as the driver headed back to his truck. The letter had her name and address handwritten in a neat scrawl, but there was no return address. Walking to the dining table, she ripped it open and pulled out a cream piece of colored stationary. There was another item wrapped in bubble paper, and she slid that out.

She read the note.

Dear Madison,

I am glad to hear you made it home and pleased your stay in jail was not overly long. I have included something for you I think you need. It came in handy before and I think it will again. Wear it when you can and remember our conversation. You are stronger than you think, know more than you realize and can take your power back whenever you're ready. Don't forget it.

Trust your instincts. They will help you during this difficult time. And remember, you have more help at your fingertips than you believe.

There is more to tell, but that is for another time. Right now, you have other forces to fight.

Until we meet again, dear.

Sonia

P.S. I talked to a few friends about your plight, and they offered to post your bail. I hope you don't mind, but they and I agreed it was for the best.

Madison reread the letter twice more, amazed at what this strange woman had done for her and wondering why she'd appeared in Madison's life. How did she seem to know her so well, and why did she care? And she had friends willing to post her bail? Why and for what purpose? Sonia had laughed at the notion when Madison had mentioned it during their discussion.

Confused, Madison put down the letter and picked up the item. Pulling at the bubble wrap, she ripped it off and saw the bracelet with the purplish stones; the one Sonia had slid off her own wrist and let Madison hold in jail. What had she called the stone? Fluorite? *It will help with balance and clarity.* Madison recalled Sonia's words. She could definitely use that right now.

Putting the bracelet on her wrist, Madison admired it in the sunlight. Something about it seemed calming. Realizing how stressed she'd been, she automatically took a deep breath and exhaled, allowing some tension to dissipate. Maybe there was something to these stones. Keeping the note, she threw away the envelope and stared at the bracelet again. *You have more help at your fingertips than you believe.* What did that mean?

The doorbell rang again, along with a strong knock. A male voice traveled. "Madison. Are you there?" The knocking came again.

It was Stephen.

**

Stephen knocked again, impatient. He needed to talk to Madison about what he'd learned, and he wanted an explanation.

He started to knock again when the door opened. Madison stood there with a flat expression on her face. "What is the matter? It takes a few seconds to walk to the door."

Stephen strode in, remembering their chemistry from the night before, but shoving it from his mind. He had more important problems to deal with and he couldn't let his feelings get in the way. "We need to talk."

Madison closed the door behind him. "We sure as hell do."

Stephen yanked off his tie and slid his jacket off. "I talked to my P.I."

Madison followed him into the front room. "I talked to Laura."

Stephen didn't know why that mattered. "He discovered something very interesting."

Madison smirked. "What a coincidence. I discovered something interesting too."

"I'm serious, Madison."

"I'm serious, too, Stephen. I didn't know you were a liar."

Stephen cocked his head. "Excuse me?"

"I saw the yearbook at Laura's."

"What yearbook?"

"Oh, the one with the pretty pictures of you and Laura in an embrace. The one where you wrote how much Laura helped you through your days and nights. That yearbook."

Stephen tried to make sense of what she was saying.

"What's the matter? Cat got your tongue? You don't recall your relationship with Laura?"

Stephen frowned. "That was ten years ago."

"And you didn't think maybe you should have told me you had an affair with my best friend? Don't you think you should have mentioned it before you slept with me last night?"

Stephen shot out a hand. "It's water under the bridge. It was a long time ago."

Madison turned red. "What the hell does it matter how long ago it was. You and Laura were a couple. How could neither of you have mentioned it to me?"

"Because it has nothing to do with where we are right now. I'm not attracted to her anymore. Why does it matter?"

"And if I told you I'd slept with your best friend ten years ago, and chose not to mention it, do you think you might have some reaction to that? Especially after last night."

Stephen considered that. "I'll do you one better. How come you didn't tell me you had an affair with Karl Scott? You want to explain that one to me? That would have been nice to know. Who's the bigger liar here? I specifically asked you if you had a connection to Scott and you told me no."

Maddie went still and the color in her face drained away. "What are you talking about?"

"Perhaps when you go to hotels with your lover, you should do a better job of concealing yourself. My guy talked to some hotel staff that remembered you and Karl."

Madison lost the remaining color in her face until she was as white as the kitchen tile. She held her stomach.

"What?" asked Stephen. "Cat got your tongue, Madison?"

Madison walked to a dining chair and sat down. "I don't want to talk about it." She spoke quietly.

Stephen dropped his jaw. "You don't want to talk about it?" His voice raised. "Well, you better prepare yourself, because if the prosecution gets ahold of this, and they will, you're looking at a second murder charge. And I don't know how much I can help you with this one. A jury doesn't take too well to liars."

Madison winced. "It...it was a mistake."

Stephen paced. "Why the hell didn't you tell me?"

Madison held her head and bit her lip, and Stephen sensed she was trying not to cry. "I...I was embarrassed."

"Jesus, Madison. This is a big problem. If those two cops that you talked to are still nosing around, and it sounds like they are, it's only a matter of time before they learn this just like I did, and if they turn it over to Biggles, it's case closed. You won't make bail again."

Madison buried her face in her hands. "I didn't think anyone would find out. We told no one, and it didn't last long. Just last summer. I ended it though. I knew it was wrong."

Stephen cursed. He took the chair across from Madison and sat. "I have to ask you this. Did you kill him? Did you kill Karl Scott?"

Madison looked up, her eyes wide. "No. I told you. I didn't kill him. I didn't kill anybody."

"You also told me you had no connection to him. I don't know what to believe anymore." He stood and paced, his mind whirling. He knew he needed to calm down, but he couldn't help but feel betrayed. He wondered how long he had before they came to arrest her again. His frustration grew, and he kicked out at the chair, knocking it over. "I don't know if I can save you from this one."

Madison sat there, as still as a corpse and about as lively as one. "Well, Laura says you're the best, which she should know. Maybe you two can put your heads together and figure it out. You'll make a great team."

"Oh, come on. Don't be a smart ass." He paused. "Did she know about this? Laura? Did she know you slept with Karl?"

"No. I never told her. I told no one. The only thing she knew was that she slept with you. Apparently, I'm not the only one good at keeping secrets."

Stephen ran a hand through his hair. "Yeah, well, we could all work on the 'keeping it secret' part. We suck at that."

"Secrets always come out at some point. I should have known that."

"Yes. You should have. Damn it." Stephen paced again, unsure of what to do now. He realized his anger was not helping, and that he needed to stop yelling and get the facts from Madison. The when, where, what and when. He needed to get on top of this before the prosecution, and worse the press, got ahold of it.

Taking several deep breaths, he forced himself to gain control. Picking up the chair, he righted it and sat again. "I need you tell me everything."

Madison looked over, her eyes weary and bloodshot. "I don't think I want to."

Anger flared, and he pointed. "You don't have a—"

Second Slice

The doorbell rang again.

NINETEEN

....

Madison moaned. "Now what?"

Stephen looked toward the door. "You expecting someone?"

"I don't know. Maybe the Angel of Death? The timing would be perfect."

Stephen stood and walked over to the door, peering out the peephole. He cursed softly. "It's those two detectives." He returned to the table. "I suspect your secret is out. Stay quiet. They'll go away. Now is not the time to talk to them."

Madison sighed, wanting to cry. "Is Biggles with them?"

"No. Not that I could see."

The knocking came again. "Madison Vickers?" said a male voice from the other side of the door. "It's Detectives Daniels and Remalla. We'd like to talk to you."

Stephen made the "shh" sign, and Madison groaned inwardly. Things could not be much worse. She sat up from her slump and rubbed her arms, touching the purple bracelet. She thought of Sonia. *Trust your instincts.* Taking a deep breath, she tried to quiet the chatter in her head and relaxed. Tired of feeling scared and having someone else telling her what to, she closed her eyes. A quiet calm came over her and she heard Sonia's voice in her head.

Opening her eyes, she knew what had to be done. Without thinking twice, she stood and walked over to the door.

"Madison, what are you doing?" asked Stephen.

"What I should have done years ago. Listening to me for once." She opened the door. Remalla and Daniels stood outside the door, looking much the same except one had a bandage on his head and the other gripped his chest and his face held a pinched look. "Detectives."

"Mrs. Vickers," said Daniels.

"I told you. Call me Madison."

"Madison. We'd like to ask you a few questions," said Remalla. "Do you have a few minutes?"

Madison swung the door wide. "Sure. Come on in." She could almost hear Stephen cursing her from behind.

The men entered the house and saw Stephen.

"Counselor," said Daniels. "I'm glad you're here."

Stephen spoke flatly. "Somehow I doubt that. Something tells me you'd love to talk to my client without my presence, much like you did in jail."

"Your client knows her rights," said Remalla.

Madison shut the door. "She sure does." She returned to the table. "Can I get you two something to drink?" Stephen glared at her.

"Water would be great, thanks," said Daniels.

"Two waters coming up." She headed for the kitchen as Stephen followed her.

"What do you think you're doing?" he whispered in her ear.

She opened the fridge and took out two water bottles and handed them to Stephen, then took out two more. "You wanted me to tell the truth? Well, here goes."

"You and I need to talk first before we talk to them. I need to know what to expect."

Madison closed the fridge, feeling strangely empowered. "No, you don't."

He started to reply, but she walked past him back into the dining area. "Here you go." She handed each a bottle. "Have a seat."

Stephen came into the room. "Madison, we need to talk, please."

Madison gave him a sly smile. "Later." She took a water from him and sat in her chair.

Remalla and Daniels glanced at each other, but then sat, Daniels with a groan as he clutched his chest.

"You okay, Detective?" asked Madison.

Daniels eased into the chair, looking pale. "Just fine. It only hurts when I move."

"You two look like you've been in a bar fight," said Madison. "Sure you don't want anything stronger?" She waved her water bottle.

Rem shrugged. "No bar fights. Just a Big Foot. Daniels used to wrestle. Thought he could take him."

Daniels rolled his eyes.

"Brave man." She eyed Remalla. "You try to intervene? That's a nice bandage. You get stitches?"

"Eight. One for every missed punch," said Daniels.

Madison narrowed her eyes. "You tried to punch a Big Foot?"

"He was much faster than he looked," said Remalla.

"Ok, gentlemen. You've had your fun. Aside from this absurd story, why don't you tell us why you're here?" asked Stephen. He took a seat at the table.

Daniels spoke first. "We wanted to clarify a few things. When we talked to you earlier, we told you we would stick around and do a little more digging. We wanted to learn a little more about Donald and Karl."

"And what did you learn?" Madison twisted the cap off of her water bottle.

"We saw two withdrawals from your account. Twenty thousand to Karl Scott and a ten thousand cash withdrawal. You know anything about those?" asked Remalla.

Madison thought back. "The twenty-K was part of Donald's investment. Karl suckered him in to paying more. The ten-K cash was me. I withdrew it."

"What was it for?" asked Daniels.

"Lucy had just discovered she was pregnant. She'd been seeing a reproductive specialist and he was expensive. Angie had just learned her brother had relapsed and her mother had called, desperate to get him back in to therapy. I'd sold a few pieces, so I loaned them both five thousand."

"Good friend," said Remalla. "They pay you back?"

Madison studied her fingers. "Not yet, but they will."

Remalla nodded. "We also noticed several charges on Donald's credit card at a place called Lou's Inn. You heard of it?" He opened his water and took a swig.

Madison made eye contact with Stephen. "I have. Donald went there?"

"He did," said Daniels. "Many times. We drove there today, hoping to find out if he went there with anybody else. Was it you?"

Madison pushed the bottle cap along the table. "No. It wasn't me. But he was there with someone?"

"He was," said Daniels. "We're hoping to get a court order to view the recordings. Lou's Inn has cameras."

Madison shifted in her seat. "It does?"

"It does," said Remalla. He leaned forward. "Interesting thing though, while we were there. One of the staff recalled Karl Scott also being there. Recognized him from his infomercials. It was last summer. And this staff member swears he was there with you."

Madison gripped the water bottle.

"Perhaps I can advise you not to say anything, Madison?" asked Stephen. His water bottle remained untouched. "That woman could have been anybody. I'm sure there are women out there who match Madison's description. This supposed staff member could have been wrong, or maybe even under the influence of something. We know nothing at this point."

"Once we get access to the footage, then we'll know," said Remalla.

Stephen smiled. "Good luck with that. I think we all know that hotels rarely save footage going back a full year. You'll be lucky to get the last three months." He sat back with a smug look.

"It was me," said Madison.

Stephen's smug look vanished.

Madison set her jaw. "Sorry, but at some point, as you said, secrets come out. There's no point in hiding it anymore."

"We heard someone else had been asking around," said Remalla. "I assume it's someone you hired?" he asked Stephen.

Stephen glared, but didn't answer.

"I'll take that as a 'yes,'" said Remalla. He looked toward Madison. "I'm guessing Lou's Inn was not the only place you two went?"

Madison cleared her throat, remembering last summer. She and Karl never went to the same place twice so as not to attract attention. Apparently, that didn't work. "No. It wasn't."

Stephen flattened his palms on the table. "Madison—"

"Stephen, please. What's the point? As you said, it's only a matter of time before the prosecution gets this."

"I'd rather it take more time than less, and certainly not straight from the lion's mouth."

"I did nothing wrong, well, nothing against the law at least."

Daniels shifted with a grimace. "Why don't you tell us exactly what went on between you and Karl Scott."

Madison sighed, wishing she could forget. "It was stupid. I knew it the moment it started."

"What started?" asked Rem.

Madison looked at him, feeling weary, yet defiant. "My affair with Karl."

"Shit," said Stephen. "I'm advising you at this moment to not say another word."

"I hear you and I am choosing to ignore it. I may have slept with the man but I didn't kill him."

"How did it start?" asked Remalla. He scratched at his bandage.

Madison rubbed her temples, feeling the beginnings of a headache. "Last summer. June, I think." She sighed as she recalled that first encounter. "Karl and I had known each other a while. Sharie and I were friends. I mean we live on the lake. Everyone knows everyone on the lake. We did picnics, parties, fishing, boating. We see each other a lot, especially in the summer." She took a sip of her water. "It had been a hot day. We were swimming. Karl and Sharie were having a get together, and Donald and I attended. The men were all talking about their recent investments and Karl was bragging about his latest and the money to be made. I didn't pay much attention to that stuff. My art was selling, and that's really all I cared about. Donald didn't care though. We'd had a fight earlier that day. He'd shoved me and I'd hit the wall hard. I had a big bruise on my shoulder. I told everyone I'd slipped on the dock and fell on a pier support beam. We'd all been drinking plenty, and I needed to use the restroom. I went back to the house. Donald cornered me in the bathroom and accused me of flirting with every man there. Said I was drunk and embarrassing him. I told him to F-off, and he pushed me. Karl walked in and told Donald to get his hands off me. Donald blamed me, but left the bathroom, and then the party. I stayed, but then when everyone started leaving, I went outside to walk home. Karl met me and asked me into the guest cottage. It's just off to the side of the main house. I hesitated, but then told myself, what the hell. Why not?"

Madison fiddled with the label on her water bottle, peeling it off. "I was drunk, and so was he. He asked about Donald and I told him a few things. He was kind and compassionate. He told me how if I was his, how well he'd treat me. He'd shower me with everything I desired. I guess he made me feel special, which Donald never did. Next thing I know, he kissed me, and I kissed him back."

Madison took a deep breath and wrapped her fingers around her bracelet. She felt shaky, and the bracelet helped to relax her.

"How long did it last?" asked Daniels.

Madison shook her head. "Mid-August, I think, before Labor Day. It was a bad idea. I knew that. But it made me feel strong. Like I was getting back at Donald for all the crap he'd done to me. Every time I was with Karl, it was like shooting the finger at Donald. I was drinking the whole time though. As much as I wanted to hurt Donald, I was also dying inside, and I think drinking helped me to ignore that. To look the other way."

"That argument Donald had with Karl. Was that about you?" asked Daniels. "Did Donald know?"

"I never told him, but I think he suspected. Karl and I were very discreet. I told no one, and neither did he. Not even Sharie that I know of. At least she never let on if she knew. We went to different motels and hotels, and even though I should have stayed out of sight, I didn't. It was almost as if I was daring someone to discover our affair. Maybe then I would have had the courage to leave Donald."

"But you didn't?" asked Remalla.

"No, I didn't."

"How did it end?" asked Daniels. He'd pulled out a small notepad and was jotting notes.

"That party, where Sharie said I disappeared, and so did Karl. I'd been drinking, and Karl had confronted me at the party. He was drunk too, and maybe even on something. He wanted to have sex there, in his house, while Sharie was there. I said no, but he kept pushing. Eventually we ended up back in the guest cottage, and I gave in. Karl grunted and had his fun and almost passed out on me. I shoved him off and went into the bathroom and looked in the mirror. My hair and makeup were a mess, and Karl was snoring on the bed. Never in all my life, even in all my years with Donald, did I feel as alone as I did in that moment. I hid in the closet and cried. Eventually, I pulled myself together, vowed to never have another drink again, or ever sleep with Karl again. And I left. I didn't break those vows until yesterday, when I had a drink with my friends."

Thinking back, Madison wished she had a drink right then. Remembering hiding in that closet filled her with regret and brought back the painful memories she'd tried to discard. Tears threatened again, but she swallowed them down.

"Did you see Karl again after that?" asked Remalla.

"Yes. I saw him. It was hard not to. He tried to pick things back up. Couldn't understand why I stopped everything so suddenly. He called and texted, but I made sure that he and I were never alone. I avoided certain parties, and the not drinking helped. It kept me aware, so I didn't make the same mistakes."

"Did he get angry that you stopped seeing him? Did he get violent?"

"No, never. That wasn't Karl's style. He persuaded with charm and charisma, gifts and alcohol. He could be very disarming and convincing when he wanted to be."

"And Sharie never knew?" asked Remalla.

"Not that I know of, although she made a comment to me once, that made me wonder."

"What was that?" asked Daniels.

"It was after the affair ended. We were having dinner. I think it was at Angela's place. Karl had been distant, distracted, not his usual vivacious self. He ended up leaving early. I asked Sharie if he was okay and did she need to leave to check on him. She said something to the effect that it wasn't her he wanted, and she gave me a look, which made me wonder. Was she talking about me? I had no idea."

"When was this?" asked Daniels, scribbling notes.

"I think it was just after Labor Day." Madison picked up her water but didn't drink from it.

"I think Madison has been more than open about this. But there is still nothing here to link her to Karl Scott's death," said Stephen. He watched Madison, his eyes unreadable. Madison fiddled with her bracelet.

"On the contrary," said Remalla. "She lied to us about her relationship with Scott from the beginning. She had an affair with a man who was later murdered. She says she had no more contact with him, but how do we know she's not lying about that. No one can verify her account of the relationship with Scott, except Scott."

Madison held her head. "I'm sitting right here, and I'm not lying."

"So you say," said Remalla. "But if we took this to Biggles, they'd have probable cause and would probably issue an arrest warrant within the hour."

"Are you going to take this to Biggles?" Madison clenched her hands together.

Remalla hesitated and Daniels put his pen down. "There are a few more questions we'd like answered."

"Like what?" asked Stephen.

"Like who is the mystery woman Donald was with? He was at that hotel with someone, and we'd like to know who." Remalla spoke to Stephen. "Your P. I. friend have any luck with that?"

Stephen paused, as if deciding whether to answer. "He went to several hotels up and down the area near Lou's. He flashed pictures, and that's how he learned about Madison and Karl. Donald had been to a few other places, but his lady friend never left the car. No one knows who she is."

Remalla raised a finger. "Which brings us to another question. Donald's phone. His cell showed nothing out of the ordinary, but if he's seeing someone on the side, you know they're communicating. So how? He must have had another phone. One you don't know about. Do you have any idea where he might have hidden it?"

Madison frowned. "You think Donald had another phone?"

"Probably a burner," said Daniels. "One that he could toss if needed. Our guess is, though is that it's still around, but probably somewhere where you won't go looking for it. Which means it might still be in this house."

"The police searched the house," said Madison.

"I'm sure they searched the obvious areas, but could there someplace else he might have hidden it? A hole in the wall, a loose tile in the ceiling?" asked Remalla.

Madison considered that. Was there some place Donald would have hidden a phone? She tried to mentally walk through the house, but nothing came to mind. "I can't think of one."

"If we can find it, and we can find this mystery lady, it might go a long way to helping you, so look around if you can," said Remalla.

"And she's supposed to turn it over to you?" asked Stephen.

Remalla glanced at Daniels. "Sure. Why not? Something wrong with that?"

"We're pretty nice guys, Counselor," said Daniels.

"We helped raise money at the policeman's charity picnic. He did the dunking booth." Remalla pointed at Daniels.

"He did the pie in the face and the potato sack race," said Daniels. "And won both."

"How do you win a 'pie in the face,'" asked Madison.

Daniels held his ribs. "He raised the most money. Everyone wanted to hit him with a pie."

"I can believe that," said Stephen. "But I will advise my client to hand that phone over to me first."

"I don't care if she gives it to a circus clown first." Remalla nodded toward Stephen. "No pun intended." Stephen knitted his brow. "We just want to know what's on it."

"I sure as hell won't be giving it to Biggles," said Madison. "I'll bring it to you."

"Madison—"

"Stephen, what are you worried about? There's nothing incriminating on it about me. I'm not the mistress."

Daniels took a swig of his water and put it down. "He's worried if Donald used the phone to talk to you, or he texted you with it, it might have captured you saying something that could be used against you. Like 'I wish you were dead' or 'I hate you.' Attorneys hate that."

"But it's not like you won't hear it anyway," said Madison. "You could get that crap off his regular phone."

"True," said Remalla. "He's just trying to be a good defender."

"At least somebody understands that," said Stephen, scowling at Madison.

Madison squared herself in her seat, eyeing Stephen. "I guess maybe I have a few trust issues. You should have told me."

Stephen shot out his hands. "Oh, come on. It was ten years ago. And it has nothing to do with this case, or my ability to defend you."

Madison spoke sharply. "She's my best friend."

The group went quiet. Madison tapped at the table. Stephen picked up his water and gripped it.

Remalla raised a brow. "Somehow I don't think we're in Kansas anymore."

Daniels shifted with a grunt. "Me either, but I think somebody's been wearing some ruby red slippers."

"On the wrong feet," added Remalla.

"He slept with Laura," said Madison.

"Madison, that's enough," said Stephen.

"Okay, I think maybe we're a bit out of our range here. We only care about investigating a murder, not current relationship issues. So maybe you can talk about this later?" Daniels asked.

"I don't know," said Remalla. "This is getting interesting." He sat back, holding his water.

Madison held her tongue, knowing it would be unwise to go further. With Stephen fuming, she spoke to Remalla, asking a more pertinent question. "So why haven't you gone to Biggles yet? Why are you here? You could have easily turned this information in and walked away. I'm sure you have things to do back at home. Why are you helping me?"

Remalla paused and then touched his head, as if his wound pained him. Daniels sucked in a breath, his injury clearly bothering him.

"What is it?" asked Madison. "Do you believe me?"

"Let's just say we think there's someone else involved. And we want to know who." Daniels stood, his face pale. "Sorry. It hurts less when I stand."

"What exactly happened to you two?" asked Stephen. "And don't tell me it was Big Foot."

Daniels regarded Remalla, and an unheard communication passed between the two. Madison could sense it. She straightened. "You saw him, didn't you?"

"Who?" asked Stephen.

Madison's heart thumped. "The man in the woods. Outside Laura's. The man who was watching me." She waited. "I'm not crazy, am I?"

Remalla cleared his throat. "Let's just say he was not a figment of your imagination. And he bears a slight resemblance to Rutger Hauer."

"Rutger who?" asked Stephen.

"Never mind," said Daniels. "We chased him into the woods outside our cabin last night, but he got away."

Stephen placed a hand on the table. "You saw the man who'd been watching Madison, and he did this to you?"

Remalla squirmed. "Our egos hurt worse than our injuries."

"Tell me about it," said Daniels, his arm against his ribs.

Madison stared in disbelief. She suspected these detectives were quite capable of defending themselves. So how had the man gotten away? "How did you know it was him? Could it have been some local kid curious about the cops hanging out in the neighborhood?"

"No. It was not a local kid. I can assure you of that." Remalla drank from his water bottle. "His skills were far superior. He said something to me. I heard it."

Madison waited to hear what it was. "Well?"

"He said 'I did it for her.'" Remalla looked at Madison.

Madison went cold. It was what the man had said to her, only in her head.

"Are you saying there's a madman running around, accosting cops and stalking women?" asked Stephen. "Did you tell Biggles?"

"No," said Daniels.

Stephen pushed his chair back and stood. "Why the hell not? This could be a break in the case. This might explain Donald's death, and maybe Karl's."

"Because we *are* the cops. We kind of do this thing already," said Remalla.

"Biggles should still know. If there's someone out there, other people could be in danger," said Stephen. He found his jacket and pulled out his cell.

"You also want to tell him why we're still here, and what we found out about Madison and Karl? You bring him in, and you tell him everything. There's no way around it," said Daniels.

"The guy's got shit for brains. You know it and I know it. He just wants to close this case, regardless of Madison's guilt or innocence," said Remalla. "Something tells us this creep in the woods is interested in Madison. No one else is in danger. If we thought they were, we'd call out the cavalry. You bring in Biggles and he starts talkin' to the neighbors, and this guy goes to ground. We'll never catch him. And if he did do something, we'll never know, and Madison here will go to jail, maybe for something she didn't do."

"I told you. I didn't kill anyone," said Madison.

"So we wait and do nothing?" asked Stephen. "How does that help Madison? This guy got the drop on you. How do you know he won't hurt her?"

"We need to figure out who he is," said Daniels. "And why he's here."

"How are we going to do that?" asked Madison.

Remalla leaned in, his elbows on the table. "He made contact once. He'll do it again. Daniels and I have somehow raised his interest. We suspect he'll be back."

A chill ran through Madison, and she remembered her walk in the woods. "I think he's been watching me. I can't be sure. I haven't seen him. But I think he has."

"Why?" asked Daniels. "What's his interest in you?"

Madison closed her eyes, remembering her dreams. "I think he knows me. Somehow, we're connected." She held her bracelet, trying to focus. Images flashed in her mind, as they had when she took Sonia's hand in jail. Two figures emerged again. A man and a woman, still shrouded in fog. But this time, the woman stepped forward. She held out a rose. An unseen man's voice echoed in Madison's mind. It was the same voice from the other night in Laura's yard. Hearing the words, she abruptly opened her eyes.

"Madison, what's the matter? Do you know how he knows you?" asked Stephen.

Madison shook her head. "I heard it again in my head. The same man's voice. 'I did it for you.' But he added something."

"What?" asked Daniels.

"He said, 'Tell JJ.'"

Remalla's face fell.

TWENTY

....

Daniels went still. Watching his partner, he saw Remalla do the same. "Excuse me?"

"I heard it. He said 'Tell JJ.' There were two other people, shrouded in fog. I can never see their faces. The woman held out a rose, and that's when I heard the voice. It was the man from the woods," said Madison.

"And you just see this in your mind?" asked Daniels.

"Yes. I do. But it's not like I'm imagining it. It's very real. It's hard to explain." Madison leaned in. "Who's JJ? That's the first I've heard that name."

Remalla had gone quiet, and Daniels could almost hear his partner's brain trying to rationalize this. "Would you excuse us for a second?" He grabbed Rem's elbow, but Rem stood, his face no longer impassive.

"What are you doing?" he asked. "Are you trying to play us for a fool?" He scowled. "Tell JJ? Do you think we're that dumb?"

"Rem, let's talk," said Daniels.

Rem pulled his arm away. "I think she's yanking our chain. She knows about the Artist and she's using that to create doubt and spread blame."

Madison straightened. "No, I'm not. I'm telling the truth."

Rem pointed. "All this 'I heard a voice in my head' business. You know exactly what you're doing." His face scrunched. "Are you in cahoots with him? You know Rutger, don't you?"

Daniels tried again. "Rem, let's go outside. We need to..."

Madison slammed her bottle on the table. "I don't know him. I'm not in cahoots with anyone."

Stephen stood. "I think maybe you need to listen to your partner, Detective. If my client says she doesn't know him, then she doesn't know him."

"Then you're as blind as Biggles," shouted Rem.

"Rem. Outside. Right now." Daniels raised his voice to reach his partner, who finally looked back at him.

Rem gestured at Madison. "You're not buying this, are you?"

"We need to talk in private." Daniels motioned to Rem, who shook his head in anger but Daniels sensed his underlying unease. Daniels slid open the back door and stepped outside. Rem followed and Daniels slid the door closed. He headed down to the dock, away from the windows.

Rem flung out his hands. "What the hell was that?"

"I don't know."

"Did you hear her?" Rem began to pace.

"Yes. I heard her."

"Tell JJ?" He stopped. "She's talking about Jill. She knows about the Makeup Artist and she's playing us for fools."

"We asked her before. She said she heard about it on the news, like everyone else."

"That's bullshit. That part wasn't in the news. But somehow she got a hold of it." Rem set his jaw. "I think this chick is messing with our heads. I questioned her guilt, but now I'm not so sure. Seeing things in her mind? Hearing voices? This whole thing is nuts, and I think she is too." He paused. "Somehow, she knows about the Artist. She and the man in the woods are working together. They got some details, maybe from some cop friend. And now she's using it to throw us off the scent while she plays the innocent victim and he goes around killing people that piss her off." He resumed his pacing. "It's a perfect plan, especially if she knows I've been dating Jill."

Daniels let his partner vent. "You sure about that? It's a stretch, although, I agree this is strange."

Remalla froze. "Strange? She's certifiable." His eyes widened. "Her and Rutger? I'll bet my badge those two are laughing at us behind our backs."

Daniels held his aching ribs. "I admit. That could be possible."

"Possible? So far, I think that's the most logical answer. Why didn't we think about it before?"

Daniels hesitated. "There's something else to think about, Rem. I know she just threw us for a loop in there, but let's take a second. You saw what that man did to us in the woods. He's not your ordinary stalker."

Rem raised a brow. "I didn't see a thing. All I know is that he disarmed you and knocked me out."

Daniels scowled. "Wait a minute. You think I threw myself into a tree? Did I throw a rock at your head at the same time? And oh, I just tossed my gun at an unknown assailant in the woods." He pointed. "You know what happened is unexplainable. Don't pretend it didn't happen."

Rem started to answer, but Daniels curtailed him. "Not only that, but Jill has some weird abilities too. She saw things in her head. Sensed the killer and his actions. Did you doubt her?"

Rem tried to answer again, but Daniels continued. "This isn't the first time we've encountered weird things. We've had odd occurrences happen on this job. The guy who lifted the car off his pinned wife on the highway. The EMTs who swear they heard a woman's voice in a canyon calling for help only to find a long dead mother behind the wheel of a wrecked car and her toddler, still alive, strapped into the car seat. How do you explain it? I don't know."

"So you believe her psychobabble? You think Madison Vickers just told us to tell Jill Jacobs, the woman who was stalked and almost killed by the Makeup Artist, that she heard in her head 'I did it for you.' The same phrase the Makeup Artist used to taunt Jill. Is that what you're saying?"

"I'm not saying we should tell Jill anything. We need to keep her out of this."

"You think?" asked Rem.

"But we need to think this through. Donald is still a possible suspect in Karl's murder. And if Madison is telling the truth, then it's possible Rutger killed Donald to protect her. We can't go off half-cocked and getting angry won't help."

Rem huffed. "Then what do you want to do, Kemosabe? How do we prove if Madison is playing us?"

"We need to just work the case, like we always do. We can check the angle that maybe Madison and Rutger somehow are in this together. If she's trying to throw us off, confuse us, then maybe we let her think it's working. But we watch her to see if we can catch them together."

"How are we going to do that? Unless we bring Biggles in. He'll have more manpower."

Daniels groaned and held his aching ribs. "I know we probably should, but something tells me if we do, it will be like having a shark in that lake."

Rem crossed his arms. "He'll scare away all the fish, plus somebody will get eaten."

"Probably us."

"Shit. This is a mess." Rem rubbed his face. "Ok. Let's think. How do we watch Madison without notifying Biggles? And let's keep in mind our time frame here. We can't do this forever. At some point, Lozano will want us back. We're stretching it thin as it is."

Daniels studied the area. Spying a ramshackle cabin set back in the woods, he hit Rem in the shoulder. "Hey. What's that?"

"What's what?" He stared where Daniels nodded. Spying it, his face dropped. "That thing? It looks like something straight out of an eighties horror flick."

"It's an old fishing cabin. Probably hasn't been used in years. It's on Madison's property and it's got a view of the grounds."

Rem stared at him like he was a trout that just walked out of the water. "I think your head is more damaged than mine. Are you serious? I doubt that thing has any running water or electricity."

"We're not going to need either. It would draw attention anyway." Daniels studied the decrepit house and its proximity to Madison's home. It would be close enough for a stakeout, but not too close to be noticed. They could stay in the woods at night and watch Madison's place without being seen. "I say we sneak in late. We give it the weekend. Let's see if Rutger shows his face. By Monday, we can check the tapes at the hotel. See if we can figure out who Donald was sleeping with. If we get nothing by Monday, we'll turn over what we know to Biggles. We'll have done what we can. It will be up to Stephen and the D.A. to take it from there. Unless Lozano wants us to stay, then we'll stay."

Rem squinted. "We are going to sneak in there tonight? In the dark? How do you know Rutger isn't already staying there himself?"

"Then it will be the shortest stakeout on record. And a successful one. Something tells me if we find him, we break this case wide open."

Rem put his hands on his hips and stared back toward the house; his face clouded.

"What's twirling around in that head of yours?" asked Daniels. "It's a good plan."

"The plan is fine, although staying in Hill House over there gives me the heebie-jeebies. I think we're more likely to run into Big Foot than find Rutger."

"We're more likely to see a ghost than run into a Big Foot."

"That doesn't help." He rubbed his bandage. "I guess what's eatin' me is this whole "'I did it for you' thing. You remember what I told you about what the Artist said to Jill? He blamed her for killing Henderson."

Daniels recalled how after killing the Makeup Artist, Rem had told him that the killer had not taken credit for killing one victim, a police officer named Rick Henderson. "You thinking maybe he was telling the truth? And now Henderson's killer has made his way to Silent Lake, and he's killing again?" He sighed. "That would be a helluva stretch. And why? What's the connection between Rick Henderson, and the murders of Karl Scott and Donald Vickers?"

Rem sighed. "Probably nothing. But if there is...then maybe this rabbit hole goes way deeper than we think." He eyed Daniels. "Rutger Hauer could be a dangerous man."

Daniels nodded. "It didn't go well on our first encounter. And he sought us out. He could have easily stayed behind the scenes. Something about us drew his attention, and he was cocky enough to confront us."

"Which means we need to be careful."

Daniels eyed the gloomy cabin. "I'm always careful."

"Since when?"

"Since I met you, partner." He smacked Rem on the arm and winced with the movement. "Come on. We've got things to do."

TWENTY-ONE

....

Sonia Vandermere sat quietly on the ground, her legs crossed, eyes closed, and her mind still. Breathing deeply, she didn't move. Soft ocean sounds of waves lapping against a shore played from her phone, helping to drown out other distractions.

Peter closed the door behind him after entering the room, careful to make as little noise as possible. Sonia frequently sat in meditation, and he tried not to disturb her. These sessions often resulted in her ability to access important information.

A few minutes passed and Peter stared at the bag of chips and soda he'd purchased at the vending machine. His stomach rumbled, but he held off on opening either. As the time passed though, he debated going out into the hallway to eat, when Sonia sucked in a breath, and opened her eyes.

"What is it?" asked Peter. He opened the bag of chips and popped the soda open.

Sonia blinked several times. "I saw him."

"You did? Did you get a location?" He munched on a chip.

"No. He's too smart for that. He is here, though." She rose from her cross-legged position with more dexterity than Peter would have expected from a woman her age, but Sonia never ceased to surprise him. She walked to a nearby chair and sat, rubbing her temples. "But he's taking risks."

"Since when does he not take risks? Everything he does is meant to shock us. Show us who's in charge."

"This is different. I haven't felt this before from him." Sonia eyed his chips. "You going to share?"

Peter remembered the bag of chips in his pocket. "Oh, sorry. Here." He pulled them out and handed them to Sonia, who opened them.

"My doctor would not approve, but such is life." She ate a chip. "I need to ground myself. I went especially deep today."

"What did you see?" asked Peter.

Sonia stared off, lost in thought as she ate. "Much the same as usual. He's watching Madison, just as he watched Jill. He's taunting her, confusing her. He's enjoying the game he's playing. But this time, he actually spoke to her about Jill. He's never done that before."

Peter stopped in mid-chew. "I thought that's the last thing he wanted."

"I thought so too, but perhaps the game is shifting." Sonia held a chip, but didn't eat it. "Maybe he's changing the rules, or at least considering it. Plus, those two detectives..." She shook her head.

"What about them? Once they finish their investigation, they'll move on."

Sonia sighed and leaned back. "He engaged with them, and I don't know why. Now he's delivering messages to Madison about Jill, and including the detectives. It's like he wants them involved."

"You saw that?" Peter ate the last chip and sipped from his soda. "You did go deep."

"I think he wanted me to. He's laughing, knowing there's nothing we can do about it."

"There is something we could do. We could tell Madison, and Jill, and those detectives, who we are. Maybe that will bring him out into the open. Plus, the other one. What's his name? Jace? He'll likely be the next target. We could bring them all in and tell them who they are."

Sonia shook her head. "It would be too dangerous. It could put their lives at risk. And I don't want to be responsible for that."

"Lives are already at risk. Look at Donald Vickers and Rick Henderson."

Sonia closed her eyes. Putting her chips down, she rested her arm over the back of the chair. Peter let her take a moment. He knew this game weighed heavily on her. After a few seconds, she opened her eyes. "I know. Don't think I haven't thought about that. But unfortunately, we are not in a position to confront him. If we jump too soon, it could backfire on all of us. I have to trust my senses. There will be a time and a place, but it isn't right now."

Peter put his soda can on the coffee table. "What about the Council? Should we talk to them about it?"

"I've told them what they needed to know. But they put me in charge and told me to do what I think is best, and that's what I'm doing. They're not out here in the field. They don't sense him the way I do. And they still have the goal of keeping this quiet, of apprehending him before, well, the you-know-what hits the fan. I have to see if I can make that happen." She stood and went to her purse. "I need some of my lavender oil."

Peter watched as she found a small vial and opened it. Shaking out a few drops, she rubbed some on her temples and the back of her neck, then rubbed her hands together, brought them to her nose, and breathed in the scent.

"Does that help?"

"Yes. Would you like some, dear?"

"No. Thanks. I'll stick with my All Spice."

She put the oil back in her purse. "As you wish."

"Why do you see him?" asked Peter. "What is it about you that makes him want to torment you? You've never told me."

Sonia returned to the bag of chips and picked them up. Popping one in her mouth, she chewed and checked her reflection in a mirror that hung on the wall in the hotel room. Her eyes softened as she adjusted the necklaces around her neck. "Really? I never mentioned it to you?"

"No."

She turned from the mirror. "Probably because I helped raise him and failed miserably at it."

Surprised by her answer, Peter held his soda but didn't drink.

Sonia sighed. "You know, I think I'll take a nap. I'm feeling a little sapped from that meditation. Would you mind waking me in an hour?"

Peter nodded. "Sure. No problem."

Her face weary, and her shoulders low, Sonia turned and left the room.

**

"Gin." Lucy put her cards down with a satisfied smile.

"Whatever," said Angela. She took a sip of her white wine. "This card game sucks."

"Then why are we playing it?" asked Lucy.

Angela cocked her head. "Because Laura won't tell us what happened between her and Maddie, and she's trying to occupy us."

Laura gathered the cards and reshuffled them, offering Angela an annoyed look. "I told you. There's nothing to tell. We had an argument. No big deal. We'll make up, eventually."

"This happened yesterday?" asked Lucy.

"Afternoon, yes," said Laura.

"It's been over twenty-four hours and you two haven't spoken?" asked Angela. "When's the last time that happened?" A breeze blew, and she ruffled her long hair in the wind. The sun dipped lower in the sky as the heat dissipated.

"I can't remember. It's been a long time," said Laura, taking a sip of her own wine. Staring out at the lake, she sighed as a boat raced by. "We'll talk soon enough."

"Are you going to make the first move?" asked Lucy. "Or are you waiting for her to do it?"

"I don't know. I can't decide."

"Oh, come on. Tell us what happened. I'm dying to know. Nobody's been murdered recently and we need something to talk about." Angela leaned forward in her seat.

"That's nice," said Lucy. "We used to talk before there were any murders you know." She helped herself to a blueberry from a bowl on the table.

"About boring stuff. Apple cobbler recipes, new outfits, health scares, and the occasional affair. How dull. My two friends are fighting, and I want to know why. Especially when one of them is suspected of killing her husband."

"Maddie didn't kill him and you know it," said Lucy, her jaw dropping. "Whoever killed Karl, killed Donald too. There's a connection, I'm sure. It's crazy to think there are two murderers running around, and one of them is Madison." Lucy held her glass of wine.

"Unless Maddie killed them both." Angie sat back, munching on a blueberry. "There are rumors. Maddie may have had more than a friendship with Karl."

"Oh, for God's sake. You're drunk. This is the last thing Maddie needs. Rumors." Lucy shook her head.

"Rumors are a helluva lot more interesting than cards. I can tell you that much. Don't you think Laura? I'm sure you can agree with me on that one."

Laura sat quietly, staring out at the lake, the cards in a stack on the table. She held her wine, but had drunk little of it.

"Laura? You okay?" asked Lucy.

Laura stared at the table. "I slept with Stephen." Angela choked on a sip of wine and Lucy's eyes rounded. "That's why Maddie and I argued."

"Are you serious?" asked Angela, coughing. "Now we have something to discuss. When? Recently?"

Laura waved her hand. "No. Don't be ridiculous. This was back in law school. Stephen and I dated for a while. Then when we graduated, we went our separate ways. No big deal."

Lucy narrowed her eyes. "Then why is she upset? That doesn't seem like a problem."

Laura tapped on her glass. "Because she slept with Stephen. After our evening of martinis."

Angela's eyes widened. "Oh, shit. This is getting better and better. And she's pissed because neither of you said anything to her."

"Yes," said Laura. "I didn't tell her because it was so long ago. But then she found my yearbook and saw pictures of me and Stephen together."

"Ouch," said Lucy.

Laura shifted on her chair. "She's furious. Thinks Stephen and I lied to her." She swirled the wine in her glass.

"I don't blame her," said Lucy.

"What?" asked Angela. "Come on. That was years ago. Stephen and Laura have no obligation to tell Maddie anything."

"Laura and Maddie are best friends. And we literally sat in Maddie's living room and suggested she sleep with Stephen. Come on. And Stephen should have said something before he took her to bed." Lucy shook her head. "Men. Dangle some sex in front of them and suddenly they go stupid."

Angela sat up. "Did you really think Maddie would sleep with him? Maddie's a prude. And did she really think Stephen was a virgin? Doesn't he have a kid?"

"Not with Laura," said Lucy. "And Maddie's not a prude. She was married to a jerk, for God's sake. Cut her some slack." She pointed. "And you were just mentioning the rumors about her and Karl. Make up your mind. Is she a saint or a slut?"

Angela paused. "That's the question we all face isn't it?" She eyed her friend, but then shot a glance at Laura. "What was your response to all this?"

Laura took a healthy swig of her wine. "Pretty much what yours was. It didn't go over well."

"You should apologize," said Lucy.

"I disagree," said Angela. "Maddie should apologize. She's over-reacting."

Laura traced the rim of her glass while her friends argued. Sighing, she closed her eyes, thinking back on the encounter, when she heard the sliding glass door open. Opening her eyes, she saw Preston step out on the patio.

"You ladies enjoying this beautiful evening?" he asked. He put a hand on Laura's shoulder.

Lucy and Angela went quiet.

"You on your way to your card game?" asked Laura, taking his hand.

"Yep. Going to drink and smoke cigars. Maybe win some change from Thomas and Sam."

"Tell my husband if he loses any more money, he won't get sex for a week," said Angela. She took a drink. "Thomas sucks at poker."

"I thought you wanted him to win," said Lucy. Angela raised a brow at her. "Tell my husband if he wins, he'll be a happy man tonight." She smiled.

Angela put down her glass. "Did you just insult me?"

Preston cleared his throat. "I'll let you ladies convey those messages." As Lucy and Angela glowered, he leaned down and spoke into Laura's ear. "You all right?"

Laura squeezed his fingers and nodded.

"You should talk to her," he said. "She's your best friend."

"I know."

"You miss her. I can tell. She keeps you sane in an insane world, and I need you sane. So call her."

Laura smiled softly. "I will."

Preston kissed her on the cheek. "I love you."

"Love you, too."

He squeezed her shoulder and turned to leave. "Bye ladies." Lucy and Angela barely acknowledged his departure as he headed down the porch steps.

**

Sharie Scott pulled up in the Benoff driveway after passing Preston Benoff on the road. After their brief fling a few years back, they rarely spoke, but were cordial if they saw each other.

Glad he wouldn't be home, Sharie parked the car. Sitting there, she wondered if she was doing the right thing. She'd stopped at the police station to talk to Biggles, but had learned that he'd left for the weekend to see his ill mother in the city and would be back in the office on Monday. Debating her next move, she sought the detectives who everyone knew were still in town and staying at the Lozano cabin, but when she'd knocked on their door, no one had answered.

Her mind reeling, she decided she needed some advice. Perhaps she was being overly hasty. Was she overreacting? Reaching into her pocket, she pulled out the blue pin she'd sealed in a plastic bag and held it. Was this the connection between Madison and Karl that Biggles needed? Would this seal Madison's fate?

Sighing, she opened the door and exited the car. She needed to talk to someone. Laura was Madison's friend. Maybe she could offer some insight into Madison's mind.

Sharie went to the door and rang the bell. After a short wait, the door opened and Laura stood there, holding a glass of wine.

"Sharie?" Her brow furrowed. "How are you? Everything okay?"

"May I come in?" asked Sharie.

"Of course." Laura stood aside and Sharie entered.

"Thank you."

Sharie followed Laura through the living area and out onto the back porch where Angela Desmond and Lucy Byers sat, having an apparently heated discussion.

They went still when Sharie stepped out.

"Can I get you a glass of wine, Sharie?" asked Laura.

"No, thank you. I didn't mean to interrupt."

"Bitch," said Lucy, under her breath, narrowing her eyes at Angela.

"Slut," said Angela, sipping her wine.

"I think actually, your timing is perfect," said Laura, eying her friends. "What can I do for you?"

Sharie, curious about the argument, remembered why she was there. "Do you mind if we speak in private?"

Lucy and Angela looked up, and Laura nodded. "Not at all. Ladies, feel free to resume your petty arguing."

"Look who's talking," said Lucy under her breath.

Laura offered her a scowl before guiding Sharie back into the house and closing the door behind her. "Sorry about that. I think they've had a bit too much to drink."

"We've all been there, haven't we?"

"I suppose so. Have a seat."

Sharie sat on the couch, and Laura sat beside her, putting her glass down on the coffee table. Sharie hesitated, unsure of what to say.

"Sharie, what is it?" asked Laura. "Is something wrong?"

Sharie's eyes clouded as she thought of Karl. "I was going through Karl's things."

Laura's eyes softened. "Oh, Sharie. I'm sorry. That must have been hard."

Sharie nodded. "I've been trying to clean things out, because you know, I can't keep it all forever. I'm planning on donating a lot of it."

"Of course."

Sharie sniffed. "I found a jacket, and I went through the pockets, and I found something."

Laura waited. "What did you find? Was it bad?" She paused. "Sharie, you know Karl had multiple vices."

Sharie shook her head. "No. It was nothing like that. It's this." She pulled out the pin in the plastic bag and showed it to Laura. "It belonged to Madison." Laura took the bag and held it. "I know because I complimented her on it. Told her it was beautiful and asked her where she got it." She clenched her hands together. "And now I find it in Karl's pocket. I put it in a plastic bag, because that's what they do on those detective shows, to preserve evidence or something. Right?"

Laura held the pin through the bag, her face unreadable. "This doesn't mean Maddie killed Karl, Sharie. There could be a number of reasons why this pin was in his pocket. Maybe it fell, and he picked it up, meaning to give it back to her. You don't know."

"I've considered that. How could I not? But it could also mean they were involved. There was someone he was seeing over the summer that he wouldn't talk to me about. Now I'm thinking it was her this whole time." She paused. "I tried to take it to Biggles, but he's out of town, and I tried to find those two detectives, but they're not home." She wrung her hands. "And now I'm wondering if I'm doing the right thing. This could sentence Madison, and Biggles told me he was looking for a connection between Karl and Madison. This could be it."

Laura handed the pin back to Sharie. "It's a stretch. A good defense attorney could make mincemeat of this. There's no way to know why this was in Karl's pocket."

Sharie studied the pin. "I realize that, but there's something else. I heard something this morning that could change everything."

Laura widened her eyes. "What?"

"I'm sworn to secrecy, but I have to tell someone, especially now that I have this pin." She leaned in. "My friend, Lou Felder, she owns a string of hotels in and around town. She called me this morning. Told me the cops want video footage from one of her hotels. Says Donald took a mistress there, and maybe Karl too. She's expecting them to get a court order. Says it could reveal the murderer."

Laura's jaw dropped. "Are you serious? Has she seen the tapes?"

Sharie shook her head. "No. She couldn't care less. But if the cops show Monday, she won't have a choice but to pull it. She asked me if I wanted her to look first, to get a heads up, in case Karl's on it, but I said no." She held her hand to her heart. "I don't think I could handle it right now."

Laura stared. "My, God. I don't know what to think." She held her head. "They think Donald had a mistress too?"

"Yes. I think so, but does that really surprise you?"

Laura made a sad sigh. "No. I suppose it doesn't." She regarded Sharie. "And you think Maddie slept with Karl and is on the tapes, which is why her pin is in his pocket?"

"It's the logical conclusion."

"Well then, these tapes could also prove her innocence. What if she's not the one with Karl?"

Sharie put the pin on the coffee table. "I asked that, but Lou says one of her people thinks it was Maddie."

Laura scoffed. "Eyewitness testimony is usually faulty. We can't be sure until we see the tapes."

"Exactly, but I think I'm seeing writing on the wall. Madison was sleeping with Karl. Maybe Donald was having an affair too. Karl broke it off with Madison. She got angry and killed him, and then she finished off Donald when he wouldn't break off his own affair. It almost seems obvious now."

"Sharie, that is totally circumstantial. You don't know if any of that is true."

Sharie rubbed her head. "Well, I'm hoping the tapes will tell the tale, and that, combined with this pin, will be the nail in the coffin." She took a deep breath. "I think I'm feeling better about my decision now. Thanks for listening to me. I needed to talk it through."

"Sharie, wait," said Laura.

The door opened, and Lucy and Angela walked inside.

"We need more wine," said Angela.

Lucy rolled her eyes. "And I can't stay out there with her anymore. Plus, we want to know what all the secrecy is about." She eyed the bag on the table. "What's that?"

Sharie reached for the pin on the table and put it back in her purse. "It's nothing." She stood. "Thank you, Laura, for talking to me. I'll be bringing this to Biggles on Monday."

"Sharie—"

Second Slice

"Enjoy your evening." Sharie walked to the front door and left.

**

Laura stared at the closed door.

"What was all that about?" asked Angela, rummaging through the wine cabinet.

"Whose jewelry was that?" asked Lucy. "Was it Sharie's? It looked familiar."

"Shit," said Laura.

TWENTY-TWO

....

"**W**hat the hell is that?" Remalla jumped up and swatted at his pants.

"It's a dust bunny," said Daniels, sitting in a folding chair and watching Madison's home out the dilapidated window. The glass had long since shattered and now hung in solitary shards.

"A dust bunny with legs." Remalla stood and checked his clothes. "How much longer do we have to stay out here?"

"It's only been twenty-four hours. We told Lozano we'd give it the weekend."

"How 'bout we go back to the cabin, pop a few beers, and tell him we stayed. I don't think I can handle another night in this place."

"It was fine last night."

"Fine? There were things moving around out there. And something crawled over my face. I didn't sleep a wink."

Daniels shifted in his seat. "A few deer walked by. Hardly dangerous. And a curious bug won't hurt you."

Remalla grabbed the second fold-up chair, opened it up next to Daniels, and sat in it. "Somehow I think I got the short end of this stick."

"I gave you the choice of shift. You could be sleeping." He checked his watch. "It's not your turn for another hour."

Remalla rested his feet on an old wooden crate he'd found in a corner and pulled toward the window. "It might as well start now. I'm not sleeping in this spook house. And you realize it's supposed to rain tonight. Did you see the forecast?" He scratched his neck. "And I'm fairly sure something poisonous bit me. I'm expecting the seizures to start at any second."

Daniels hid a smile. "I'm sure you're fine, but we have some antibiotic ointment if you need it." He opened a jug of water and drank from it. "And the roof should keep out most of the rain."

Rem studied the structure. "You call that a roof?" He shook his head. "How are you so comfortable out here? You're a city boy, just like me."

"I was a dedicated Boy Scout. Earned all my badges, plus Dad took me camping. While you were learning to steal cars, I was learning to build a campfire." Holding his ribs, he rested his feet next to Remalla's. "It comes in handy in moments like this."

Remalla grumbled. "That's great. If we get chilly, you're the guy, but if we need to get out of here fast, I'm all over it. I'll take the latter any day."

"You planning on going somewhere fast?"

Remalla pulled a granola bar out of his pocket. "If there was a cheeseburger in the vicinity, I'd beat the Roadrunner in a foot race." He opened the package and took a bite and grimaced. "I thought you said this would be good." He spat the unchewed remains on the floor. "That's awful."

"You need the nutrition. If Rutger shows, you might face that foot race."

"Just give me a candy bar and a soda. That's all the energy I need." He found his canned drink and drank from it. "Besides,

Rutger won't show. It's a long shot. All we saw last night were creepy crawlies, spooky trees, and what you say was a deer."

"You never know. We have to at least try. This may be the only way to see if Madison has some connection to him."

"Two days out here is not near enough to find out. I think Rutger is way more careful than that. If Madison knows him, it may be impossible to prove it."

Daniels nodded. "She's the one with everything to lose though. If they're in this together, I doubt she'd be okay with going to jail for murder while Rutger hangs out in the woods."

"If they are in it together, then to keep her out of jail, they would have to make Rutger look like the bad guy. Which is why I think he came after us. We can corroborate her story and provide reasonable doubt for a jury. It's perfect. Who better to back up your story about a madman stalking you than two cops?" Remalla stretched on the chair. Watching the house, he saw exactly what he'd seen on his last watch, nothing.

"Or, Rutger killed Donald and Karl and is making Madison the scapegoat. She doesn't know him, but maybe he knows her. Either way, if he's around, maybe we'll see him. Then if we can catch him, we can ask him." Daniels capped the water and put it down, then pulled a banana out of a bag and peeled it.

Rem scratched his head. He'd taken the bandage off, but the stitches were still in. He'd have to visit his doctor in two weeks to have them removed. "Something tells me he's not going to be open to talking. What happens then?"

Daniels glanced at him. "Don't think I haven't considered that. He made us look stupid the last time." He adjusted his position in his seat with a grimace. "I don't think we can take another encounter like that."

"So what do we do the next time around, if there is one? If he has these weird abilities, he'll use them again. We're good in a fight, but we can't defend ourselves against that."

"Maybe try talking. See if he'll open up. He spoke before. Maybe he'll speak again."

"Talking. There's an idea. Why didn't I think of that?" asked Rem.

"I think that's our best angle. Other than wrestling him to the ground and hoping he doesn't toss us around like toothpicks."

"And hoping. There's another thing to hang our hat on. Let's hope he doesn't kill us." Rem swatted at a mosquito. "Worst comes to worse, we could shoot him." He eyed Daniels.

"Let's hope it doesn't come to that," said Daniels.

"There's that hoping again. I don't want that either, but if he threatens either of us, I'm taking him down."

Daniels held his banana. "And I'll be right there with you."

Rem cracked his knuckles. "Let's assume that doesn't happen though, and this guy wants to talk. It's this whole 'I did it for you' thing that is making me squirm. He smiled when he said it." Rem sighed. "I still think he and Madison are messing with us, but if they're not, I'm worried there's more going on here."

"Maybe you should reconsider talking to Jacobs about it." Daniels took a bite of his banana. "She might know something."

Rem frowned. "You think if she thought someone else killed Henderson that she wouldn't be busting down whatever doors were in her way? You know how intense she can be." He kicked at a broken piece of glass. "She'll think I'm nuts."

"Since when do you care about that? Everybody thinks you're nuts. Even I think you're nuts. I just put up with it because it comes in handy when my life's at stake."

Rem picked up a bag of food and dug through it. Finding some trail mix, he pulled it out. "Remind me not to let you do the shopping for stakeouts."

"Sorry. There are no Taco del Fuegos in the area."

Rem opened the trail mix and ate some nuts. "I'll think about asking Jill, but let's see how this stakeout goes first. If Rutger doesn't show, and we never see him again, then what's the point? Do we chalk it up to some nutcase wandering the woods? If Madison's telling the truth and he's as big a mystery to her as he is to us, then we have no way of finding him."

"We could do a sketch. Show it around. We know what he looks like."

"Lozano would love that. Let's spend even more time here. Looking for a mystery man who taunts people and throws cops and rocks with his mind. That will go over well."

Daniels took the last bite of his banana and tossed the peel in a bag of trash. He rubbed his ribs, chewed and swallowed. "You really want to say that to the Captain?"

Rem massaged his temples. "What I really want is some sleep. That would do wonders right now." He grabbed another handful of trail mix. "We hear anything about that court order for the video at Lou's?"

"Should have it tomorrow morning. Cap's going to see if he can send Mel and Garcia to check the tapes. Give us more time here."

Rem turned in his seat. "More time here? If nothing happens tonight, then we're out. This survival stuff is killing me. I'd rather choke down one of your green drinks than stay out here another day."

"Which is exactly why I agreed to it. If nothing happens, then we can go back to the cabin and sleep, or would you rather drive to Lou's and review hours of video footage?"

Rem sank back into his seat. "Oh. That's a good idea."

"I occasionally have them. If Mel and Garcia find something, then we can turn everything over to Biggles and head home. We will have done what we can here. Madison's attorney will have to take it from there."

"If we see nothing this weekend, and Madison's on those tapes with Karl, she's screwed."

"I agree. It doesn't look good." He pushed up with a groan, trying to find a more comfortable position.

"Why don't you go get some rest. I'll take it from here," said Rem.

"You sure? You still have some time."

"Nah. It's not like I'll get any sleep. I'll take the rest of the day. Go get some shuteye. Rest your ribs."

Daniels nodded. "I'll take you up on that. Wake me when it's my turn." He stood slowly.

"Don't worry. The first sliver of moon appears, the shadows come out, and I hear anything moving, or Rutger pops out and winks at me, believe me, I'll let you know."

Daniels yawned. "Thanks, partner."

"You're welcome." Finding his thermos of coffee, Rem unscrewed it and sipping the hot brew, settled back, popped some trail mix in his mouth and watched Madison's house.

TWENTY-THREE

....

Laura scrubbed the potatoes and washed them under the running water from the kitchen sink. Her mind preoccupied, she stared out the window at the night sky. The sun had gone down, and the crescent moon appeared above the trees. Not hearing the back door open, she jumped when she felt a hand on her back, dropping the potato. "Shit."

"Hey, it's me," said Preston. "Didn't mean to scare you. I thought you heard me."

"No. I didn't." She held the side of the sink, wiping the water from her face that had splashed up when she dropped the potato.

"You okay? You seem tense." He put his briefcase down in a dining chair and slipped off his jacket. Since he'd been working on the weekend, he was dressed casually. "I thought you were out tonight."

Laura picked up the potato and resumed her scrubbing. "Me, too. Plans changed."

"You making dinner?"

"Yes. Is that a problem?"

"No. Not at all. What are you making?"

"Chicken with potatoes."

"Sounds good. What's the occasion?"

Laura put the potato in a pot on the stove and picked up another. "Does there have to be an occasion to make chicken and potatoes?"

Preston leaned against the counter beside her. "No. It's just you rarely cook on the weekend. We're more of a 'let's order out' couple."

"We order out too much. We're both capable of cooking. Our current financial state being what it is, we should be more frugal." She threw the next potato into the pot.

Preston watched her for a second. "You sure you're okay?"

Laura scrubbed the next potato. "Sure. I'm fine."

"How many potatoes are we eating?"

She stopped scrubbing. "Really?"

Preston held up his hands. "Sorry. But it's just the two of us. Are we expecting someone?"

Laura finished scrubbing the last potato and turned off the sink. "I considered asking Maddie over."

Preston nodded. "Did you? Is she joining us?"

"No. I haven't asked. Not yet, at least."

"It's a good idea. You should."

"You want me to?"

"Why not? You two need to talk."

Laura added the last potato to the pot and grabbed a towel to dry her hands. "I suppose."

Preston turned toward her. "Full disclosure. I stopped by her place on the way home."

Laura held the towel. "You did what?"

"I wanted to talk to her. Find out what all this mess was about."

"I told you what it was about."

"I know. But I thought maybe I could grease the wheels a bit with Maddie."

"I didn't ask you to do that, Preston." She threw the towel on the countertop.

"I know, but she's our friend. I thought it might help. We've known each other a long time. This is a silly disagreement and misunderstanding."

"Silly?" asked Laura. She leaned her hip against the counter and crossed her arms. "Why is it silly?"

"You two have known each other too long to stay angry at each other."

Laura cocked her head. "You know, I never got your take on all of this. I told you what happened. Whose side are you on?"

"Side? I'm on both your sides. I want you two to be friends again. And she's torn up about the argument too, but she's hurt. She just feels she should have been told."

Laura raised a brow. "So, you're on her side?"

"I'm not taking sides. I'm only telling you what she said. I see your point too. Your thing with Stephen was way under the bridge. I get it."

Laura frowned. "What is this really about?"

"What do you mean?"

"You're mad because I didn't tell you, either. Is that it?"

Preston pushed off from the counter. "I never said that."

"But you're thinking it."

Preston paused and studied the floor before looking up. "I'll admit. I think it's odd you brought in Stephen as Maddie's attorney, and you never told me you used to date him. But I'm not mad about it. I just think it's strange. Why not tell me? We've never kept secrets with each other."

Laura went still. "We've never kept secrets from each other?"

He stared back. "Forget it. It's not a big deal. You dated him in law school. You're not dating him now, are you?" He smiled.

Laura tensed. "And what did you tell Maddie on your little stop over?"

"I told her what I'm telling you. That you two need to work this out. Your friendship deserves another chance, and I don't want you two to hold on to this resentment. She needs you, especially with everything she's going through. There's no better friend than you, and she knows that. I almost invited her over to dinner myself, but thought I'd better ask you first."

Laura nodded, but said nothing. She walked to the fridge, opened it, and pulled out the defrosted chicken and put it in the sink. Opening the drawer beside her, she flipped on the water, pulled out some kitchen gloves, and put them on.

"You don't have anything to say?" asked Preston.

Laura opened the bag, dumped the chicken out and started to clean it. "You want me to say something?"

"Yes. I do. You're mad. I can tell."

Laura scrubbed the chicken, opened it, and pulled out the insides. "Do you like Maddie?"

"What kind of question is that? Of course, I do."

She scrubbed harder. "You two are very flirty together. Do you want to sleep with her?"

Preston's jaw dropped. "What kind of question is that?"

Laura grabbed a brush, yanked on the chicken legs, and continued to clean the bird. "Don't be stupid, Preston. I see the way you look at her."

Preston straightened. "What the hell are you talking about? I don't want to sleep with Maddie."

"Is that what you were doing over there today?"

Preston's eyes widened. "No. Where is this coming from? I would never do that to you. Nor would she."

"She slept with Karl. Did you know that?"

Preston shook his head. "What? How do you know that's true? And what does that have to do with me sleeping with her? This whole conversation is outrageous." He stopped for a moment and went still. "Did you take your pills today?"

Laura stopped scrubbing and put the brush down. The sink continued to run. The blood rushed through her ears, and everything went numb. "Did I what?"

Preston narrowed his eyes. "You are not making any sense. You accuse me of having an affair with Maddie and her of sleeping with Karl. What is going on?"

"Are you saying you've never slept with her?"

"Of course I haven't."

"You've never cheated on me?"

He hesitated, and she saw the slight tick in his cheek. "Why would I cheat on you?"

Laura made an angry chuckle. "Do you really think I'm that stupid? You think I don't know about Sharie? Oh, and that chick at your office?"

Preston's face went white. "I never..."

"You never what?"

"Laura—"

"What? Are you going to tell me it never happened? Or wait. That it did happen, but it didn't mean anything?"

Preston held his breath. "It didn't."

Laura pursed her lips. "I see. At least you're not denying it."

"It was stupid. Sharie was just an escape. We were going through that rough patch, and you were seeing the shrink..."

"You're blaming me?"

"God, no. I just want to explain. The girl at the office. It was just a one-time thing."

"Uh-huh."

"Laura, please. I didn't mean to hurt you."

Laura stared out the window, her mind racing. The water still ran, and she reached over and turned it off. "It's okay, Preston."

His face scrunched in confusion. "It's okay? No, it's not. I lied to you, I cheated, and I'm sorry."

Laura picked up the chicken and placed it on a cutting board already on the counter. Then she opened a drawer below. "You're sorry? That's sweet. But it's too late for that. To be honest, I don't really care. I haven't cared in a long time."

"What do you mean?"

"You're not the only one who slept around. You were just too stupid to see it. Did you really think I only had eyes for you?"

Preston sucked in a hard breath. "What?" His eyes shifted as the news settled. "Who—?" His eyes rounded with understanding. "Karl? Did you sleep with Karl? No."

Laura nodded. "Yes. I did."

"Laura, what are you telling me? Do you want a divorce?" He shook his head in disbelief. "What is happening here?"

Laura pulled a knife from the open drawer, put it next to the cutting board, and then slid the drawer shut. "You know what, Preston. I've had a lot of time to think about that. I've wondered about many things lately. You, Maddie, Stephen, Karl. I have a lot going through my mind. And then to add to all of that, your stupid financial decisions. I can't believe I trusted you. I could have made double the money you lost in the same amount of time. I trusted Karl, but he betrayed me too." She picked up the knife. "I taught him a lesson, and now I guess I have to teach you, too." Moving closer to Preston, she gripped the knife.

Preston watched her with uncertainty. "Laura, what the hell are you talking about?" He stepped back as she neared, but bumped into the kitchen counter, his hands up. "What are you doing?"

"Doing what I should have done months ago."

"Come on. Be serious. Put that thing down."

Laura hesitated, lowering the knife. Blinking her eyes, she stood there warily. "Did I scare you?"

Preston flicked his eyes between the knife and her eyes and let his hands relax. "Jesus. Yes. You scared the hell out of me." He let go of a held breath. "You got me and I deserved it. Now put that thing away."

Laura tilted her head. "With pleasure." Stepping close, she jabbed the knife deep into his belly, removing and jabbing again, several times, as blood spurted from his stomach. Stunned, Preston pushed away from her, yelping and grabbing at his injuries, blood gushing through his fingers. He collapsed to the ground, falling forward, with a pitiful moan.

Laura dropped the knife on the floor, removed her gloves, scrubbed them clean in the sink with soap and water, dried them, and returned them to the drawer. Leaving the chicken and Preston where they were, she went to the bathroom where she carefully changed her clothes, and put the bloody ones in a garbage bag. She took a quick shower, put on a fresh outfit, and grabbed the garbage bag. Going to the front closet, she opened it and put on her jacket. Spying an old purse on the shelf above, she took it down, reached into it and pulled out a gun. She slid the gun into her pocket and put the purse back on the shelf.

Returning to the kitchen, she was careful not to step in the growing puddle on the floor. Preston did not move. "I have to go now, honey. As you say, Maddie and I need to talk. Watch the house for me, will you?" With a last glance at the house and Preston, and holding the garbage bag, she turned and left.

TWENTY-FOUR

....

Madison flipped on the outside lights as the moon rose. It was a quiet but beautiful night. In the distance, thickening clouds and a flicker of lightning threatened rain, but for now, a light wind ruffled the trees and the lake sat still; disturbed only by the slight ripples in the water from falling leaves or a gliding bird. The boaters and skiers had gone home for the day.

She took a seat in a lounger on her back porch, thinking about her day. Compared to yesterday, it had been uneventful. After their conversation with the detectives, she and Stephen had talked briefly, but Madison didn't want to talk about the case or about what had happened between them, and Stephen didn't seem interested in apologizing, only explaining. Madison had suggested he leave, and he did. He'd called this morning and had been all business, so she'd acted the same.

All they could do was wait. Remalla and Daniels, after Remalla's outburst, decided they would look for the mysterious man in the woods. But Madison knew once they got the court order to view the footage at the motel, and if she and Karl were on it, then it would only be a matter of time before Biggles arrived to arrest Maddie for Karl's murder. The one hope was that Donald would also be on the tapes, and maybe also the mystery woman, and if they found her, then maybe they'd have another suspect. It was all pure conjecture at this point. Stephen would talk with his investigator and inquire about him continuing to check the surrounding hotels and restaurants and ask about Donald. It was a long shot, but it couldn't hurt to try.

Madison sighed and rubbed her temples, seeing the paint on her hands. She'd spent the afternoon working in her studio. It had been a while since she'd had the urge to create, but that morning, it was all she could do. She'd spent hours at her easel, allowing all the anger and pain to jump from her to the canvas. Before she'd known it, she'd blinked, and it was dinner time. Her stomach growling, she'd put down the brush, and found something to eat.

She'd been about to jump in the shower, when Preston had stopped by on his way home. He wanted to talk about what had happened between her and Laura. He knew the details, and Maddie appreciated his efforts to help, but she'd told him she'd expected more from her friend, and had been disappointed in Laura's response.

The conversation had ended well, and Preston had given her a hug and told her he'd talk to Laura and see if he could help. Madison had encouraged him to let it be and that they would work it out. Remembering her and Laura's angry words, she sat back, and considered calling her, but decided not to. Preston would be home by now and maybe he and Laura were talking. She'd let it alone until tomorrow.

Hearing the crunch of leaves, she looked up and scanned the property. Darkness had descended, and the lights made it hard to see beyond a certain distance. Madison wondered if the man in the trees was there, watching her. She stood and went inside, locking the back door behind her. Flipping off the outside lights, she stared out the window, but only saw the distant flicker of lightning. A low rumble of thunder joined it.

Shaking her head, she walked away from the door and down the hall toward the guest room, ready for that shower. Seeing the door to the master, she paused. Her heart rate jumped, recalling the night she found Donald.

Swallowing, she moved closer to the door and put her hand on the wood. The images flared, and she took a deep breath. Feeling the terror of that night, she fought the urge to run, but she did the opposite. She opened the door.

Pushing it wide, she looked inside, but it was too dark to see. Her hands shaky, she stepped inside and felt along the wall for the light switch and flipped it on. Light illuminated the room, and she froze. The furniture remained, but the bed was gone. After forensics had cleared it, Laura had had it removed. Madison took a step into the room.

Emotions swirled, and she forced herself to breathe normally. The floor was clean, but Madison could see Donald's lifeless eyes in her mind and all the blood in the sheets. A chill rushed through her, making the hair on her arms stand up. Forcing herself forward, she entered the bathroom, remembering the bloody knife on the ground, and her staring at it, trying to comprehend what it was.

Another impulse rushed through her to flee this room and never return, but she fought against it and walked into the master closet instead. Her clothes hung from the hangers and her shoes sat in their cubbies. Across from her things were Donald's slacks and shirts. They took up less space, but were also hung neatly. She saw his suits and ties, and his shoes lined up along the floor. Staring at his things, a crazy rage bloomed inside her. Recalling his treatment of her, and his lies, she grabbed at his shirts and yanked them down. She kicked at his shoes, and yelling epithets, she cursed his name. She knocked over a jewelry box containing his cufflinks, and she opened his drawers and pulled out undershirts, socks, and briefs, and threw and stomped at them. Pulling all his clothes down, she piled them up, determined to get rid of all of them. She wanted Donald erased from her mind and her memory. There would be no trace of him left in this house when she was done. It would be as if he never existed.

Breathing hard, she put her arm against the wall and rested, her rage spent, but her anger remained. Donald had made her life a misery, but she was mad at herself too, because she'd allowed it.

Disappointed but determined to never go down that road again, she decided that if she could get out of her present mess, she would figure her shit out. Men would never be the answer. No one would. Only she, herself, had the cure. She would have to be enough. It would be a long road though. Thinking of Stephen, she realized she'd followed the same pattern. She'd looked to him to make it better, and she'd expected him to understand. But falling into bed with a man would never be a long-term solution. She had to learn that.

Feeling a little better, she stared at the pile of clothes on the floor. She'd bag it up tomorrow and give it to charity. At least someone could benefit from it. Turning to leave, she stopped when she caught sight of a depression in the wall. It was on Donald's side of the closet, now exposed with the clothes removed. Moving closer, Madison studied it.

It was a small door with hinges on it she never knew existed. Pushing on it, it swung open revealing a small space behind the closet wall. Looking closely, she reached in, and pulled out a cell phone.

TWENTY-FIVE

·······································

Daniels snored lightly as Remalla continued to watch the Vickers' house. Little had happened since Remalla had started his watch hours earlier. The only activity of interest had been Preston Benoff. He'd stopped by about thirty minutes earlier but had only stayed about twenty minutes. After he'd left, Madison had come out on her front porch and sat for a while and then went inside. If she hadn't flipped on the outside lights, he would not have been able to see her. The sun had descended, and the moon provided only a minimal light.

Soon, though, the moon would be higher and he would be able to see a little better. Not that it mattered much because there was nothing happening. He stood from his seat and stretched. His stomach growled, and he dreamed of a giant pizza and a beer. There were sandwiches in a cooler and he debated eating one.

Daniels snored again, and Rem wondered how his partner could sleep so well in such an uncomfortable area—a sleeping bag on a hard and dirty floor. Since the windows were busted, a cool breeze chilled the room, and Rem had shivered the previous night. He'd been on unpleasant stakeouts before, but this one was one of the worst. He couldn't wait to sleep in a bed.

Knowing he wouldn't be getting any rest, he let Daniels sleep and resumed his position in the chair. For the umpteenth time, he thought of Jacobs. Should he tell her about Rutger and what he had said? Was Rutger responsible for killing a man assumed to be a victim of the Makeup Artist? Someone close to Jacobs? And if that was the case, then why? And why was he here now, bothering Madison Vickers? What was the connection?

Once this case was over, he and Jill had plans to see each other over a long weekend. He'd planned to take her here, but after all this, he might consider another destination. Once they were together, then he could decide what to tell her. A lot would depend on what happened with this case. If Rutger never showed again, it would be pointless. They'd have to chalk him up to being a nut job who liked to scare women and detectives in the woods. There would be little else they could do.

Rem ran his hands through his long hair, ruffled his locks, and stretched his neck. Since Madison had returned inside and flipped off the lights, it had been silent, other than a rumble of thunder. He'd checked his phone, and the forecast had been correct. A storm was rolling in. The only sounds now though were the crickets chirping and the occasional footfall of the nocturnal animals leaving their dens to search for food. This was the part Rem liked the least. He couldn't be sure what was walking around out there. A fox, a deer, a bear, a human, Big Foot. It was all the same to him. His instincts would be the only way to distinguish between them. They hadn't let him down yet. He'd have to continue to trust them.

Digging through a bag of food, he found a bag of chips. Sitting down, he opened them and began to munch. His coffee was long since gone, and he was considering popping a soda when he heard a crunch of leaves. He stopped chewing, listening intently. Was it an animal? Not hearing anything, he started to chew when the noise came again, this time closer.

He froze in his seat, waiting to see if something would walk out into his line of sight. It had to be an animal, but something about the sound made it seem bigger. Standing slowly, he dropped the bag of chips to the ground. Reaching to his waist, he unsnapped his weapon from its holster and rested his palm against the handle. Stepping closer to the window, he looked outside, scanning the area. Although it was dark, his eyes had adjusted to the light. The shadows of the trees in the remaining moonlight swayed against the ground and Rem swallowed his mouthful of chips. He saw nothing, but the hair on his neck raised.

"Daniels," he whispered.

Daniels didn't stir, but snored again.

"Daniels," he said again, slightly louder.

Daniels came awake with a start, attuned to the sound of his name spoken in a certain tone. Shaking the sleep away with a rub of his eyes, he was up with a groan, but despite his ribs, he was standing beside Rem in seconds. "What is it?"

Rem didn't move. "Something. We're not alone."

Daniels did the same with his weapon—unsnapping it and having it at the ready. "What'd you hear?"

"Someone's walking around out here."

"You sure it's not a deer?"

"It's not a deer."

The noise came again, only now from behind them. They both swiveled, their weapons now in their hands. The small fishing cabin had another broken window on the opposite side and Rem watched and waited, expecting at any moment to see someone walk past.

"Definitely not a deer," whispered Daniels.

"Nope."

They walked silently to the window, careful not to step on any debris. Daniels went to one side and Rem to the other, both looking out.

"Anything?" asked Daniels.

"Nothing."

They waited for the sound to come again. Rem held his gun, pointing it toward the ground. The shadows of the trees continued to sway, and the crickets still chirped, but nothing else moved. Rem had the strange feeling that they were being watched, but he couldn't tell from where.

"You think it's him?" asked Daniels.

"I think—"

A figure darted out from a tree, running through the brush. Rem and Daniels reacted instantaneously, both heading for the door and sprinting through it, Daniels behind Rem. Rem jumped over a fallen log and dodged a shrub, determined not to lose sight of the man in the woods. He could hear Daniel's footfalls behind him and knew his partner was close.

Breathing hard, Rem ran deeper into the woods. He swiped at low-hanging branches and one scratched his face, but he kept up his pursuit. The man ahead kept up a steady pace, seemingly comfortable running through the dense trees at night.

"Stop. Police," he yelled, but the man showed no sign of hearing or stopping. Rem kept up the pace, doing his best to dodge shrubs, vines and trees, with Daniels following.

The man suddenly picked up his speed, made a sharp turn right, and disappeared into a thick grove of foliage. Rem darted in to follow, ran through and narrowly missed a twisted branch hanging at eye level, and stopped when he found himself in a small, circular clearing. It was maybe ten feet wide with nothing but dirt, surrounded by heavy trunked trees and tall grass. Daniels shot through and narrowly missed running into Rem. Both men stood there, trying to catch their breath.

"Where'd he go?" asked Daniels.

Rem swiveled around. "I don't know. He was right in front of me."

They stood for a moment, listening. Rem waited to hear footsteps, but didn't. "He has to be near. We'd hear him running away."

Daniels turned, his weapon raised. Rem did the same. The woods were thick and hard to see beyond them. Clouds had rolled in, obscuring the light even more. He squinted, trying to see. His skin prickled, and he shivered. "He's here. He's watching us."

Daniels, his eyes alert, trained his gun along the perimeter of the clearing. "He's playing with us."

Rem considered their options. There weren't many. Either give up the chase and let Rutger be, or see just how far they could go. "We know you're out there," he said to the trees.

Daniels followed his lead. "Show yourself. You got us out here for a reason." A twig snapped and he and Rem turned toward the sound. "Who are you?" asked Daniels.

Nothing moved, and it was silent, but the crickets had stopped chirping. Rem aimed his weapon but saw nothing. The only noise was their breathing and another rumble of thunder.

Getting impatient, Rem debated charging forward, hoping to flush the man out, when a male voice spoke from the darkness.

"I did it for her."

**

Madison held the phone in her hand, her mind reeling. Was this the phone the detectives were looking for? Did Donald use this to communicate with his mistress? Instinctively, she knew it was. Why else would he hide it?

She tried to turn it on, but the battery had long since died. After studying the phone, she realized she had a charger for it. Turning, she left the closet, walked out of the bathroom and exited the master, closing the door behind her. Holding the cell, she passed her studio and entered a small office off the hallway. Donald had occasionally used it when he worked from home, and she used it to talk with art dealers and potential customers. Her laptop sat on the desk.

She opened the top drawer and rummaged through it, finding the cord she sought. After trying it to see if it fit the phone, Madison sighed in relief when it did. Plugging it in to an outlet, she laid the phone on the desk to let it charge.

It would take a few minutes before she could access the information, and Madison paced the room, wondering what to do next. Should she turn it over to the police? Would it hurt for her to look first, or could that somehow be used against her? Maybe she should have never touched it, because now her fingerprints were on it. Stephen. She had to talk to Stephen. He would tell her what to do.

She left the office and headed to the kitchen where she found her cell. Finding his number, she punched it and waited for him to pick up, but it went to voicemail. At the beep, she left a message, telling Stephen what she had found and to please call her as soon as possible. Hanging up, she put her phone down, considering what to do next. What would it hurt if she checked the phone? Could anyone blame her for that? The identity of Donald's lover was likely on it. She decided she'd give it fifteen minutes. If Stephen didn't call her back by then, she'd access the phone.

Tapping her fingers against the kitchen counter, she waited, feeling as if time had slowed considerably. Surely it had been fifteen minutes by now. Checking the clock though, she saw it had only been five.

"Screw it," she said to herself. She started to head toward the office when the doorbell rang. Hesitating, she wondered who would stop by now, but wondered if it could be Stephen. Maybe he'd heard her message, and he'd been in the area. She jogged to the door, and checked the peephole. But it wasn't Stephen, it was Laura.

**

The voice made Daniels' blood run cold. He stared in the direction from which it had come but he didn't see anyone. Large trees and the cloudy sky made distinguishing anything almost impossible. His ribs hurt, but the adrenaline had almost numbed the pain.

Rem swung his gun and aimed it toward the voice, as did Daniels. They made eye contact and Daniels cocked his head. Rem nodded, and he took some steps to his right and Daniels moved to his left, both ready to fire.

"What did you do?" asked Rem. He moved toward the edge of the clearing as Daniels moved opposite him, allowing them to cover both sides in case their perpetrator darted out.

There was no reply, and Daniels stepped closer. Rem did the same.

Daniels debated whether to say something when the man answered. "You know what I did." His voice was deep and gruff. "They all do."

Daniels' heart raced. Until the man had spoken, he couldn't be sure if they were speaking to Rutger, or some big teenager playing a prank, but now it was a certainty that this was Rutger.

"Who's they?" he asked. Moving closer, he reached the edge of the clearing. His next step would be into the brush.

"The ones who know who I am. They know what I did, and why."

The direction of the voice was difficult to discern. Rutger was definitely behind a tree, but he couldn't tell which one.

Rem reached the edge of his side of the clearing, and he took a small step into a thick hedge of high grass. "You say you did it for her. Who's her?"

A quiet chuckle echoed through the trees. Daniels' hair stood on end.

"I did it for both of them."

Rem and Daniels shared a glance. "Both of them?" asked Daniels.

"Jill and Madison."

Even in the dark, Daniels could see Rem's eyes widen. "Did you kill Donald Vickers?"

"They needed me. I helped them."

Daniels swallowed. "Do they know who you are?"

A brief pause. "They will. All of them will. When it's time."

Rem ducked under a branch. "I thought you said they knew what you did and they know who you are. Now you're saying they don't know who you are? You're not making sense, Rutger," said Rem. He moved further from the clearing and deeper into the woods. Daniels did the same.

"It's not for you to understand."

"You brought us into this," said Daniels. "We have questions."

"And we want answers," said Rem.

"You will know only what I need you to know. You serve a purpose. You will go in the direction I you need to go."

"Last I checked, we already have a boss. We don't need another." Rem swiveled and aimed behind a tree, but no one was there.

"Why don't you come out," said Daniels. "Let's talk face to face."

"There will be a time and a place, but not yet."

"We've come this far. Why not reveal yourself? You showed yourself before. We saw what you could do. You want to try it again?" asked Rem. He nodded his head at Daniels, and Daniels nodded back. They would move deeper into the trees and come around Rutger from the side.

The chuckle traveled again. "You do not understand who or what you're dealing with. None of them do." Lightning flashed, and with the brief light, Daniels stepped over a bulging root and moved around a thick tree. He kept scanning with his eyes, searching for any movement. He could make out Rem moving slowly in the same way, but on the opposite side, away from the clearing. A crack of thunder made him jump. "Why are you here tonight?" asked Daniels. "Did you plan to meet Madison?" He moved closer.

"I am here for you."

"We're flattered, but let's be honest. I'd rather meet over a beer. You got a reason you prefer the woods at night?" asked Rem.

Rutger didn't answer, and Daniels heard the crunch of leaves. He moved quickly forward, expecting to see something, but only the leaves moved with the wind. *Who was this guy?* He saw Rem take several steps forward, his gun extended.

Another crunch of leaves. "I prefer my secrecy. It serves me well, as it serves you."

Daniels saw Rem come up on another large tree and swing around it, his gun raised. Daniels made a similar move around a tree near him. At some point, they would flush this guy out. He had to be close.

"How does your secrecy serve us?" asked Daniels.

"I'm finding it to be a pain in the ass," said Rem.

"The less you know about me, the better."

"Are you saying you're protecting us? You broke my partner's ribs and gave me stitches. Care to explain that?" asked Rem.

"It was necessary. You need to know what I'm capable of. If I wanted to kill you, I could do it right now. Your guns won't stop me."

Daniels approached an area thick with foliage, and he swiveled around it, but no one was there. He saw Rem disappear into a grove of trees. Daniels stepped up to keep pace with Rem, and expected to see him come around the other side, but heard a shout instead, and a figure flew out from the grove, landing sideways in the dirt, barely missing a large rock jutting from the ground. Daniels rushed forward, seeing Rem lying on a bulging root. He still held his gun. Daniels made it to his side, squatting next to him. "You okay?"

Rem grunted and struggled to sit up. "I'm okay. Got the wind knocked out of me."

"What happened?" Daniels kept his gun raised, watching the area, careful to cover his partner while he was down.

Lightning flashed and an immediate low boom of thunder followed it.

"I'm what happened." Rutger stepped out of the shadows and Daniels took aim.

TWENTY-SIX

....

Madison opened the door. Laura stood there, wearing a sweatshirt and jeans under an oversized trench coat with a hood over her head. Her hands were in her pockets.

Madison stood for a moment, as did Laura. Lightning flashed and thunder rumbled.

"Hey," said Madison.

"Hey," said Laura. "Can I come in?"

Madison nodded. "Sure." She stepped aside as Laura entered. "Thanks."

Madison closed the door and followed Laura, who walked into the living area, pushing her hood back. Once there, she turned, facing Madison. "I heard Preston stopped by."

Madison nodded. "He did."

Laura looked around the room, took her hands out of her pockets and crossed her arms. "What did he say?"

"Just that he didn't like us fighting. I told him how I felt, and why I was angry. He said he would talk to you about it, but that he knew our friendship was stronger than a silly disagreement."

Laura stared at the ground. "I didn't ask him to do that."

"Would you have preferred he hadn't?"

"I don't like people fighting my battles for me. I'm a big girl."

"He cares about you."

Laura looked up at Madison, her eyes round. "He cares about you too."

"He doesn't want us to fight. He doesn't like it."

Laura squinted. "You seem to know him pretty well."

"I should. He's your husband. You and I have been friends for years. You knew Donald pretty well."

At the mention of Donald's name, Laura straightened. "What are you saying?"

Madison picked up on Laura's tension. "I'm not saying anything. Merely that we all know each other." She paused. "What's going on Laura? Why are you here?"

Thunder rumbled again. "I think it's going to rain," said Laura.

"Sounds like it."

Laura walked toward the window, staring out. "We could use some rain. The lake's a little low."

Madison studied her friend. "Laura, you didn't come here to talk about the weather."

"No, I didn't." She turned back toward Madison, and cocked her head. "I know you're mad I slept with Stephen."

"I'm not mad you slept with him. You dated him in law school. I just don't understand why you didn't tell me."

"People keep secrets. Surely you understand that."

"But we're friends. And he's my attorney, and..."

"And what? I should have known you were going to fuck him?"

Her language startled Madison. Laura rarely cursed, and something about her body language put Madison on edge. "Laura, what's wrong?"

Laura smiled, and a shiver ran through Madison. This conversation was not going in the direction she was expecting.

"You're trying to tell me you don't have secrets of your own? Is that what you're saying?" asked Laura. She took a step forward. "How come you didn't tell me you were sleeping with Karl?"

Madison froze, her blood running cold. "Who told you that?"

Laura rolled her eyes. "You're such an idiot. Karl did."

"Karl what?"

"You think you were the only one sleeping with him?"

Madison's heart flipped in her chest. "You had an affair with Karl? When?" A flash of lightning and a boom of thunder made Madison jump.

"After you ended it with him. He was upset, and sought out my affections. I responded in kind. But he never got over you. Did you not know that?"

Madison shook her head. "What are you saying? What is all this about?"

"This is about you, Maddie. You always try to come across as some goodie-two-shoes, but you're not."

"I'm not trying to be anything. What happened with Karl was a mistake. I just fell into a hole and I dug it deeper. I was drinking too much, and Donald—"

"Donald. Yes. Let's blame him for everything."

Madison dropped her jaw. "You know what he did to me."

"I know what you said he did to you."

Madison set her jaw. "Are you saying I lied about his abuse?"

Rain began to fall and Madison could hear it hit the roof. Laura walked away from the window, and rested her hip against the kitchen counter. "I talked to Donald many times. He told me how dramatic you could be. That you liked attention. And when you didn't get it, you said what you had to to get it."

"And you believed him?"

Laura went still. Her eyes were as chilly as the night breeze, and Madison gripped the back of a dining chair. It was obvious Laura was not here to apologize. Madison could deal with Laura's defense of her relationship with Stephen, but not of Donald's abuse. Anger made her stomach clench.

"I did sleep with Karl," said Madison. "I told no one. It was awful, and I broke it off. No matter how badly Donald treated me, I couldn't stomach having an affair. I did it for all the wrong reasons. I was using sex and alcohol to deal with my misery. I hated my husband, but I couldn't leave him. He was verbally and physically abusive and you know it. Now you're trying to tell me you believed him instead of me? Are you insane?"

Laura face hardened. "I don't think this little talk is helping."

"No, it isn't. I think you should leave."

Laura cocked her head and slid her hands into her pockets. "I think you're right."

The doorbell rang, there was hard knock on the door, and a voice rang out. "Madison, are you there? It's Stephen."

**

Remalla held his chest, trying to catch his breath. He'd been approaching an alcove cloaked in shadows, when there'd been a tingling in his chest, and he'd been pulled back violently, landing sideways in the dirt. Daniels was there in an instant. The figure stepped out from the darkness. Although still obscured, a flash of lightning briefly illuminated his face. He recognized him as the same man from the other night.

Daniels squatted next to Rem, but aimed his weapon at Rutger. "Don't move."

Getting to his knees, Rem swiveled around, turning and aiming his gun as well. He took a shaky breath. "You take one step and you're a dead man."

Rutger raised his arms, palms out. "Relax. I have no intentions of harming you, unless you give me no choice."

Without the flicker of lightning, Rutger was almost impossible to see.

"Keep your hands up," said Daniels. Pushing up, he got into a standing position. Rem joined him, the tingling in his chest subsiding.

"Get down on your knees," said Rem. The wind picked up and a cold raindrop hit his face.

Rutger kept his arms raised. "I'm not going anywhere. I have more to do."

Daniels straightened his aim. "Do as he says. Get down on your knees and lay flat, arms out."

Rutger chuckled. "What exactly are you arresting me for? Running through the woods?"

"Assault of a police officer," said Rem.

Another flicker of lightning revealed Rutger's smirk. "You're going to tell your fellow officers that I disarmed your partner, threw him into a tree and knocked you out with a rock, all without touching you? How well do you think that will be received? Sheriff Biggles will laugh you out of the station."

"Maybe so, but it will give us time to figure out who you are and why you're here, and what your connection to these murders are, and how you know Jill and Madison," said Rem. Another raindrop hit his arm.

"The timing of that will be up to me, not you."

"We'll see about that," said Daniels. A louder clap of thunder boomed, and the rain picked up. "Now, step out and keep your hands up." He took a step closer and Rem did the same.

Rutger didn't move, but as Rem and Daniels encroached, Rem could make out Rutger shifting and looking slightly away, as if distracted. A second passed before Rutger spoke again. "I have to go now, and so do you. You're about to learn the truth. It's why you're here."

Rem blinked the rain from his eyes. "You're the reason we're here. You're a suspect in Donald Vickers' death. You come peacefully, and you won't be hurt."

They stood for a second, no one moving, when Rutger moved his hands, as if waving.

The tingles returned, and Rem's palms burned. Daniels cursed and started to cock his gun when their weapons flew from their grips. They traveled through the air and landed at Rutger's feet.

The rain started to fall in torrents, and Rem stood in shock, unsure of what to do.

Rutger took a step out of his hiding place, now in full view of the detectives. "I told you your guns were useless. When I'm ready, I'll find Madison and Jill, but I have to help Jace next and then we will see what happens."

Daniels wiped the rain from his face. "There's no winning this. We'll catch you eventually."

Rutger stared with unflinching eyes. "I'm not here to win, detective. I'm here for revenge, and when I'm done, everyone one will pay. And the only ones left will be my family. Then they will know my name."

"Your family?" asked Rem. The rain was falling so hard now, he could barely see. His clothes were soaked and he shivered.

Daniels yelled over a rumble of thunder and the torrential rain. "Family? Who's your—"

A shot rang out in the distance and Rem and Daniels instinctively turned toward the sound. It came from the direction of Madison's home. Turning back toward Rutger, Rem saw no one. The man had disappeared.

**

Laura eyed the door. "Speak of the devil. He always did have good timing." She sighed. "That's one of things I like about him." She paused. "Are you going to let him in?"

Madison watched her friend, the knocking coming again.

"Madison, I got your message. Open up. It's pouring out here."

She turned and went to the door and let Stephen in. He rushed inside, shaking out his wet jacket. His hair dripping and his shoes soaked, he stood in the foyer. "Thank you. It's a mess out there. The rain came out of nowhere."

He slid off his jacket. "I got your message. Where is..." He stopped when he saw Laura. "Oh, I'm sorry. I didn't realize you had company."

"Company? Is that what I am?" Laura pushed off from the counter. "Come on, Stephen. We're much more than that." She walked over and put her hands up around his neck. "Right, honey?" Pressing her lips against his, she kissed him.

Stephen pulled back immediately. "What the hell are you doing?"

Laura gestured toward Madison. "Madison and I are truth-telling. Don't you think it's about time we told her everything?"

Stephen stared at her like she'd grown wings and just dropped out of the stormy sky. "What are you doing?"

"Like I said, I'm telling the truth." She turned toward Madison. "Stephen and I have...well...rekindled our romance. When I called him about your case, it was if the time that had passed vanished, and we were back in school again. Right, Steve?"

Stephen's mouth fell open, and he shook his head. "Stop it." He looked at Madison. "Don't listen to her."

"It's too late for that. She is listening, and she knows I'm telling the truth. Don't you, Madison?"

Madison still stood by the front door. Her blood rushed down into her toes, and her head spun. "Is that true?"

Stephen stammered, his face red. "It was stupid. It just happened. I...I'm sorry. I...I...should have told you."

Madison could hardly breathe. My God. Stephen and Laura had picked up where they'd left off. Her best friend and her attorney, the two people she trusted the most, had lied to her, but it was far worse than she'd thought.

Her thoughts scattered; she couldn't think of anything to say. She thought of the phone in the office. Laura and Stephen stood facing each other; Laura with a cold stare of satisfaction, and Stephen, his face white with shock. Without thinking, she turned and left the room, walking down the hallway, and into the office.

"Madison, wait," said Stephen.

Madison ignored him, and kept moving. Once in the office, she heard him speak to Laura. "You bitch."

Laura responded, but Madison tuned them both out. Grabbing the cell, she checked the display, which lit up when she hit a button. Unplugging it, she held her breath when she saw the request for a password.

The arguing continued from the front room, but Madison focused on the phone. Something nagged at her, and a troubling thought occurred to her. If Laura could do this to her, what else could she do? Who was this person she had considered to be her best friend?

Making an assumption, she used Donald's birthdate as the passcode, and groaned in relief when the home screen appeared. Donald was not a complicated man, and he had a horrible memory. His birthday was the most logical option.

Madison quickly pulled up the text messages, and sucked in a breath when she read them. They were all sexual, and Madison had a difficult time reading them. She didn't recognize the number he'd been texting, but she suspected his mistress also had a burner phone.

Madison flipped through several texts discussing where and when they would meet, what they would do to each other, and re-calling previous satisfying encounters. Those were the easy ones. The worst were the pictures. Madison closed her eyes, barely able to breathe. Unsure if she could continue, she realized she had to; she had to know the identity of the woman, and she feared she already knew. Opening her eyes, she flipped through the messages, and stopped on one.

None of the pictures showed the couple's faces, but this photo was of the woman, bare from the midriff up, her breasts perky, and her back arched. A mirror in the background showed the back of her bare shoulder. A small tattoo of a parakeet, wings outstretched, caused Madison to drop the phone onto the desk. Putting a hand to her mouth, a clap of thunder shook the house. She knew that tattoo. She'd held Laura's hand in the tattoo parlor and had tried to distract her from the pain.

Laura had been sleeping with Donald.

Everything spun. Madison grabbed onto the side of the desk. Her best friend had been screwing her husband, and Stephen, and Karl. What else had she done?

Realizing the implications of what she'd learned, she knew she needed help. Laura was unstable and in Madison's house. She needed to call the police. Reaching for the phone on the desk, she started to pick it up when a shot rang out from the front room, and Stephen yelped in pain.

....

TWENTY-SEVEN

D aniels leapt over a large rock and Remalla pushed back a low-hanging branch. The weather had deteriorated rapidly. Rain made visibility poor and the lightning and thunder came in rapid succession. Daniels ran toward the main house, careful to avoid obstacles, but the thick woods made it difficult. He heard Rem curse behind him.

"You okay?" he yelled over the downpour.

"I can barely see. You know where you're going?"

A flash of lightning illuminated their surroundings and Daniels saw the lights of the house appear in the distance. "Yes. We're almost there." He held his gun after he and Rem had retrieved their weapons from where Rutger had left them.

He almost tripped and side-stepped a spindly tree. Seeing the old fishing cabin, he took a left and headed toward the main house.

"You sure you know where you are?" asked Rem from behind him.

The rain smacked against his face, and he pushed his wet hair off his forehead. Another flash of lightning made him slow and stop behind a large oak. Breathless, he crouched low. His ribs ached, but he ignored it. Rem squatted beside him, holding his side and breathing hard. "Are we close?"

"Yes. About fifty yards."

Rem leaned around the tree. Lightning lighted the area and Rem pulled back. "Okay. I see it." He wiped his eyes. "How do you want to handle this?"

Daniels thought about it. "One of us goes to the front and the other to the back. We go in at a set time."

Rem shook his head. "I don't like it. Not in these conditions. We can barely tell where we're going. We separate, we could put the other at risk. We need to stay together. We don't know what we're dealing with."

Daniels watched the house. "Okay. We go around to the back. There are windows. We can try and see in, then make our move based on what we find."

"For all we know, that shot could have been a neighbor firing at a possum, or some other creepy crawly. It might not be anything."

"Is that what you think it is?"

Rem squinted in the deluge. "No. But I can hope."

Rem checked his weapon, and Daniels did the same. "You ready?" asked Daniels.

Thunder rumbled and Rem wiped the water from his face. "Lead the way."

**

Madison froze. For an instant, her body would not move. And then the fear shifted from immobilizing her into shocking her into action. She reached for the landline on the desk and listened for a dial tone, but she heard nothing. Phones around the lake were notoriously bad in this kind of weather. So was the electricity, but that still worked, and she counted her blessings.

Dropping to the floor, she grabbed for the cell she'd dropped, and punched 911, but there was no connection. She tried again, but it didn't work.

Desperate, she searched the room, looking for anything that might help her. Nothing on the desk would be of any use as a weapon, unless she had the chance to stab Laura with a pen, but if Laura had a gun, that would be useless.

Her search stopped on the window. Rain pounded against the pane and lightning flashed. If she could get outside, she could run for it and try and make it to a neighbor where she could get help. She dashed toward it, unlocking it and gripping the ledge and pulling. The window barely moved, but with a groan, it gave way, and opened. Rain spattered the inside edge and she started to lean out when she heard the cock of the gun behind her.

"One more step and I'll shoot you in the back."

Madison turned to see Laura standing in the doorway with a gun aimed at her. Ice cold fear raced down her spine. "Laura, what are you doing? Put that down."

The thin thread of whatever sanity Laura had left snapped and a maniacal grin enveloped her face. "Come with me. We're not done here yet."

"Laura—"

"I said come with me. Now." Laura yelled at her and Madison jumped. Laura waved the gun. "Move."

Madison bit her lip, and held up her hands. "Okay, okay. I'm coming. Don't shoot."

Laura stepped aside from the door as Madison walked past, but kept her weapon on Madison. Madison turned down the hall, walking slowly, but as she neared the front of the house, she saw Stephen sprawled on the floor in the fetal position. Blood pooled beneath him. Fearing the worst, she ran toward him and kneeled beside him. "Stephen. Oh my God." His pale face scrunched in pain and he moaned. "Stay still. We'll get you help. Don't move." She put a hand on his shoulder. "Laura, he needs a doctor. We have to get an ambulance."

Laura didn't acknowledge her worry and showed no concern for Stephen. "Leave him alone. Get up and sit in the chair."

"But he needs help—"

"I said get up."

Madison rose and went to the chair, but didn't sit. She noticed the blinds on the windows were lowered, preventing anyone from seeing in, not that much could be seen with the heavy rain. Trying to stay calm, she eyed Stephen on the floor, and watched Laura hold the gun on her, and remembered the pictures and texts on Donald's phone. Waves of anger surfaced. This woman had claimed to be her friend. Madison had shared her deepest secrets with her, had confided in her, trusted her, laughed and cried with her, and Laura had betrayed her. Madison didn't understand. Despite the danger, rage bubbled up.

"Who are you?" she asked. "You shot Stephen. Why?" She shook her head. "I don't understand. How could you do this? You were my friend. I relied on you, told you everything, trusted you. And you lied about everything. You slept with Donald. I saw the texts."

Laura narrowed her eyes. "You're so dumb. I can't believe you never suspected. But I guess I shouldn't be surprised. You've always been so smug. So high and mighty. I trusted you too. But you didn't tell me everything. Karl told me about your fling with him. He pursued me after that, and I thought it was because he wanted me, but then I realized he wanted you, and I was just a way for him to get closer to you. I didn't give up though. Secretly, I'd hoped he'd dump Sharie. Then I could enjoy his money since Preston lost ours. But he just used me until the day he told me he couldn't see me anymore. That I wasn't what he wanted, because he couldn't stop thinking about you. It made me sick. I wanted to hurt Sharie too. Preston cheated on me with her, but Karl didn't care when I threatened to tell her. Said she wouldn't care either. He kept talking about you. I took it as a challenge. I've always been able to wrap men around my finger, but Karl wouldn't bend."

Laura glanced at Stephen and snickered. "That's when I told Donald about you and Karl."

"You told Donald?" asked Madison.

"That's what the fight was about. Donald confronted Karl, but Karl told him it was over. I think I wanted Donald to kill Karl, but he didn't have the balls. Donald wanted to confront you too, but I convinced him there were better ways to deal with you. A week later, I saw Karl again. He was angry I'd told Donald. He told me it was a mistake to start something with me. He'd done it for all the wrong reasons. He regretted it." She raised the side of her lip. "Can you believe that?" Her smile grew. "I gave him something to regret. A knife between his shoulder blades."

Madison held her stomach, the realization stunning her. "You killed him. You killed Karl."

"Don't play stupid. I know you know. You knew all along. After Karl's death, it gave me an idea. I suggested to Donald that if you were to have an unfortunate accident, then Donald would have the house and the money. Unfortunately, you took care of him first. Smart."

Madison dropped her jaw. "That's not true. I didn't kill anyone. Why would I go to jail for a crime you committed?"

"You were never going to go to jail, and you know it. That was your plan all along. I can see right through you. It might have taken me some time but I figured it out."

"You figured what out?"

"You killed Donald, knowing Karl's killer would be the obvious suspect. Eventually, it would come out that you slept with Karl so you had to have another target. I was the obvious choice. You would be accused of murder initially, but you planted the seeds well. Convincing those detectives to stick around. The pin in Karl's jacket, Donald's cell phone. I knew you had it. And you'd find it at just the right time to accuse me." She set her jaw. "I'd hoped at first that maybe we could share our secret together. You killed Donald. I killed Karl. We could protect each other. But I knew, once Sharie told me about the pin, what your plan really was."

Madison tried to keep up. Most of what Laura said made no sense. Laura thought she'd killed Donald, and was staging an elaborate plot to expose Madison as the killer of both men. She held her breath and tried to think. "Laura, I didn't kill Donald."

Laura cackled. "You can stop with the stories, Madison. It's just you and me right now. No detectives. No Biggles. Maybe Donald beat you and treated you like shit, and you killed him. I don't blame you. He never laid a hand on me though. I'd have killed him first if he had. But he told me how miserable his marriage was with you. I felt sorry for him. Seducing him was easy. Although he was lousy in bed. I wanted so much to confide in you after his death. But I realized it was safer for us to play dumb."

Madison concluded her friend had fallen down a hole she would not climb out of. Using logic would not work. Laura had somehow convinced herself that Madison, not her, had killed Donald. Madison tried to keep her talking.

"You said Sharie found a pin. What pin?"

Laura sighed with impatience. "You know what pin. The pin you gave me. The blue turquoise pin you wore, and I admired. You gave it to me on my birthday in front of Angie and Lucy. Sharie found it in Karl's jacket and thinks it's yours. She's bringing it to Biggles, hoping it will seal your fate. But you expected that, didn't you? All you have to say is that you gave it to me. Lucy and Angie can confirm that, and then the suspicion shifts to me. But that won't happen. By the time Monday rolls around, the murder suicide that occurred here will stun the neighbors. No one will care about that pin then."

Madison's stomach dropped and she clenched her hands. "What are you talking about?"

Laura straightened her aim. "You. You killed Stephen and then shot yourself. After you stabbed and killed Preston in my home. And almost killed me. But I managed to escape and run into the woods. It's tragic how you went on a killing spree."

Madison tried to draw a breath, but her chest constricted in terror. "Preston? No."

"He's lying on my kitchen floor, bleeding out, stabbed by your knife from this kitchen. I took it when I made the martinis."

Madison swallowed. Her mind swirled and she winced. "No, Laura. This won't work."

"Yes, it will. I'll shoot you in the head, put the gun in your hand—it's Donald's gun by the way; he kept it in his sock drawer. Those idiot deputies didn't find it, but I did." She straightened her aim. "Then I'll shoot Stephen again, and I'll walk out of the woods, injured and terrified, telling how you went nuts, came into our home, and attacked Preston and then came after me, but I got away. Biggles won't even bother to get a second opinion. The pin won't matter, and hopefully with a little luck, the videos will show you and Karl together. It'll be open and shut."

"Laura, please. Think about what you're doing."

"That's all I've been doing for the last twenty-four hours. It's perfect." Her face dropped. "Now sit down."

Madison realized her time was up. Either she did something now, or she would die, and this story would hold up. She scanned the room, looking for anything that might help. Her body shook with adrenaline and fear. This couldn't be the way it ended. Her mind clamored for ideas. She had to get the gun. *Focus, Madison.*

Focus. The fleeting thought rushed her mind. *Trust your instincts. Use your strengths.*

Laura encroached. "I said sit down." Her voice rose.

Madison backed away from the chair. "No."

Laura's face darkened. "Do as I say, Madison. I promise. It will all be over quick."

Thunder boomed, and Madison stepped back, catching her reflection in a mirror across the room. Her ashen face and wide eyes made her look like a ghost. Beside her, on a side table against the wall, sat a picture of her and Donald from happier times. Seeing it, the anger and betrayal surfaced. Donald's abuse, her father's disdain, Stephen's lies, Laura's hatred and betrayal, and Madison's acceptance of all of it. She might die tonight, but she wouldn't make it easy. The disgust and fury building, she took the offensive, and advanced on Laura. "You want to kill me, then do it. But you'll have to look me in the eyes when you pull the trigger."

Madison's approach surprised Laura, but not for long. She aimed the gun at Madison, and Madison braced for the boom, when the picture beside her flew off the table, sliced through the air, and hit Laura square in the shoulder. Laura deflected, causing her to swing the gun. A shot rang out and hit the wall behind Madison.

Torrents of rain shook the house, and Madison dove beneath the dining table as two male voices shouted from behind her.

"Freeze! Don't move!"

Madison looked to see Detectives Daniels and Remalla, drenched, enter the front room, their guns raised, aimed at Laura. Another flash of lightning flickered, thunder cracked, and then the lights went out.

TWENTY-EIGHT

···

Remalla blinked water from his eyes. After running through the woods in a downpour, they'd approached the home, but the closed blinds prevented them from seeing anything. One window had allowed enough of a view that they could see Laura Benoff in the dining area, holding a gun.

The doors were locked, but by some miracle, they'd found an open window, and climbed inside. They were in a small office. Cautiously, Rem crept down the hall, water dripping from his clothes. Daniels followed on the opposite side of the hall. Hearing voices, they slowed and stopped before entering the main area of the house. Stephen, Madison's attorney, lay unmoving on the floor near the kitchen, a puddle of blood beneath him.

Madison's voice traveled. "You want to kill me, then do it. But you'll have to look me in the eyes when you pull the trigger."

Rem made eye contact with Daniels, using that silent communication they'd relied on throughout their partnership. They would have to go in, but before they could move, a shot rang out. Instinctively, they jumped out, guns raised, yelling to freeze. Rem saw Madison on the floor behind the dining table, but she appeared unharmed.

Laura Benoff swiveled, holding her own gun, when the lights flickered and went out.

Rem dropped to the floor, and Daniels did the same, scrambling behind the table for cover. He could have taken the shot, but hesitated. If there was a way to take Laura alive, he had to try. He knew Daniels would feel the same.

A brief flash of lightning revealed Madison beside him. He put a finger to his lips to tell her to stay quiet.

"Laura?" said Daniels. "It's Detectives Daniels and Remalla."

Laura's voice shook. "Stay where you are."

"We're not moving. We just want to talk," said Daniels.

"There's nothing to talk about."

Rem tried to see where she was, but the house was dark. Only the occasional lightning flash revealed her location, which meant it could reveal theirs too, although the tabletop helped to conceal them. He heard footsteps and knew she was moving. He rose up into a squatting position, ready to move fast. Daniels kept up the conversation.

"Yes, there is. We want to help you. There's still a chance to do that."

"I don't want your help. I don't need it. Once I'm done here, I'm free. Madison and Preston will be dead, as will you."

"Listen, Laura. Think this through. You're going to kill two cops? How will you explain that?"

"I didn't kill two cops. Madison did. It's just a matter of staging."

Rem wiped his wet face with his shoulder. He listened to Laura's voice to pinpoint her location. The lightning and thunder lessened as the storm drifted away. He didn't hear her moving, kept his gun raised, and slid silently forward, around the other side of Madison, giving himself a more direct line of fire. He said nothing, keeping his own position unknown.

Daniels kept trying. "Laura, this is not necessary. You don't have to kill anyone."

She chuckled. "It's a little late for that. I killed Karl, and Preston is probably dead by now. Stephen, too. But I'm not alone. Madison killed Donald. Right, Madison? And before this night is done, I'm going to kill her."

"Why?" asked Daniels. "You're her friend."

The lightning had not flickered in several seconds, and Rem listened, keeping his gun trained in Laura's direction. If she started firing, he'd have to return fire.

"I thought we were friends, but she used me, just like Karl. Just like Preston. Just like Donald. Just like..." She paused. "Everyone has their own agenda. Well, now I have mine."

Her voice traveled, but Rem could not hear footsteps. He waited for another flash of lightning, but none came. He held his breath, fearing his breathing would give away his position.

Daniels kept his voice calm. "Laura, what about your family? What about our families? What about Stephen's family? Have you thought about them?"

Laura's voice tensed. "Family? What the fuck do I care about your *families*? Nobody cared about mine. Nobody cared about *me*. Your families will move on. Life goes on. Who gives a shit?"

Lightning flashed, and Rem got a glimpse of the room. Laura stood closer than he realized, her gun pointed at the table. As the light returned, she swiveled, aiming toward Daniels. Rem raised up on his knees, prepared to fire, when a vase from the kitchen counter slid across it, flew up and hit Laura in the back. The lights flickered, came back on and the house lit up again.

Daniels jumped out from his hiding place along with Rem. Laura stumbled forward from the impact. Caught off guard, she stumbled into a dining chair, lowering the gun. For a split second, Rem saw Madison kick out at the chair, causing it to slide and hit Laura's hand. The gun almost fell from her grasp, but she managed to hold onto it. Daniels yelled at her to freeze, but she ignored him.

Rem lowered his weapon and reached for Laura, hoping to get to her while she was distracted, but she was a split second faster, and she rose up, gun in hand, swiveling it between Rem and Daniels.

He and Daniels backed off. Daniels had his gun raised. Rem did not. He let his grip go loose, his gun swinging from his trigger finger, and he held up his hands in a gesture of surrender, knowing his partner would shoot if needed. "Easy. Take it easy," he said.

Her face tightened and her eyes flicked between the both of them. "Stay back."

Rem didn't move. "Laura. I'm staying right here. We don't want to hurt you."

She took a couple of steps back into the living room. Daniels kept his gun raised. Laura swiveled toward him.

"Laura," said Rem, hoping to talk her down. "Think this through. Put the gun down and let us help you."

"You can't help me. No one can."

"Laura, please," said Madison from beneath the table. "Listen to them."

"Shut up," said Laura. "Just shut up." Her jaw clenched, and her hands shook.

"Laura, just stay calm," said Rem.

Laura shifted her attention back to him, the gun following. Rem could sense Daniels' tension on the trigger. If Laura didn't back down soon, his partner would have to shoot. They could have justifiably shot her before now, but neither wanted that.

"Please. We can figure this all out. If Madison is guilty, we will bring her to justice. I promise. She won't get away with anything."

Laura's face was paper white. Her lips pulled back into a garish gaze, and a single tear escaped and ran down her cheek. "It doesn't matter anymore." She moved the gun off Rem, and pointed it toward her head.

"No!" yelled Rem.

"Don't—" yelled Daniels.

The gun discharged, and Madison screamed.

TWENTY-NINE

....

Madison sat on a bench alongside the walkway to her door, a few yards from the front entrance. Lights from various vehicles flickered, illuminating her driveway and her house. A blanket had been placed over her shoulders and she held her head, as police and members of a crime scene and coroner's unit, came and went. The rain had ended, and a cool breeze ruffled her hair.

She couldn't be sure how long she'd been sitting there. It felt like hours. After Laura had pulled the trigger, Madison had lost it. Daniels and Remalla had pulled her away and out of the house, but the image of that moment played repeatedly in her head. How would she ever have another night's sleep without remembering? Laura had shot and killed herself.

Daniels and Remalla had called Biggles, as well as their own captain, the local deputies, and an ambulance for Stephen, who was still alive. Within an hour, her home had more lights on it than the main square at Christmas time, and Stephen had been taken to a nearby hospital. He'd lost a lot of blood, but he was conscious when they'd taken him away. Preston Benoff had been found dead in his kitchen, with several stab wounds to his chest and abdomen.

Madison rubbed her temples. She'd finally stopped crying, but a full-blown headache throbbed. She had no idea what time it was or where she would sleep tonight. She could barely count straight from exhaustion and shock.

A hand touched her shoulder. "Madison, you okay?"

She looked up to see Daniels beside her. He'd dried off with a towel, but his clothes were still damp. She shook her head.

"Is there anyone you can stay with tonight? A friend or relative?"

She nodded absently. "I'm sure there is."

"You want me to call someone for you?"

Tears threatened again, but she swallowed them back. "I don't know."

He sat beside her, pausing before he spoke. "This isn't your fault."

She sniffed. "How did I not see this? She was my friend."

He leaned forward, his elbows on his knees. "She obviously had a lot of issues, most of which you knew nothing about. I'm sure after we do a little digging, we'll find out what they were. I think, in her own way, she was your friend, but her demons got the best of her in the end."

Madison dropped her head back down. "I just can't believe this happened." Fresh tears fell. "She killed Karl, Donald, and Preston and almost Stephen." She looked over. "She kept saying I killed Donald, but I didn't. Why would she say that?"

Daniels sighed. "I don't know. If she was having a psychotic break, she likely created a story in her mind, which helped her cope. She'd made you into a person she admired, and then, when she saw you as competition, maybe it helped her to think that you were like her, so she told herself you killed Donald, but when that story unraveled, so did she. She had to make you the villain then, to get herself out of the hole she'd dug for herself."

"How did she maintain this sane persona for so long?"

"I wish I knew. I'm sure a doctor could explain it better than me. But we've seen some crazy things in our line of work, and this will only get added to the list."

Remalla walked over and joined them. "A press van just pulled up. Things are about to get even crazier. You want us to get you out of here?"

Madison wiped a tear from her face. "I have no idea where to go."

Remalla squatted in front of her. "We can take you to a hotel until you can figure out what you'd like to do."

Madison pulled the blanket closer around her. "I suppose."

"Okay." Remalla hesitated and glanced at Daniels. "Listen, before we go, I know this may be bad timing, but I'm not sure I'll get the chance to ask this again."

"What is it?" asked Madison.

He eyed her warily. "In the house, the vase, it flew off the counter..." He paused. "I'm wondering how that happened."

Madison swallowed. She studied her hands, which still tingled. Closing her eyes, she recalled the vase, and the picture frame, both flying up and hitting Laura. She couldn't be sure, but she knew she'd caused it. She'd been angry and scared, and then something had moved up and through her, like she'd been shoving a heavy weight off of her body. Her hands had tingled and then the vase had shot forward, like the frame. Madison thought of Sonia. *You don't know what you're capable of.*

She grasped her hands together and spoke softly. "I don't know what you're talking about." She met Remalla's gaze. "I don't remember anything like that. Do you?"

Remalla narrowed his eyes, then glanced at Daniels, who shrugged. Remalla sighed. "Yeah. That's probably for the better. At least for the reports we'll have to file."

Madison didn't answer. There would come a time when she'd have to deal with whatever she'd done, but it wouldn't be while she was sitting on this bench. "I think that's for the best."

"For now, at least," said Daniels.

Madison studied the vehicles on her property, noting the reporters across the street. "I should go now, I think." She rubbed her neck.

"Madison. Madison?" Lucy and Angie tried to push their way past a uniformed officer.

"It's okay," said Daniels. "Let them through."

The officer let them pass, and the two women rushed over. "My God," said Lucy. "Are you okay?"

"We heard it was Laura? She killed Karl and Donald. Is that true?" asked Angela, breathless. "Did she shoot herself? Jesus. What the hell?"

"Ladies, I think Madison needs some space. She's had a rough night," said Daniels. He stood and Lucy took his place on the bench.

"You poor thing," said Lucy, putting her arm around Madison. "You're lucky to be alive.

"I'm okay. Really." Madison didn't know how true that was, but it felt good to say it.

Remalla moved out of the way when Angie almost knocked him over. He stood next Daniels. "Madison needs a place to stay. Could one of you help her out tonight."

"Of course," they both said at once.

"You can stay in our guest room," said Lucy. "For as long as you need."

"I have an extra room too. You're more than welcome," added Angie.

Madison nodded. "That would be great. Thanks." She stood and Lucy and Angie helped her up. "I'm okay." She got her bearings and took a deep breath. Pausing for a moment, she spoke to Lucy and Angie. "Can I have a few seconds? I'd like to talk to the detectives."

Angie and Lucy eyed Daniels and Remalla. "Take your time. We'll be right over there when you're ready," said Lucy.

Angie pointed a finger at Daniels and Remalla. "You be nice," she said before walking away.

Remalla shot up his hands. "What? Are we not nice?"

Daniels agreed. "We saved her life. I think we're pretty nice."

Madison walked up, thinking about what to say. "I want to thank you. You guys could have walked away from all of this, and left me holding the bag, and I'd likely be dead right now."

Their postures relaxed, and Remalla nodded. "That's our job. It's what we do. No thanks needed."

"Regardless, we all know that it would have been easy for you to leave, but you didn't, and I appreciate it."

"You're welcome," said Daniels. "We were happy to help, I'm just sorry it ended the way it did."

"Me, too," said Madison. "Me, too."

"You're free and clear now though, and hopefully Stephen will pull through," said Remalla. "Biggles will be taking over from here. We'll just add our report, but we'll be around if you need anything."

Madison nodded. "Okay." She paused, thinking. "There's one more thing."

"What's that?" asked Daniels.

She crossed her arms, keeping the blanket around her. "What about Rutger?"

Daniels and Remalla regarded each other. Remalla raised a brow. "That's a great question. You want to take that one?" he asked Daniels.

Daniels huffed and stared off, as if recalling something. "I think we'll have to table that for a bit. Like that flying vase, I don't think there's much to say about it. At least not right now."

"But if that changes, we'll be in touch," said Remalla. "Believe me. Rutger is a man I'd like to find."

"Me, too," said Daniels, setting his jaw. "But for now, I think you're safe. Focus on taking care of yourself. Don't worry about Rutger."

Something told Madison there was more to the story, but as they said, now was not the time. For the moment, she'd settle with figuring out the next step. It was all she could handle. Maybe when she could put her life back together, then there would be time to search for answers to several questions.

She went quiet, her mind too tired to argue. "You two okay? Everybody keeps asking me that question, but nobody's asked you. You saw the whole thing."

Remalla sighed. "I doubt I'll be sleeping well anytime soon, but I'll live."

"We'll be fine. Don't worry about us," said Daniels. "Go get some rest."

Madison fought a wave of fatigue. "You guys deserve a raise. I'll call your captain."

Remalla chuckled. "I'd like to see how that goes over."

"We're staying in his cabin. You may have met him. Frank Lozano?" asked Daniels.

Madison recognized the name. "Oh, yeah. I think he's the guy that fell out of his fishing boat. Had to be rescued by Mrs. Huggins."

Rem's eyes widened. "What? Who's Mrs. Huggins?"

"Our oldest resident on the lake. She's 85. Lozano fell out of his boat, and couldn't get back in. Alice Huggins went out on her pontoon and threw him a life preserver, then dragged him back to shore. I think it was last summer."

Remalla dropped his jaw. "Everything that's happened on this case is now worth it based on that alone. He never told us."

"Gee. I wonder why," said Daniels, shaking his head.

"Well, he should wear a life jacket next time," said Madison.

"We'll be sure to tell him," said Daniels. "Over and over."

Madison smiled, feeling guilty at the same time. It didn't feel right. "Is it okay to laugh?" she asked, her smile fading.

The moment of brevity passed. Rem studied the ground, his voice quiet. "It will be uncomfortable, almost painful, but eventually it will be normal again, but to be honest, it will always feel strange." He looked up, and Madison thought she detected a slight shine to his eyes.

Daniels patted his partner's arm, regarding Madison. "Just be patient with yourself. Talk to someone. It will help."

Madison wiped away an unshed tear. "I will. I think I need to do a lot of talking."

They stood silently for a second. "Your friends are waiting," said Remalla. "Try and get some sleep."

She nodded. "You, too. And thanks again. You guys come back to the lake, let me know. I'll make you dinner."

"You're on," said Daniels.

Madison swallowed, feeling the urge to cry again. A strange melancholy enveloped her at the thought of saying goodbye, but realizing her body and her mind's need to rest and recuperate, she turned and walked away.

THIRTY

D aniels shut the door behind them. Rem collapsed on the sofa and Daniels joined him, barely able to keep his eyes open. "What time is it?" he asked.

"I'm too tired to look. Probably close to five a.m." Rem yawned.

Daniels nodded. "I talked to the hospital. Did I tell you?"

"Yeah. Stephen's out of surgery. Should be fine."

Daniels closed his eyes. "That's good." He felt a swat on his arm.

"Hey, don't fall asleep. We need to hit the hay. This couch will kill our backs."

Daniels cracked an eye open. "Okay." He forced himself to sit up. Rem did the same. Daniels rubbed his face. "Lozano said we could take the day. Get some rest. What time do you want to head back?"

"I don't care."

"If you don't mind, maybe we can get a few hours of shut eye, and then pack up and go. I'd like to see Marjorie and JP."

"That's fine with me. I sleep better in my own bed anyway." He blinked tired eyes.

They sat, neither moving. Although Daniels could barely think straight, he knew there were issues to address. "Before we crash, you want to talk about it?"

Rem made a groaning noise and leaned forward, holding his head. "Talk about what?"

"You know what. Rutger? In the woods? What he said? Pulling our guns out of our hands? Laura Benoff blowing her head off in front of us? How about that?"

"Just another day on the job."

"I wish, but it's not. There's stuff going on here. You know Laura didn't kill Donald. Rutger did."

Rem stretched his neck. "I know."

"And he likely killed Rick Henderson."

"I know."

"Shit." Daniels rubbed the tight muscles in his shoulders.

"I know."

"Perhaps there's more you can contribute?"

Rem sighed. "I wish I could. We've got a madman out there who can somehow control inanimate objects and throw them around like a juggler, who also seems intent on killing men connected to certain people in his life."

"Not certain people. He called them 'family.'"

Rem raised a brow. "And that makes no sense. Madison and Jill have no connection. They don't even know each other."

"But you saw what happened with that vase at Madison's. It's the same shit that Rutger pulled with our guns, and with me."

"And with that rock," added Rem, touching his head. "If there is a connection, though, then Madison and Jill are not aware of it."

"But he is. And now he's looking for someone else. What name did he say? Jace?"

Rem threw out a hand. "God knows who Jace is. Could be a nickname. Could even be a man or a woman. There's no way we could find anyone based on that alone. All we can do is wait."

Daniels studied the floor. "You plan on telling Jill?"

Rem shook his head. "At this point, I don't think I have a choice. She deserves to know."

"We could be wrong. Rutger could be just a psychopath yanking our chain."

Rem looked over. "You believe that, after all we've seen?"

"No."

"Neither do I. Something's going on here, and for some reason, I think Rutger likes us, or at least needs us involved."

"He's using us. He called them family. We protected Jill from the Artist, and Madison from Laura."

"If he's so interested in protecting them, then why is he killing the most important people in their lives?"

"He must believe, in some way, that's he's helping them. Donald abused Madison."

"But Henderson was a stand-up guy."

"Maybe not in his eyes."

Rem went quiet. "Well, we're not going to solve this tonight. We need to get some rest. We can deal with it tomorrow."

"It is tomorrow."

"Then the tomorrow after that." He stood with a groan, held out a hand and helped Daniels up. "Come on, partner."

Daniels held his chest. The night had been so crazy, he'd barely noticed his damaged ribs, but now, as he stood, the pain returned with a flare and he winced.

"Take some aspirin. It will help. It's going to ache tomorrow."

"You mean today."

"Whatever," said Rem. He pulled on his shirt sleeve, seeing something on it.

Daniels saw it, too. It was blood. "You should throw that in the sink tonight. Let it soak."

"Yeah." He continued to stare.

Daniels' mind flashed back to Laura pulling the trigger. "Lozano wants us to talk to the department shrink, about what we saw."

Rem dropped his arm. "I know. He and I are on a first name basis though, so no big deal."

"A woman shot herself in the head in front of us. It's kind of a big deal."

Rem closed his eyes, then opened them. They were red with fatigue. "I get it. I'm not making light of it. Believe me, I'll be seeing that in my mind for a long time, and so will you, but it'll eventually take its place with the other horrible things I've seen, and they'll all get together once in a while and have a beer. And I'll disappear and drown my sorrows in some bourbon. But then I'll pop back up and keep right on truckin'. It's what I do."

Daniels regarded Rem. He knew of the demons that plagued his partner and wished he could offer some pithy comment to lighten the mood, but nothing came to mind. "Well, when you're ready to hit the bourbon, let me know, and I'll be right there with you. You don't have to drink alone."

"I know that. I've always known that. We've shared plenty of drinks. This job does that to you."

Daniels pointed. "We find Rutger, and I'll close down the bar with you."

Rem grinned. "We find Rutger, I'll buy a distillery, we'll make our own bourbon, get drunk every day, and we'll die fat and happy with a belly full of Taco del Fuegos."

Daniels rolled his eyes. "Speak for yourself."

"You don't know what you're missing."

Daniels turned toward his room. "How about we catch a few hours, and I'll buy you breakfast on the way home? No Taco del Fuegos, though."

Rem headed toward his room, stifling a yawn. "You're on." Pushing open his door, he disappeared inside.

"Hey," said Daniels.

Rem poked his head out.

"Once we put this case to bed, how about we look for someone named Jace?"

Rem stared at him. "It's a long shot."

"Long shot is my middle name."

"I thought it was Oliver."

Daniels squinted. "That's just between you and me. And Marjorie."

Rem rested a hand on the doorframe. "Lozano will have questions."

"Lozano doesn't have to know. We can do it on our own time."

Rem tipped his head. "We could also check the mug books for Rutger."

"We could."

They regarded each other. "Looks like we have a new case," said Rem.

Daniels nodded. "Looks like it."

Rem patted the door. "Get some sleep."

"You, too."

Rem went into his room and closed the door, and yawning, Daniels did the same.

THIRTY-ONE

....

S onia Vandermere stared out the window, paying no attention to the view. Her mind raced with the events of the
day.

The door to the room opened and Peter spoke from behind her.
"We're all checked out."

Sonia nodded. "Okay."

"You need anything else?"

"No. I just need a few minutes."

"I'll take the bags. Meet you downstairs."

"Thank you, dear."

She heard the door close and she continued to stare, reflecting
on her early morning meditation. Feeling conflicted and sad, she'd
needed it after hearing about Madison's frightening night, and
Laura Benoff's death.

Closing her eyes, she took a deep breath. It had been her most
disturbing meditation yet. He'd come to her almost immediately,
smiling at her, knowing that he was ahead of her in this game. It
was a rare moment. No matter how many times she'd tried to reach
out to him before, he'd denied her, but now, he'd openly confronted
her. It had taken a lot of control for her to stay calm. She'd almost

pulled out of the connection, but she'd stayed. She had to try to communicate with him.

Allowing her shield to fall, she'd opened up, hoping he would feel her regret and willingness to help, but he'd rejected her advances, and instead sent his own wave of energy back to her. The intensity of it had startled her, and she couldn't help but break the link. With a sharp intake of breath, she'd opened her eyes. Her hands were clenched and she'd had to force herself to relax.

Now, looking out the window, she couldn't forget his eyes, and the feeling that had come over her. Anger, no fury, had pulsed from him, and all she could see was fire. And she knew that's what he intended. To burn everything. Right down to the ground. And it wouldn't matter who he took with him. Whether it was her or even those nice detectives. Perhaps that's what disturbed her the most. It was one thing for him to come after her, but to hurt those who had no blame in this, that was the most difficult to accept.

Sighing, she turned from the window, and found her purse. Digging through it, she found her favorite piece of rose quartz and held it in her hand until the heavy energy began to lift. Then, with a last glance out the window, and a deep sigh, she closed her purse, checked her hair in the mirror, walked to the door and left.

ACKNOWLEDGEMENTS

······································

Thank you to my family, friends, coworkers and fans, all of whom make this possible. I wouldn't write if it weren't for you and your continued support and encouragement. I hear it, I see it, and I thank you immensely.

ABOUT THE AUTHOR

Born and raised in Dallas, TX, J. T. Bishop began writing in 2012. Two years later, the Red-Line trilogy was complete. She's not done though. J. T. continues to create new characters and story lines to entertain her fans.

J. T. loves stories that explore characters' unique abilities and origins. It's a theme she finds intriguing and provides a wealth of inspiration for her books. Drama, angst, passion, and humor all add to the fun. A little bit of romance doesn't hurt either.

J. T. loves to spend time with family and friends, traveling whenever she can, and spending time in nature (despite the heat in Texas). Getting up in the morning with a cup of coffee, ready to write is the start of a perfect day.

ENJOY AN EXCERPT OF J.T. BISHOP'S NEXT BOOK – THIRD BLOW

....

Jace awoke with a start, blinking his eyes, trying to focus. Pictures of space and the planets drifted and changed on his monitor and a puddle of drool had collected on the files beneath him. Rubbing his face, he looked around his office and checked the time. Four a.m. He'd fallen asleep at his desk.

The couch against the wall beckoned. He kept a blanket and pillow for nights like these when he didn't want to go home. Home was too quiet and he would only return here tomorrow. His friends had left the bar around midnight, his girlfriend, Devyn, included.

He spied a water bottle and took a sip, his fingers shaking. The dream still lingered and he took a deep breath, trying to shake it off. He had never been one to have nightmares, but for the last two months, he'd been dreaming the same dream.

He remembered most of it. Two women and a man. The women were running toward him, trying to find Jace. Jace could see them, but couldn't reach them, no matter how hard he tried. He knew they needed help. A man chased them; his face cloaked but his eyes gleaming. And he smiled. It was more of a leer than a smile, as if the man knew Jace's torment. The women got closer and Jace was close to reaching them, but the man would get to them first.

Screaming, the women fell to the ground, writhing in agony, grasping for help, while the man grinned, and Jace would wake up, breathless and sweating.

He had no idea what it meant. God knows he'd been to enough shrinks in his life that he could probably be one himself, but it didn't make sense. In the dream, he knew the women. They were important to him, but when he woke, he had no idea who they were or their connection to him.

He took another swig of the water; his heart rate slowing. The dream tonight had changed. The women were running, but this time, Devyn was with them. She'd run to him and he'd grabbed her. But her face fell into a grimace, and she'd said I'm sorry and she'd been yanked from his grasp, and the man had been there, rising up in Jace's face and he'd spoken. I did it for you.

Jace exhaled and rubbed his face as the dream faded, but he still heard the man's voice in his head.

Pushing back from the desk, he put his hands on his knees and debated calling Devyn, but she would kill him if he woke her from her sleep, especially when she had to get up in two hours.

Deciding to shake it off, he stood to get the blanket and pillow, when his cell phone rang. He picked it up from the desk, and eyed the caller id. It was Justin, his best friend. He'd been in the bar earlier playing cards.

Wondering why his friend was calling him at four a.m, he answered, trying not to think the worst, but also feeling an uncomfortable twist in his gut. "Justin? What's up, brother? You okay?"

There was quiet at first, but then he heard heavy breathing. For a minute, he thought Justin was playing with him when he heard Justin whisper. "Jace."

That twist in his gut became a spike. "Justin, what's wrong?"

Justin gulped in air and he sounded terrified. "Jace?" His voice was high pitched, as if he was on the verge of tears.

"Justin?" Jace's heart rate tripled. "Tell me what's wrong."

"I...I...I'm sorry." He could barely get the words out.

Jace grabbed his jacket and keys, planning to go to Justin's apartment. "Justin, I'm heading over. Stay put."

"Please," said Justin, but distant, like he'd turned from the phone. Was he speaking to someone else?

"Is someone else there? Justin?" Jace left the bar without even locking the door behind him.

Justin's voice returned. "I'm...so sorry. I didn't mean..." A sob escaped. "...to hurt you."

"Justin, what are you talking about?"

Jace threw on his jacket, keeping the phone to his ear, and got on his motorcycle parked in front of the bar. "I'm coming. Whatever it is, we'll figure it out."

Justin sobbed again. "Please, I did what...no..." His voice sounded distant again. "No." It was almost a wail.

"Justin?" Jace heard a gasp and a gurgle and then the phone went quiet. Jace's heart stopped and he froze. "Justin? Buddy? Hold on."

He heard a thud and then a muffled noise, like the phone had been dragged across something. Jace waited and was about to start up the bike when another voice spoke. It was deeper than Justin's and more guttural, and it whispered. "I did it for you." Then the line went dead.

Printed in Great Britain
by Amazon

43424108R00189